The Celebrity at Home

BY

VIOLET HUNT
AUTHOR OF 'A HARD WOMAN'

FOURTH EDITION

1904

British Library Cataloguing-in-Publication Data
A catalogue record for this book is available from the
British Library

Violet Hunt

Isobel Violet Hunt was born on 28th September 1862 in Durham, England. Her father was the artist William Albert Hunt and her mother the translator and novelist Margaret Raine Hunt.

Hunt's family moved to London in 1865 where she grew up among the Pre-Raphaelites of the 'Rossetti Circle'. She knew John Ruskin, William Morris, and it is even rumoured that Oscar Wilde asked for her hand in marriage in Dublin in 1879.

Hunt covered several literary forms, including short stories, novels, memoirs, and biographies. Her first published work was her novel *The Maiden's Progress* (1894) which fell into the New Woman genre and represented her ideals as an active feminist. These political views led to her founding the Women Writer's Suffrage League in 1908. Feminism however, was by no means her only subject matter, with works like *Tales of the Uneasy* (1911) being a collection of supernatural fiction short stories.

Although Hunt produced many works, her reputation is as much for the literary salons she held at her home in Campden Hill as it is for her writing. She would entertain guests such as Rebecca West, Ezra Pound, Joseph Conrad, D. H. Lawrence, and other important writers of the time. She also had several famous lovers, including H. G. Wells and Ford Maddox

Ford. Ford was married but lived with Hunt at her home, South Lodge between 1910 and 1918 and collaborated with her on several works, including *The Desirable Alien* (1913). Hunt is said to have been fictionalised by Ford, becoming the scheming Florence Dowell in *The Good Soldier* (1915) and the shrewish Sylvia Tietjens in the *Parade's End* tetralogy.

Hunt died of pneumonia in her home in 1942 and her grave is in the Glades of Remembrance at Brookwood Cemetery, Surrey, England.

CONTENTS

THE CELEBRITY AT HOME

CHAPTER I

THEY say that a child's childhood is the happiest time of its life!

Mine isn't.

For it is nice to do as you like even if it isn't good for you. It is nice to overeat yourself even though it does make you ill afterwards. It is a positive pleasure to go out and do something that catches you a cold, if you want to, and to leave off your winter clothes a month too soon. Children hate feeling "stuffy"—no grown-up person understands that feeling that makes you wriggle and twist till you get sent to bed. It is nice to go to bed when you are sleepy, and no sooner, not to be despatched any time that grown-up people are tired of you and take the quickest way to get rid of a nuisance. Taken all round, the very nicest thing in the world is your own way and plenty of it, and you never get that properly, it seems to me, until you are too old to enjoy it, or too cross to admit that you do!

I suspect that the word "rice-pudding" will be written on my heart, as Calais was on Bloody Mary's, when I am dead.

I have got that blue shade about the eyes that they say early-dying children have, and I may die young. So I am going to write down everything, just as it happens, in my life, because when I grow up, I mean to be an author, like my father before me, and teach in song, or in prose, what I have learned in suffering. Doing this will get me insensibly into the habit of composition. George—my father—we always call him by his Christian name by request—offered to look it over for me, but I do not think that I shall avail myself of his kindness. I want to be quite honest, and set down everything, in malice, as grown-up people do, and then your book is sure to be amusing. I shall say the worst—I mean the truth—about everybody, including myself. That is what makes a book saleable. People don't like to be put off with short commons in scandal, and chuck the book into the fire at once as I have seen George do, when the writer is too discreet. My book will not be discreet, but crisp, and gossippy. Even Ariadne must not read it, however much of my hair and its leaves she pulls out, for she will claw me in her rage, of course. Grammar and spelling will not be made a specialty of, because what you gain in propriety you lose in originality and *verve*. I do adore *verve*!

George's own style is said to be the perfection of nervousness and vervousness. He is a genius, he admits it. I am proud, but not glad, for it cuts both ways, and it is hardly likely that there will be two following after each other so soon in the same family. Though one never knows? Mozart's father was a musical man. George says that to be daughter to such a person is a liberal education; it seems about all the education I am likely to get! George teaches me Greek and Latin, when he has time. He won't touch Ariadne, for she isn't worth it. He says I am apt. Dear me, one may as well make lessons a pleasure, instead of a scene! Ariadne cried the first time at Perspective, when George, after a long explanation that puzzled her, asked her in that particular, sniffy, dried-up tone teachers put on,—"Did she see?" And when he asked me, I didn't see either, but I said I did, to prevent unpleasantness.

I do not know why I am called Tempe. Short for temper, the new cook says, but when I asked George, he laughed, and bid me and the cook beware of obvious derivations. It appears that there is a pretty place somewhere in Greece called the Vale of Tempe, and that I am named after that, surely a mistake. My father calls me a devil—plain devil when he is cross, little devil when he is pleased. I take it as a compliment, for look at my sister Ariadne, she is as good as gold, and what does she get by it? She does not contradict or ask questions or bother anybody, but reads poetry and does her hair different ways all day long. She never says a sharp word—can't! George says she is bound to get left, like the first Ariadne was. She is long and pale and thin, and white like a snowdrop, except for her reddish hair. The pert hepatica is my favourite flower. It comes straight out of the ground, like me, without any fuss or preparation in the way of leaves and trimmings.

I know that I am not ugly. I know it by the art of deduction. We none of us are, or we should not have been allowed to survive. George would never have condescended to own ugly children. We should have been exposed when we were babies on Primrose Hill, which is, I suppose, the tantamount of Mount Täygetus, as the ancient Greeks did their ugly babies. We aren't allowed to read Lemprière. I do. What brutes those Greeks were, and did not even know one colour from the other, so George says!

I am right in saying we are all tolerable. The annoying thing is that the new cook, who knows what she is talking about, says that children "go in and out so," and even Aunt Gerty says that "fancy children never last," and after all this, I feel that the pretty ones can never count on keeping up to their own standard.

I cannot tell you if our looks come from our father, or our mother? George is small, with a very brown skin. He says he descends "from the little dark, persistent races" that come down from the mountains and take the other savages' sheep and cows. He has good eyes. They dance and flash. His hair is black, brushed back from his forehead like a Frenchman, and very nice white teeth. He has a mouth like a Jesuit, I have heard Aunt Gerty say. He never sits very still. He is about thirty-seven, but he does not like us chattering about his age.

Mother looks awfully young for hers—thirty-six; and she would look prettier if she didn't burn her eyes out over the fire making dishes for George, and prick her fingers darning his socks till he doesn't find out they are darned, or else he wouldn't wear them again, and spoil her figure stooping, sewing and ironing. George won't have a sewing machine in the house. Her head is a very good shape, and she does her hair plain over the top to show it. George made her. Sometimes when he isn't there, she does it as she used before she was married, all waved and floating, more like Aunt Gerty, who is an actress, and dresses her head sunning over with curls like Maud. George has never caught Mother like that, or he would be very angry. He considers that she has the bump of domesticity highly developed (though even when her hair is done plain I never can see it?), and that is why she enjoys being wife, mother, and upper housemaid all in one.

We only keep two out here at Isleworth, though my brother Ben is very useful as handy boy about the place, blacking our boots and browning George's, and cleaning the windows and stopping them from rattling at nights—a thing that George can't stand when he is here. When he isn't we just let them rave, and it is a perfect concert, for this is a very old Georgian house. Mother makes everything, sheets, window-curtains, and our frocks and her own. She makes them all by the same pattern, quite straight like sacks. George likes to see us dressed simply, and of course it saves dressmakers' bills, or board of women working in the house, who simply eat you out of it in no time. We did have one once to try, and when she wasn't lapping up cocoa to keep the cold out, she was sucking her thimble to fill up the vacuum. We are dressed strictly utilitarian, and wear our hair short like Ben, and when it gets long mother puts a pudding basin on our heads and snips away all that shows. At last Ariadne cried herself into leave to let hers grow.

The new cook says that if we weren't dressed so queer, Ariadne and me, we should make some nice friends, but that is just what George doesn't want. He likes us to be self-contained, and says that there is no one about here that he would care to have us associate with. Our doorstep will never wear down with people coming in, for except Aunt Gerty, and Mr. Aix, the oldest friend of the family, not a soul ever crosses the threshold!

I am forgetting the house-agent's little girl, round the corner into Corinth Road. She comes here to tea with us sometimes. She is exactly between Ariadne and me in age, so we share her as a friend equally. We got to know her through our cat Robert the Devil choosing to go and stay in Corinth Road once. At the end of a week her people had the bright thought of looking at the name and address on his collar, and sent him back by Jessie, who then made friends with us. George said, when he was told of it, that the Hitchings are so much lower in the social scale than we are, that it perhaps does not matter our seeing a little of each other. She is better dressed than us, in spite of her low social scale. She has got a real osprey in her hat, and a mink stole to wear to church, that is so long it keeps getting its ends in the mud. She doesn't like our George, though we like hers. George came out of his study once and passed through the dining-room, where Jessie was having tea with us.

"Isn't he a *cure*?" said she, with her mouth full of his bread-and-butter.

We told her that our George was no more of a cure than hers, which shut her up; and was quite safe, as neither Ariadne nor I know what a "cure" is. She isn't really a bad sort of girl. We teach her poetry, and mythology, and she teaches us dancing and religion. She has a governess all to herself every morning, and goes to church regularly. She once said that her mamma called us poor, neglected children, and pitied us. We hit her for her mother, and there was an end of that. We love each other dearly now, and have promised to be bridesmaids to each other, and godmothers to each other's children. I am going to have ten.

Ariadne went to her birthday party at Christmas, and did a very silly thing, that Mother advised her not to tell George about. Every one at home agreed that poor Ariadne had been dreadfully rude, but I can't see it? I adore sincerity. When Mr. Hitchings asked her what she would like out of the bran-pie when it was opened, same as they asked all the other children, Ariadne only said quite modestly, "A new papa, please!"

Their faces frightened her so, that she tried to improve it away, and explain she meant that she should like an every-day papa, like Mr. Hitchings, not only a Sunday one, like George. I know of course what she meant, a papa that one sees only from Saturdays to Mondays, and not always then, is only half a papa.

Ariadne's real name is Ariadne Florentina, after one of George's friends' books. She has nice hair. It is reddish and yet soft, but it won't curl by itself, which is a great grief and sorrow to her. But at any rate, her eyelashes are awfully long and dark, and she likes to put the bed-clothes right over her head and listen to her eyelashes scrabbling about on the sheet quite loud. She has big eyes like nursery saucers. The new cook calls them loving eyes. On the whole, Ariadne is pretty, she would think she was even if she wasn't, so it is a good thing she is. She considers herself wasted, for she is over eighteen now, and she has never been to a party or worn a low neck in her life. We have neither of us ever seen a low neck, but we know what it is from books, and from them also we learn that eighteen is the age when it takes less stuff to cover you. The new cook says that all her young ladies at her last place came out when they were only seventeen. What is outness? I asked George once, and he said it was a device of the Philistines. I then told him that the new cook said that Ariadne would never be married and off his hands unless he gave her her chance like other young ladies, and he said something about a girl called Beatrice who was out and married and dead before she was nine. Her surname was Porter, if I recollect. The new cook said "Hout!" and that Beatrice Porter was all her eye and just an excuse for selfishness!

Anyhow it is Ariadne's affair, and she doesn't seem to care much, except when the new cook fills her head with ideas of revolt. She walks about the green garden reading novels, and waiting for the Prince, for she has a nice nature. I myself should just turn down the collar of my dress, put on a wreath and go out and find a Prince, or know the reason why!

We keep no gardener, only Ben. Ben is short for Benvenuto Cellini, another of George's friends. He is thirteen, old enough to go to school, only George hasn't yet been able to make up his mind where to send him. It is a good thing Ben has plenty of work to do, for he is very cross, and talks sometimes of running away to sea, only that he has the North border to dig, or Cat Corner to clear.

That is the corner George calls The Pleasaunce—it is we who call it Cat Corner. Not only dead cats come there, but brickbats and tin kettles with just one little hole in them, and brown-paper parcels that we open with a poker. I hope there will be a dead baby in one some day, to reward us. The trees are so dirty that we don't like to touch them, and the birds that scurry about in the bushes would be yellow, like canaries, Sarah says, only for the dirt of London. I hardly believe it, I should like to catch one and wash it. In the opposite corner George has built a grotto, and we have to keep it dusted, and he sits there and writes and smokes. The next garden is the garden of a mad-house. The doctor keeps a donkey and a pony. Once a table-knife came flying over the wall to us. George's nerves were so thoroughly upset that he could not bear anything but Ouida and Miss Braddon read aloud to him all the rest of the day. Mother happens to like those authors and another Italian lady's books that we are forbidden to mention in this house. She never reads George's own works; she says she has promised to be a good wife to him, but that that wasn't in the bond. She knows them too well, having heard them all in the rough. Behind the scenes in a novel is as dull as behind the scenes in a theatre, you never know what the play is about. Aunt Gerty says that all George's things are rank, and quite undramatic, and George says he is glad to hear it, for he doesn't like Aunt Gerty.

The other persons in the house are George's cats. There are three. The grey cat, the only one who has kittens, I call Lady Castlewood, out of *Esmond* by Thackeray. George sometimes says "that little cat of a Lady Castlewood"—it occurred to me that "that little Lady Castlewood of a cat" just suits ours, for she is a jealous beast, a cantankerous beast, and goes Nap with her claws all over your face in no time! She hates her children once they are grown up, and is merely on bowing terms with them, or you might call it licking terms—for she doesn't mind giving them a wash and a brush-up whenever they come her way. Robert the Devil was the one that stayed away a week. He is very big and mild; he can lie down and wrap himself in his fur till he looks all over alike, and you couldn't find any particular part of him, no more than if he were a kind of soft hedgehog. George talks to them and tells them things about himself.

"I am sure they are welcome to his confidence!" that is what the new cook said. She likes them better than she likes him. She is quite kind to cats, though she gives them a hoist with her foot sometimes, when they get in her way. They are valuable, you see. I wish I was, for then people care what you eat and give you medecines, which I love. It isn't often you are disappointed in a new bottle of medecine, except when there's gentian in it.

CHAPTER II

YOU don't get a very good class of servant down this way, my mother says, but then she is so particular. She is the kind of mistress who knows how to do everything better herself, and that kind never gets good servants; it seems to paralyze the poor girls, and make them limp and without an idea in their heads, or what they choose to call their heads, which I strongly suspect is their stomachs. You can punish or reward a servant best through its stomach, and don't give them beer, or beer-money either! Beer makes them cross or cheeky, depending, I suppose, on the make of the beer. Mother never gives it. They buy it, I know, but I never tell. It would be as much as my place (in the kitchen) is worth, and I value my right of free entry.

Mother is terribly down on dust too. She has a book about germ culture, and sees germs in everything. It doesn't make her any happier. But as for dusting, so far as I can see, what they call dusting is only a plan for raising the dirt and taking it to some other place. It gets into our mouths in the end. I do pity Matter that is always getting into the wrong place, chivied here and there, with no resting-place for the sole of the foot. For whenever Mother sees dust anywhere, or suspects it, she makes a cross with her finger in it, and the servants are supposed to see the cross and feel ashamed. Though I don't believe any servant was ever ashamed in her life. 'Tisn't in their natures. They just grin and bear with it—with the dust, and the scolding too.

"It's 'er little way," I heard Sarah say once, not a bit unkindly or disagreeably, though, after Mother had come down on her about something. But once I caught the very same girl shaking her fist at George's back and calling him "an old beast!"

"Sarah," I said, "whom are you addressing?"

"The doctor's donkey, miss," she said, as quick as lightning, pointing to it grazing in the doctor's garden next door. People were always overloading that donkey, and shaking their fists at it.

I must get to the new cook. The last one gave Mother notice, and I never could find out why, because she was fond of Mother and could stand the cats.

"Oh, I like *you*, ma'am," I heard her say, just as if she disliked some one else. Mother took no notice, but left the kitchen, and Cook took a currant off her elbow and pulled down her sleeves, and mumbled to Sarah, "It isn't right, and I for one ain't going to help countenance it. A-visiting his family now and then between jobs, just like a burglar—or some-think worse!"

What is worse than a burglar? I was passing the scullery window, and Sarah had just thrown a lot of boiling water into a basin in front of them both, so that it made a mist and she didn't see me. I knew, though, she was saying something rude, for when Sarah told her she "shouldn't reely," she muttered something more about a "neglected angel!" I did think at first she meant me, or perhaps the doctor's donkey as usual, but then the words didn't fit either of us? I asked her straight if she did mean the donkey, just for fun, and she said the poor beast was minding his own business and I had better do the same.

She left us next month, crying worse than I ever did in my life for really serious things. Mother patted her on the back as she went out at the back door, and she kept saying, "A poor girl's only got her character, mum, and she is bound to think of it—" and Mother said, "Yes, yes, you did quite right!" and seemed just to want her out of the house and a little peace and quiet and will of her own. The very moment Sarah's back was turned, she set to work and turned everything into the middle of the room and left it there while she and Cook swept round into every corner. Ariadne and I rather enjoyed clearing our bed of the towel-horse before we could lie down in it, and having dinner off the corner of the kitchen-table because the dining-room one was lying on its back like a horse kicking.

Of course George wasn't allowed home all this time. Mother wrote to him where he was staying at the Duke of Frocester's for the shooting (George shooting! My eye!—and the keeper's legs!) and said he had better not come home till we were straight again. I was in no hurry to be straight again. It was like Heaven. When I was a child I always built my brick houses crooked, and Ariadne called me Queen Unstraight, and that made me cry. But she liked this too. We made all the beds, and didn't bother to tuck them in. It isn't necessary to do so when we turn head over heels in the bed-clothes onto the floor every night three times to make us dizzy and sleepy. We washed up everything with a nice lather of three things mixed that occurred to me, Hudson's, Monkey Soap, and Bath Eucryl. In the end there wasn't a speck of dirt, or pattern either, left on the plates. It looked much cleaner. Why should one eat one's meat off a fat Chinese dragon or have bees all round the edge of one's soup plate ready to fall in? It is a dirty idea. We basted the joints turn and turn about, and our own pinafores. They couldn't scold us for not keeping clean, any more than they can pigs when they put them in a sty. We asked no questions or bothered Mother at all, but we black-leaded the steps and bath-bricked the grates, and washed down the walls with soda-water. The wallpaper peeled off here and there, but that shows it was shabby and ready for death.

Mother said afterwards that she couldn't see any improvement anywhere, but anyhow we enjoyed ourselves and that is everything. We spent money on it, for we bought *décalcomanie* pictures, and did bouquets all over the mantelpieces, but Mother insisted we should peel all these off again before George came back. He couldn't come back till we got that cook, for George is most absurdly particular about our servants. Sarah has got used to him, and there seems to be no idea of her going. She has to valet him, for he is always beautifully dressed. She has to take the greatest care of her own appearance, and get her nails manicured and her hair

waved when he is at home. That is about all for her. But
the cook he calls the keeper of his conscience, that is to
say, his digestion. His digestion is as jumpy as he is.
Sometimes it wants everything quite plain, and he will
eat nothing but our rice-puddings and cold shapes of
tapioca, etc.; at another time he calls it "apparition," and
says the very name of it makes him shiver. I am used to
cold shapes, alas! He sometimes brings things down from
town himself—caviare and "patty de foy." Children are
not supposed to like that sort of thing, but we do, and
George gives them us; he is not mean in trifles.
Sometimes it is pheasants and partridges, that he has
shot himself on ducal acres. They are shot very badly, not
tidily, with the shot all in one place as it ought to be: Mr.
Aix explained this to me. They are not to be cooked till
they are ready, and when they are they are a little too
ready for Mother and us, so Papa and Mr. Aix have to eat
it all. George belongs to the sect of the Epicureans; I
heard him tell the cook so, also that he is the
reincarnation of a gentleman called Villon.

For a month Mother "sat in" for cooks, and all sorts
of fat and lean women came and went. Our
establishment didn't seem attractive. George bespoke a
fat one, by letter, but Mother inclined to lean. These
women sat on the best chairs and prodded the pattern of
the carpets with their dusty umbrellas, and asked tons of
questions,—far more than she asked them, it seemed to
me, and this one that we have at last got was the coolest
of all, but in rather a nice way. She was tall and thin,
with a long nose with a dip in it just before the tip,

which was particularly broad. Ariadne said afterwards that a nose like that seemed to need a bustle. She said she was a north-country woman, and that is about all she did tell us about herself, except her name, Elizabeth Cawthorne.

She sat and asked questions. When she came to the usual "And if you please, ma'am, how many is there in family?" Mother answered, "Myself and my son and my two daughters,—and my sister—she is professional—and is here for long visits—that is all."

"Then I take it you are a widow, ma'am?"

Mother, getting very red, explained that George is very little at home, so that in one way he didn't count, but in another way he did, for he is very particular and has to be cooked for specially. Being an author, he has got a very delicate appetite.

"A proud stomach, I understand ye. Well, I shall hope to give him satisfaction." She said that as if she would have liked to add, "or I'll know the reason why."

She seemed quite to have settled in her own mind that she was going to take our place. She "blessed Mother's bonny face" before that interview was over, and passed me over entirely.

She came in in a week, and the first time she saw George she was "doing her hall." Ariadne and I were there as George's hansom drove up and he got out and began a shindy with the cabman.

"Honeys, this will be your father, I'm thinking!" she said.

Perhaps she expected us to rush into his arms, but we didn't; we knew better. We just said "Hallo!" and waited till he was disengaged with the cabman, who wanted too much, as we are beyond the radius. George didn't give it to him, but a good talking to instead. The new cook stopped sweeping—servants always stop their work when there is something going on that doesn't concern them, and looked quite pleased with George.

"He can explain himself, and no mistake!" she said to Sarah afterwards, and she cooked a splendid dinner that night, for, says she to Sarah, "seemed to her he was the kind of master who'd let a woman know if she didn't suit him."

She doesn't "make much account of childer," in fact I think she hates them, for when Ariadne showed her the young shoots in a pot of snowdrops she was bringing up, and said, "See, cook, they have had babies in the night!" Elizabeth, meaning to be civil, said, "Dis*gust*ing things, miss!"

Still, she isn't really unkind to children, and admits that they have a right to exist. She will boil me my glue-pot and make me paste, and lets Ariadne heat her curling-tongs between the bars of the kitchen fire. She doesn't "matter" cats, but she gives them their meals regular and doesn't hold with them loafing in the kitchen, and getting tit-bits stolen or bestowed. And they know she is just, though not generous, and never forgets their supper. They were all hid, as it happened, when she came about the place, but she said she knew she had got into a cat house as soon as she found herself eating fluff with her tea, and she thinks she ought to have been told. George laughs at her and calls her "stern daughter of the north," but he wasn't a bit cross when she told him that Ben ought to be sent to school. He even agreed, but Ben isn't sent. Ben is still eating his heart out, and he keeps telling Elizabeth Cawthorne so. He is much in the kitchen. She is very sensible. She just stuffs a jam tart into his mouth, and says, "Tak' that atween whiles then, my bonny bairn, to distract ye." Ben takes it like a lamb, and it does distract him, or at any rate it distends him; he has got fat since she came.

She orders Mother about as if she were a child. Mother *does* look very young, as I have said. She ought, and so ought Aunt Gerty, considering the trouble they both take to keep the cloven hoof of age off their faces. They go to bed with poultices of oatmeal on them, and Aunt Gerty once tried the raw-beef plaster. But what she does in the night she undoes in the day, with the grease paint and sticky messes that are part of her profession.

She lives with us except when she is on tour, and is only here when she is "resting" in the *Era*, and all that time she is dreadfully cross, because she would rather be doing than resting, for "resting" is only a polite way of saying no one has wanted to engage her, and that she is "out of a shop," which all actresses hate.

CHAPTER III

I HAVE forced George's hand, so I am told, and neither he nor mother take any notice of me.

But Aunt Gerty hugged me all over when she heard what I had done, and scolded Mother for not being nice to me.

"I don't see why you need put that poor child in Coventry?" she said. "You had more need to be grateful to her than not. How much longer was it going to go on, I want to know? Hiding away his lawful wife like an old Bluebeard, and me Sister Anne boiling over and wanting to call it all from the house-tops!"

"Well, Gerty, you seem to have got it a bit mixed!" said Mother. "But, talking of Bluebeard, I always envied the first Mrs. B. the lots of cupboard room she must have had! I wonder if she was a hoarder, like me, who never have the heart to throw anything away? If I do happen to see the plans for the new house, I will speak up for lots of cupboards, and that is all I care about."

"See the plans! Why, of course you will! Isn't it your right? You must make a point of seeing them and putting your word in. Look after your own comfort in this world or you will jolly well find yourself out in the cold, and 'specially with a husband like you've got!"

"Bother moving!" said Mother, in her dreary way that comes when she has been overdoing it, as she has lately. "It is an odious wrench; just like having all one's teeth out at once."

"Hadn't need! Yours are just beautiful. One of your points, Lucy, and don't you forget it."

"The life here suited me well enough; I had got used to it, I suppose."

"You can get used to something bad, can't you, but that's no reason you are not to welcome a change? Oh, you'll like the new life that's to be spent up-stairs in the daylight, above-board like, instead of this kind of 'behind the scenes' you have been doing for eighteen years. And a pretty woman still, for so you are. Cheer up! You are going to get new scenery, new dresses, new backcloth——"

"You see everything through the stage, Gerty. I must say it irritates one sometimes, especially now, when——"

"I know what you mean. No offence, my dear old sis. And you can depend on me not to be bringing the smell of the footlights, as they call it—it's the only truly pleasant smell there is, to my idea!—into your fine new house. Pity but *He* can't get a little whiff of it into his comedies, and some manager would see his way to putting them on, perhaps? No, beloved, me and George don't cotton to each other, nor never shall. He isn't my sort. I like a man that is a man, not a society baa-lamb! Baa! I've no patience with such——"

"Sh', Gerty. You seem to forget his child sitting messing away with her paints in a corner so quietly there!"

That was me. Aunt Gerty stopped a minute, and then they went on just the same.

"We have never minded the child yet" (which was true), "and I don't see why we should begin now. Tempe is getting quite a woman and able to hold her tongue when needful. And she knows her way about her precious father well enough. What you've to think of now, Lucy, is getting your hands white, and the marks of sewing and cooking off. Lemons and pumice! Cream's good, too. You have been George Taylor's upper servant too long—Gracious, who's that at the front-door?"

Aunt Gerty nearly knocked me over in her rush to the window. We were all three sitting in the front bedroom, which is George's, when he is at home, and Mother had been washing my hair. It was a dreadfully hot day—a dog-day, only we haven't any dogs, but the kittens were tastefully arranged in the spare wash-basin all round the jug for coolness. They had put themselves there. We humans had got very little clothes on, partly for heat and also having got out of the habit of dressing in the afternoons, for no callers ever came to The Magnolias. But there were some now. There was a big, two-horsed thing at the door such as I have often seen driving out to Hampton Court, but never, never had I seen one stop at our gate before. It was most exciting. I hoped Jessie Hitchings and her mother saw.

There were two ladies inside, one of them old and frumpy, the other was Lady Scilly, whom I knew, though Mother didn't. I haven't got to her yet in my story. A footman was taking their orders, and Sarah was standing at the door holding on to her cap that she'd forgotten to put a pin in. Lucky she had a cap on at all! Mother doesn't like her to leave her caps off to go to the door, even when George isn't here, out of principle, and for once it told.

"For goodness sake get your head in, Gerty, you have got the shade a bit too strong to-day," cried Mother, pulling my aunt in by her petticoats, and nearly upsetting the mirror on the dressing-table. Aunt Gerty came in with a cross grunt, and we all sat well inside till we heard the carriage drive away and Sarah mounting the stairs all of a hop, skip and a jump.

"Please m'm!" she cried almost before she got into the room, "there's a carriage-and-pair just called——"

"Anything in it?" Mother said.

"Two ladies, m'm, and here's their cards."

I took one and Aunt Gerty the other.

"Dowager Countess of Fylingdales!" Aunt Gerty read, as if she was Lady Macbeth saying, "Out, dammed spot!"

The card I held was for Lady Scilly, and there was one for Lord Scilly, but it had got under the drawers.

"I said you wasn't dressed, ma'am," Sarah said, looking at Mother's apron all over egg, and her rolled-up sleeves.

"No more I am," said Mother, laughing. "Don't look so disappointed, Gerty. I couldn't have seen them."

"But you shouldn't have said your mistress wasn't dressed, Sarah," said Aunt Gerty. "It isn't done like that in good houses. You should have said, 'My mistress is gone out in *the* carriage.'"

"But that would have been a lie!" argued Sarah, "and I'm sure I don't want to go to hell even for a carriage-and-pair."

"Oh, where have you been before, Sarah," Aunt Gerty sighed, "not to know that a society lie can't let any one in for hell fire? Well, it is too late now; they have gone. And it was rather a shabby turnout for aristocratic swells like that, after all."

"They didn't really want to see me," said Mother. "They only called on me to please George. He sent them probably. I have heard him speak of Lady Fylingdales. He stays there. She is one of his oldest friends. She is lame and nearly blind. Lady Scilly I shall never like from what I have heard of her. Tempe, run in the garden in the sun and dry your hair. Off you go!"

"And get a sunstroke," thought I. "Just because she wants to talk to Aunt Gerty about the grand callers!"

So I stayed, and they have got so in the habit of not minding me that they went on as if I really had been out broiling in the sun.

Mother began to talk very fast about the new house, and getting visiting-cards printed, and taking her place in Society. These ladies coming had given her thoughts a fresh jog. She nearly cried over the bother of it all, and what George would now go expecting of her, and she with no education and no ambition to be a smart woman, as Aunt Gerty was continually egging her on to be, saying it was quite easy if you only had a nice slight figure, like she has.

"Bead chains and pince-nezs won't do it as you seem to think," Mother said. "And even if I get to be smart, I shall never get to be happy!"

"Happy!" screamed my Aunt Gertrude. "Who talked of being happy? You don't go expecting to be happy, unless it makes you happy, as it ought, to put your foot down on those stuck-up cats who have been leading your husband astray all these years, and giving them a good what-for. It would me, that's all I can say. Happiness indeed! It is something higher than mere happiness. What you have got to do, my dear Lucy, is just to take your call and go on—not before you've had a trip to Paris for your clothes, though—and show them all what a pretty woman George Taylor's despised wife is. There's an object to live for! That's your ticket, and you've got it. He married you for your looks, now, didn't he?"

"Nothing else," said Mother sadly.

"Nonsense! Weren't you—aren't you as good as he? You are the daughter of a respectable Irish clergyman. Whose daughter—I mean son—is he? A French tailor's, I expect. You married him eighteen years ago in Putney Parish Church by special licence, when he was nothing and nobody cared whom or what he married. Little flighty, undersized foreign-looking creature! You have been a good wife to him, borne his children, nursed him when he was ill, and kept a house going for him to come back to when he was tired of the others, and if it's been done on the sly, it hasn't been through any will of yours! And now that the matter has been taken out of his hands, and a good thing too, and he's obliged to leave off his dirty little tricks and own you, and send his grand friends to call on you, and build a nice house to put you in, you want to back out and hide yourself—lose your chance once for all and for ever! You are good-looking, your children are sweet—you'll soon catch them all up, and then you can be as haughty and stuck-up as the rest of them. If it is *me* you are thinking of, I shan't trouble you—I have my work and I mean to stick to it!"

"I shall never disown you, Gerty."

"No, I dare say not, but I shan't put myself in the way of a snub. I've got one thing that's been very useful to me in this life—that's tact. I shan't make a nasty row or a talk, but you'll not see more of me than you want to. I'm a lady—I'll never let anybody deny that—but I've knocked about the world a bit, and it's a rough place, and that soft dainty manner people admire so, rubs off pretty soon fighting one's own battles. The aristocracy can afford to keep it on. Clothes does it, largely. Where you're wearing chiffon, I'll be wearing linen, that's the diff. Now I'm off—'on' first act and share a dresser with three other cats, where there isn't room to swing one. Ta-ta! I'm not as vulgar as you think!"

She put on her picture-hat carefully with sixteen pins in it, and went away. Mother asked me why I hadn't been drying my hair in the garden all this time? Because I wanted to hear what Aunt Gerty had to say, I answered, and Mother accepted the explanation. But now I went and found a cool place and meditated on my sins.

I am not what is called a strictly naughty child. I am too busy. Satan never need bother about me or find mischief for me to do, for my hands are never idle, and I can generally find it for myself.

On the eventful morning that decided our fate three weeks before this incident, I was in the drawing-room, where we hardly ever sit, making devils with George's name with the ink out of the best inkstand. I spilt it. Why do these things happen? It is the fault of fatality.

There is nothing I hate more than the sickening smell of spilt ink, or rather, the soapy rags they chose to rub it up with, so I went up to my room quietly intending to get my hat and go out till it had blown over, or rather soaked in. Sarah was there, tidying or something, and she said immediately, "Now whatever have you been up to?" I told her that the word "ever" was quite surplus in that sentence, and that George objected to it strongly. Thus I got away from her, wishing I had a less expressive face.

I found myself in the street without an object. I have got beyond the age of runaway rings, thank goodness, but they did use to amuse me, till one day an old gentleman got hold of me and went on about the length of kitchen stairs generally, and the shortness of cooks' legs, and the cruel risk of things boiling over. He changed my heart. So this day I just walked along to a motor-car, that I saw at the end of the next street but one, standing in front of the "Milliner's Arms," with nobody in it. I expected the man was having a drink, for it was piping hot. I got into the car and sat down, and just put my hand on the twirly-twirly thing in front, considering if I should set the car going. It was the very first time I had ever been in a motor in my life, and I simply hadn't the heart to miss the chance.

A lady came out of the Public. I never saw anything so pretty, and her dress was all billowy, like the little fluffy clouds we call Peter's sheep in a blue sky, and the hem of it was covered with sawdust off the public-house floor. Yet I can't say she looked at all tipsy.

"I wanted a pick-me-up so badly, I just had to go in and get it." She said this in an apologizing sort of way, while I was just wondering how I should explain my presence in her car. She settled that for me, by saying with a little sweet smile, "Well, you pretty child, how do you like my motor-car?"

"It is the first time I——"

"Oh, of course! Would you like to be in one while it is on the move?"

I confessed I should, and she jumped in beside me, saying, "Sit still, then, child!" and moved the crissy-cross starfish thing in front, and we were off.

Mercy, what a rate! Policemen seemed to hold up their hands in amazement at us, and she looked pleased and flattered. We drove on and on, past the Hounslow turning, through miles of nursery gardens and then miles of slums, till at last the houses got smarter and bigger, and I guessed this was the part of London where George lives, only I did not ask questions. I hardly ever do. I did see a clock once, and I saw it was nearly our lunch time. I realized that I had missed rice-pudding for once, and was glad. She talked all the way along, and I listened. I find that is what people like, for she kept telling me that I was a nice child, and that she thought she should run away with me.

"You *are* running away with me," I said.

"And you don't care a bit, you very imperturbable atom! I think I shall take you home with me to luncheon. You amuse me."

She amused *me*. She was a darling—so gay, so light, as if she didn't care about anything, and had never had a stomach-ache in her whole life. If George's high-up friends are like this, I don't wonder he prefers them to Aunt Gerty. Mother can be as amusing as anybody,—I am not going to try to take Mother down—but even she can't pretend she is happy as this woman seemed to be. She was like champagne,—the very dry kind George opens a bottle of when he is down, and gives Mother and me a whole glassful between us.

We were quite in a town now, and on a soft pavement made of wood, like my bedroom floor. The streets, oddly enough, grew grander and narrower. She told me about the houses as we went along.

"That is where my uncle, the Duke of Frocester, lives," she said, and pointed to a kind of grey tomb, with a paved courtyard in a very tiny street. I knew that name—the name of the man George stays and shoots with—but of course I didn't say anything. Then we passed a funny little house in a smaller street called after a chapel, and there was a fanlight over the door, and a great extinguisher thing on the railings.

"You have no idea what a lovely place that is inside," she told me. "A great friend of mine lives there, and pulled it about. He took out all the inside of the house, and made false walls to the rooms. One of them has just the naked bricks and mortar showing, but then the mortar is all gilt. He always has quantities of flowers, great arum lilies shining in the gloom, and oleanders in pots, and stunted Japanese trees. He gives heavenly tea-parties and little suppers after the play. He writes plays, but somehow they have never been acted that I know of? Bachelors always do you so well. I declare, if I wasn't going to see him this very afternoon at my club, I would go in and surprise him, now that I have got you with me, you little elf! You have certainly got the widest open eyes I ever saw. He is probably in there now, working at his little table in the window, getting up the notes for his lecture, so we should put him out abominably. I will take you to the lecture instead. And remind me to lend you one of his books,—that is, if your mother allows you to read novels."

I explained to her that I was a little off novels, as my father kept us on them.

"Oh, does he? How interesting! I love authors! You must introduce him to me some day. Bring him to one of my literary teas. I always make a point of raising an author or so for the afternoon. It pleases my crowd so, far better than music and recitations, and played-out amusements of that kind; and then one doesn't have to pay them. They are only too glad to come and get paid in kind looks that cost nothing. The queerer they are, the more people believe in them. I used to have Socialists, but really they were *too* dirty! Some authors now are quite smart, and wear their hair no longer than Lord Scilly, or so very little longer. Now, there is Morrell Aix, the man who wrote *The Laundress*. I took him up, but he had been obliged, he said, to live in the slums for two years to get up his facts, and you could have grown mustard and cress on the creases of his collar. And I do think, considering the advertisement he gave them, the laundresses might have taken more trouble with the poor man's shirts!"

I knew Mr. Aix, of course, and I have often seen Mother take the clothes-brush to him, but I said nothing, for I like to show I can hold my tongue. Knowledge is power, if it's ever so unimportant. We didn't go far from the house with walls like stopped teeth, before she pulled up at another rather smart little door in a street called Curzon.

"Here we are at my place, and there's Simmy Hermyre on the doorstep waiting to be asked to lunch."

It was a nice clean house with green shutters and lovely lace curtains at the windows, that Ariadne would have been glad of for a dress, all gathered and tucked and made to fit the sash as if it had been a person. The young man standing at the front door had a coat with a waist, and a nice clean face, and a collar that wouldn't let him turn his head quickly. He helped us out, and she laughed at him as if he was hers.

"Are you under the impression that I have asked you to lunch? Why, I don't suppose there is any!"

Imagine her saying that when she had brought me all the way from Isleworth to have it! I didn't, of course, say anything, and she made me go in, and the young man followed us, quite calm, although she had said there wasn't anything for him to eat.

"I would introduce you to this person" (I thought it so nice of her not to stick on the offensive words little or young!) "only it strikes me I don't know her name." She didn't ask it, but went on, "It's a most original little creature, and amused me more in an hour than you have in a year, my dear boy!"

Now, had I said anything particularly amusing? I hadn't tried, and I do think you should leave off calling children "it" after the first six months. Mothers hate it.

Still, though I didn't think her quite polite, I told her my name—Tempe Vero-Taylor—in a low voice so that she could introduce me to her great friend, as we were going to lunch at the same table. I thought there wouldn't be a children's table, as she didn't speak of children, and I was glad, for children eat like pigs and have no conversation.

Her eyebrows went up and her mouth went down, but she soon buttoned up her lips again, though they stayed open at the corners, and didn't introduce me to Mr. Hermyre at all. I didn't suppose I should ever meet him again, so it didn't matter.

We went in and had lunch, and it was quite a grand lunch, hot, and as much again cold on a side-table. But I was actually offered rice-pudding! I wouldn't have believed it, in a house like this. I refused rather curtly, but she ate it, and very little else. I generally take water at home, but I did not see why I shouldn't taste champagne when I had the chance, and I took a great deal, quite a full glass full, and when I had taken it, I felt as if I could fight a lion. George often says when he comes back from London that he has been fighting with wild beasts at Ephesus. I wondered if I might not meet some this afternoon at the lecture at the Go-ahead Club? Lady Scilly (that's her name) said she must take me, and I knew I should be bored, but I couldn't very well say no.

"You may come too, Simmy," she said to the young man; "it will be exciting, I can promise you!"

"Not if I know it," he said. Then he tried to be kind and said, "What is the lecture about?"

"The Uses of Fiction."

"None, that I can see, except to provide some poor devil with an income."

"That's a man's view."

"It is," he said, "a man, and not a monkey's. You don't call your literary crowd men, do you?"

I was just wondering what he did call them, when Lady Scilly shut him up, and I thought she looked at me. Presently he went on—

"You're quite spoiling your set, you know, Paquerette. I used to enjoy your receptions."

"I don't see why you should permit yourself to abuse my set because you're a fifth cousin. That's the worst of being well connected, so many people think they have the right to lecture one!"

"All the better for you, my dear! Do you suppose now, that if you were not niece to a duke and cousin to a marquis, that Society would allow you to fill your house with people like Morrell Aix and Mrs. Ptomaine and Ve——"

Lady Scilly jumped up and said she must go and dress, and if he wouldn't come to the lecture he must go, and pushed me out of the room in front of her and on up-stairs.

"Good-bye!" she called to him over the bannisters. "Let yourself out, and don't steal the spoons."

That was a funny thing to say to a friend, not to say a relation! We went up into her bedroom, and her old nurse—I suppose it was her nurse, for she wore no cap and bullied her like anything—came forward.

"Put me into another gown, Miller!" she said, flopping into a chair. Miller did, putting the skirt over her head as if she had been a child, and even pulling her stockings up for her. Then she had a try at tidying me.

"Don't bother. The child's all right. She's so pretty she can wear anything."

I think personal remarks rude even if she does think me pretty, but I said nothing. She looked at herself very hard in the glass, and we went down-stairs and got into the motor again. Lady Scilly sat with her hand in mine, and a funny little spot of red on the top of the bone of her cheek that I hadn't noticed there before. It was real.

CHAPTER IV

WE went into a house and into a large empty room with whole streets of coggley chairs and a kind of pulpit thing in the middle. A jug of water and a tumbler stood on it. There was a governessy-looking person present, presiding over this emptiness, whom Lady Scilly immediately began to order about. She was the secretary of the club, and Lady Scilly is a member of the committee.

"Where will you sit, Lady Scilly?" said this person, and she asked a good many other questions, using Lady Scilly's name very often.

"I shall sit quite at the back this time," Lady Scilly answered. "Too many friends immediately near him might put the lecturer out!" As she said this she looked at me wickedly, but I could not think why.

We then went away and read the comic papers for a little until the place had filled. In the reading-room we met a gentleman, who seemed to be a great friend of Lady Scilly's. He spoke to me while she was discussing some arrangement or other with the secretary, who had followed her.

"How do you like going about with a fairy?" he asked me.

"I'm not," I said. "She's a grown-up woman, old enough to know——"

"Worse!" he interrupted me. "She is what I call a fairy!"

"What is a fairy?" I asked, though he seemed to me very silly, and only trying to make conversation.

"A fairy is a person who always does exactly as she likes—and as other people sometimes don't like."

"I see," I said, as usual, although I did not see, as usual, "just as grown-up people do."

"But she isn't pretty when she is old! I wonder if you will grow up a fairy? No, I think not, you don't look as if you *could* tell a lie."

"I beg your pardon," I said. He then remarked that Lady Scilly had sent him to take me into the room where the lecture was to be given, and we went. Of course I politely tried to let age go first, but he didn't like that, and said "*Jeunesse oblige*," and "*Place aux dames*," and "*Juniores ad priores*"—every language under the sun, winding up with that silly old story about the polite Lord Stair, who was too polite to hang back and keep the king waiting.

"Oh yes, I know that story," I said, just to prevent him going on bothering. "It's in Ollendorff."

The lecture-room was quite full, and we—Lady Scilly and I—squeezed ourselves in at the back in a kind of cosy corner there was, and we were almost in the dark.

"Sit tight, child, whatever happens!" she kept saying, and held my hand as if I should run away. When among a rain of claps the lecturer came in I saw why, for it was George!

Lady Scilly grabbed my arm, and said, "Don't call out, child!"

As if I was going to! But now I saw why she had kept calling him the lecturer instead of saying his name whenever she had spoken of him before. Now I saw why she was so full of nods and winks and grins, and had brought me to the lecture so particularly. Now I saw why the old gentleman had called her a fairy—that meant a tease, and I wasn't going to gratify her by seeming upset or anything. Not I! So I sat quite still as she told me, and George began.

I borrowed a pencil of the Ollendorff man, and put down some notes to remind me of what George said, for Ariadne. It took me some time to get used to the funny little voice George put on to lecture with, quite different to his Isleworth voice. Presently when I began to catch on a little I found that the lecture was all about novels and the good of them, as Lady Scilly had said. This is the sort of thing—

"*A novel,*" said my father, "*is apt to hold a group of quite ordinary, uninteresting characters, wallowing in their clammy, stale environment, like fishes in an aquarium, held together by a thin thread of narrative, and bounded by the four walls of the author's experience. His duty is to enlarge that experience, for to novels we go, not so much for amusement as for a criticism of Life. That portion of life which comes under the reader's own observation is naturally so restricted, so vastly disproportionate, to the whole great arcana.*" (I do hope I got this down right!) "*The novelist should be omniscient and omnipotent.*" (Once I got these two great words, all the rest seemed child's play.) "*A great responsibility lies with the purveyors of this necessary panorama of existence, the men who monopolize the furnishing and regulating of the supply.*" (Loud applause.) "*The right man, or peradventure, the right woman*" (he bowed at Lady Scilly), "*knows, or ought to know, so many sides, while the reader, alas, knows but one, and is so tired of that one!*"

Everybody sighed and groaned a little to show how tired they were, and George went on—

"*I see my audience is in touch with me. It works both ways.*" (What works both ways? I must have left something out.) "*A Duchess of my acquaintance said some poignant, pregnant words—as indeed all her words are pregnant and poignant*" (he bowed to an old corpulent lady in another part of the room)—"*to me the other day. She said that her novel of predilection was not a society novel. 'I know it all, don't I, like the palm of my hand?' she* objected. '*I know how to behave in a drawing-room and how not to behave in a boudoir!*' So she complained. *The substance of her complaint, as I understand it, is this;— what she wants is worlds not realized! She wants to see the actress in her drawing-room, the flower-girl in her garret, the laundress at her tub, the burglar at his work——*"

Here George made a little bob at Mr. Aix in the audience, for there he was, and there was another fit of clapping. Then he went on—

"*I mean to say that what we mostly seek in fiction is to be taken out of our own lives, and put into somebody else's— to temporarily change our moral environment. High life is deeply interested in what is going on below stairs. Bill Sykes and 'Liza of Lambeth, if they have any time for reading, want to know all about countesses and their attendant sprites.*" (Fancy calling Simon Hermyre that!) "*The Highest or the Lowest, but no middle course, is the novelist's counsel of perfection. There is no second class in the literary railway.*

"*Yet there is a serious issue involved in this proposition. If, for instance—only for instance, for I am very sure that most of us here will have to rely on imagination, not fact, to support my illustration—if our home is a suburban one, and our wildest actual dissipation a tea-party in Clapham or Tooting—even Clapham Rise or Upper Tooting—we must transport ourselves in seven-league boots to the better quarters of London, to visualize the giddy cultured throng in the halls of Belgravia, and set down accurately the facile*

*inaccuracies of the small talk of Mayfair. It is the tale of the
mad, bad great world that sets the heart of the matron of
Kennington Common aflame, and makes her waking
dreams 'all a wonder and a wild desire.' Que voulez vous?
She is our staple standing reader. She does not want to bend
her chaste thoughts towards Hornsey Rise and Cricklewood,
to envisage, stimulated by the novelist's art, its bursten
boilers, its infant woes, its humdrum marrying and giving
in marriage. No, she prefers, in her grey unlovely Jerry-built
parlour, to gloat over the morbid, rose-coloured sins that are
enacted in the halls of fashion; the voluptuous sorrows of the
Bridge-end of the week; the mystery of Royal visits postponed
are her chosen pabulum. To all these novelists whose ways
are cast in safe and humdrum middle-class places I would
say that they had best ignore their entourage as a help to
local colour. In this case, character drawing, like charity,
should not begin at Home. Go out, go out, young man, from
thy homely nest in the suburbs, where the females of thy
family hang over their flaccid meat teas in faded blouses—
—"*

I think it was about here that I half got up, quite
determined, and Lady Scilly pinched me in several places
at once.

"Don't nip me, please," I said. "I think somebody
ought to get up and tell George he's drivelling, and if
nobody else does, I will."

"Bless the child!" she said. "You may answer him when he's done, if you like, and can. It will be quite amusing."

I think that she really was a fairy, but never mind! I did think somebody ought to stop George, and take Mother's side. So I waited, though I stopped my ears and would not listen to any more till George sat down and the secretary lady asked if some one would care to answer Mr. Vero-Taylor's speech? Lady Scilly poked me up, and I got up so that George and all of them could see me, and I didn't feel a bit shy—no, for I had something to say, and off I went, to speak up for Mother who wasn't there to speak up for herself.

"Ladies and Gentlemen," I said—I noticed that George began like that—"I don't agree at all with what the gentleman—who is my father—has been saying about Tooting—Upper Tooting, I mean. He ought to be more patriotic, as he lives at Isleworth, which is pretty nearly the same thing, part of his time anyhow, and I suppose he needn't do it unless he likes. And as for what he says about Mother, why, I can tell everybody that Mother doesn't read novels about Duchesses or anybody. She hasn't time, she's much too busy in the house, bringing us up, and cooking specially for George, and so on. That's all!"

I sat down with a bump. George seemed to subside, and I lost him, but I hardly expected him to come and hug me. Lady Scilly went and comforted him, perhaps! I don't know what happened, except tea and coffee, but I didn't feel inclined, and I asked Mr. Aix to take me home.

He did, in a hansom. He held my hand all the way. We didn't talk, but I am sure he wasn't cross with me, and held my hand to show it. He seemed to know I was going to have a bad time.

I did. Even Mother scolded me.

Papa didn't come near us for a week, and when he was due I asked if I might have a cold and be in bed. God sent me a real cold to make me truthful. Aunt Gerty nursed me. It wasn't so bad. She read to me about Thumbelina and Boadicea, my two favourite heroines, one big and the other little, and poetry about my painted boy, which I love and that always makes me go to sleep. I believe it is spelt with a u, and doesn't mean a child at all. But, I like it best my way—

"We left behind the painted buoy
That tosses at the harbour-mouth,
And madly danced our hearts with joy

While I was ill, though, I missed all the discussions about moving, and the results of the lecture and all that. Ariadne reported what she could. She said that Mother and George never mentioned me, but talked as if the drains had gone wrong, or a pipe had burst, or as if George had lost a lot of money somehow. Everything is to be altered and the world will be topsy-turvey when I get down-stairs again. Though I don't suppose that even if I did get a chance of putting my word in, I could alter anything as I wished it? These grown-ups, once they get the bit between their teeth——!

CHAPTER V

IT is no fun for George now, when everybody knows he is a married man. Lady Scilly took care of that, and told everybody as a good joke, and all her friends at the Go-ahead Club told their friends how George Vero-Taylor's little girl had burst into the middle of his lecture there and given him away—such fun, don't you know! It wasn't fun for me, for I had nothing but the consciousness of a bad action to support me in Coventry, where they all put me for a month. It wouldn't have mattered so much if George hadn't been at home a good deal about that time. I think I prefer George as a visitor, and so does Elizabeth Cawthorne, though she says it is more natural perhaps for a gentleman to stop with his family, though wearing to the servants.

George is a philosopher. He has been forced to own up to a family, and thus has lost a certain amount of prestige, but he is now trying a new line. At any rate, he has been a good deal talked about, and got into the newspapers, and that will sell an edition, I should think. He has a volume on the stocks. Misfortunes never come single-handed, luckily. He settled to build a house—a house that should express him and shelter his family as well. Mother didn't want to build. If we *had* to move, she wanted a dear little house on the river at Datchet, or even at Surbiton, and she and I used to go down for the day third-class to see if there were any to let. We used to take a packet of sandwiches and a soda-water bottle full of milk for us both. Mother never hardly touches spirits.

In this way we looked over heaps of little earwiggeries trimmed with clematises and pots of geraniums hanging from the balconies, with their poor roots higher than their heads, and manicured lawns right down to the water's edge. George didn't stop our doing this and taking so much trouble; I believe he thought it amused us and did him no harm. But all the time, he was hansoming it backwards and forwards to St. John's Wood, where he meant to settle. He quietly chose a site, and bought it, and was his own architect, though a little Mr. Jortin he discovered, made the plans from his dictation. He got no credit, except for the blunders. George, being a man of the widest culture, wanted to show the world that he can do other things than write books. In *Who's Who*, he doesn't mention writing as one of his occupations, not even as one of his amusements. These are Riding, Driving, Shooting, Fishing, Fencing, Polo, Rotting and Log-rolling, or at least, that's what his friend Mr. Aix read out to us one afternoon he came to see us, out of the very newest edition, and George was in the room too, and laughed.

All this time Ariadne and I were kept hard at it copying things. George talked of nothing but atriums and tricliniums and environments. I only interrupted once, when I said that they had never mentioned a main staircase, and was it going to be outside, like those wooden ones you see in the country, with the fowls stepping up to bed on them? They thanked me, and added an inside stairs to the plan at once.

As soon as we get into the new house, George intends to raise his prices. He expects to get ten pounds per "thou." He told Middleman, his literary agent, so. Up to now his price was four pound ten per "thou." for articles, and the royalties on his last book are going to pay for the new house. Middleman says George will be quite right to charge establishment charges. Middleman is supposed to have a faint, very faint sense of humour, and that's the only way people get at him. Mr. Aix says Middleman can run up an author's sales twenty per cent. in no time, if he fancies you personally, or thinks there's money in you.

George's new book is going to be not mediæval this time; people have imitated him and *The Adventures of Sir Bore and Sir Weariful* was brought out just to plague him, so he is going to quit that for a time. He thinks that the Isles of Greece would be a good place to dump a few English aristocrats and tell their adventures on. He will go abroad soon, but is waiting for some of the aristocrats to make up a party and pay his expenses.

Meanwhile Cinque Cento House, as it is to be called, rose like a thief in the night, and as it grew higher and higher Mother's face grew longer and longer. She refused to go near it, and it was Lady Scilly who helped George to arrange the furniture.

Aunt Gerty, however, is practical, and tried to get Mother to take some interest in her own mansion.

"I do," Mother said, "but at a distance. I couldn't be of any use advising, and whatever I advised, George would still take his own way. That odious woman, whom I thank God I have never set eyes on, is always about, and would put my back up if I met her there, and I should say things I should be sorry for after. No, Gerty, let them arrange it as they like, and buy furniture and set it up. It is George's own money. He earned it."

"Not by the sweat of his brow, at all events!" sneered my aunt.

"I came to him without a penny, and I haven't the right to dictate so much as the position of a wardrobe."

"You're the man's lawful wife," said Aunt Gerty, as she always did. One got tired of the expression.

"Yes, unfortunately," said Mother. "Or I'd have a better chance! But I am *not* going to fight over George with that minx!"

How Mother did hate Lady Scilly, to be sure, a person she had never seen! I once told her she needn't be cross with Lady Scilly, and how harmless she was, and how very little she really thought of Papa—snubbed him even, and treated him like dirt; and then she was cross with *me*, and said George was a man of whom any woman might be proud.

Ariadne and I went over to the new house often, to get measurements for blinds and curtains and things at home. Mother made them, and then we took them round. Lady Scilly was always there, from twelve to two, and George generally met her and they shut themselves into first one room and then another, discussing it. Vanloads of furniture kept coming in, and all George's furniture from his old rooms in Mayfair. She kept saying—

"Oh, that dear old marquetry cabinet! How I remember it in Chapel Street, and how the firelight caught it in the evenings!" or else—"That sweet little pair of Flemish bellows? Do you remember when you and I"—something or other?

She marched about and settled everything. George took it quite mildly, and made jokes, at least I suppose they were jokes, for he made her laugh consumedly, so she said. It's extraordinary how he can make people laugh—people out of his own family!

She is very friendly to me and Ariadne, and has promised to present Ariadne at the next Court. It's to please George, if she does remember to do it. But if I were Ariadne I should refuse till my own mother had been presented first, so that she could introduce me herself. George ought to insist on it, but he always says "Let them rave!" and that means, Do as you like, but don't bother me. What he won't like will be forking out forty pounds for Ariadne's dress, and it will end by her staying at home. Ariadne wants to be presented badly; she is practising curtseys already, and longing for the season to begin. I would not condescend to owe even a pleasure to Lady Scilly, but Ariadne is so poor-spirited, and Aunt Gerty continually advises her to take what she can get, and make what she can out of George's "mash," when well disposed.

About Easter, George got his chance. Lady Scilly proposed a month's yachting trip in the Mediterranean in somebody's yacht that they were willing to lend her, on condition she invited her own party and included them. If I had a yacht, I would ask my own party, that is all I can say. She asked George to go with them—"We shan't see more of Mr. Pawky (i.e. the owner) than we can help, and you can have a study on board and write a yachting novel, like William Black's, and put old Pawky in. He is quite a character, you know, with a gilded liver, as they say—dyspeptic and all that. I can't stand him, but you might bear with him a little in the interests of Art!" George had no objection to visiting the scene of his new book at Mr. Pawky's expense, in the company of his own pals, and accepted at once. I wonder if they will batten down the hatches on Mr. Pawky as soon as they get out to sea, and keep him there for the rest of the voyage? It would be just like them.

George proposed to Mother that she should move in while he was away. He said somebody must go in to get the painters out. Then he would come home fresh and full of material, and find his study organized and everything ready for him to begin. He said there would be ructions, inseparable from a first installation, and that would put him off work abominably, and spoil the whole brewing!

"Dear," said Mother, "I fear we shall do badly without you—you are a man, at least—but I'll be good, and spare you cheerfully!"

So he went. Then Mother set to work, and was perfectly happy. There was to be a sale in this house, because the furniture in it would not go with what George and Lady Scilly had chosen for Cinque Cento House, but there were some old pieces Mother could not do without. Her nice brass bedstead, and the old nursery fender that Ariadne nearly hanged herself on once in a fit of naughtiness, and of course all the bedding and linen and kitchen utensils from "The Magnolias"—one could hardly suppose Lady Scilly had troubled herself about that sort of thing? The greengrocer "moved" us for two pounds. Mother and Aunt Gerty and the cook saw the things off at Isleworth, and Ariadne and I and Kate—Sarah had gone, and I never got any better reason than that she "had to"—received them at Cinque Cento House. Mother had stuck to it, that she would not go near the place till she went in for good, so it was to be all quite new to her and Aunt Gerty. Ariadne and I, who had been in and out for months, wondered how they would like it, and expected some sport when their eyes first fell on it.

We had a long delightful day of anticipation, and putting things where they had to go, and in the evening Mother and Aunt Gerty came. They had got out of the train at Swiss Cottage, and asked their way to their own house. Aunt Gerty had her mouth wide open; Mother had hers tight shut. She was not intending to carp or pass opinions, but the front-door knocker was a regular slap in the face, and took her breath away.

She tried to talk of something else, and whispered to Aunt Gerty, "Rather an inconvenient place for a coal-shoot, isn't it! Right alongside the front-door!"

I hastened to explain that that was the larder-window she saw, to prevent unpleasantness.

Mother shivered when she got into the hall, which is vast and flagged with marble like a church. "It strikes very cold to the feet!" she said to Aunt Gerty. "Mine are like so much ice."

"Oh, come along, and we'll brew you a glass of hot toddy!" Aunt Gerty said cheerfully. "It's a bit chilly, I think, myself, but 'ansom, like the big 'all where 'Amlet 'as the players!"

Aunt Gerty is generally most careful, but she is apt to drop a little h or so when she is excited. She could hardly contain herself, as Ariadne and I had hoped, when she saw the gilt stairs leading up into the study.

"What price broken legs? Why, I shall have to get roller-skates or take off my shoes and stockings to go up them!"

"So you will, Aunt Gerty," said Ariadne. "It is one of George's rules. He made Lady Scilly even leave off her high heels before she used them."

"Took 'em off for her himself with his lily hands, I suppose?" snorted my aunt. "Well, I don't expect you will find me treading those golden stairs very often. I ain't one of George's elect."

"Such wretched things to keep clean," Mother complained. "The servants are sure to object to the extra work, and give up their places, and I am sure one can't blame them, and such good ones as we've got, too, in these awful times, when looking for a cook is like looking for a needle in a bottle of hay. Heavens, is the girl there all the time listening to me?"

Kate was, luckily, down-stairs, showing Elizabeth Cawthorne the way about her kitchen, or else it would have been very imprudent to tell a servant how valuable she is. Mother was cowed by the danger she had escaped, but Aunt Gerty went on flouncing about, pricing everything and tinkling her nails against pots and jugs, till she stopped suddenly and put her muff before her face—

"Well, of all the improper objects to meet a lady's eye coming into a gentleman's house! Who's that mouldy old statue of?"

I told her that was Autolycus.

"Cover yourself, Tollie, I would," Aunt Gerty said, going past him affectedly. "Oh, look, Lucy, at all those dragons and cockroaches doing splits on the fire-place! Brass, too, trimmed copper. My God!"

"I shall just have to clean that brass fire-place myself," said Mother. "I shall never have the face to ask Kate to do it."

"And no proper grate, only the bare bricks left showing!" Aunt Gerty wailed. "How could one get up any proper fireside feeling over a contraption like that! The Lyceum scenery is nothing to it. It makes me think of Shakespeare all the time—so *painfully* meretricious——"

Lady Castlewood in a basket under Mother's arm, suddenly began to mew very sadly. Aunt Gerty had put Robert the Devil down on the floor, in his hamper, and I suppose a draught got to him, for he spat loudly. Ariadne and I let out the poor things and they bounced straight out on to the parquet floor, and their feet slid from under them. I never saw two cats look so silly!

"Well, if a cat can't keep his feet on those wooden tiles," said Mother, "I don't suppose I can," and she jumped, just to try, right into the middle of a little square of blue carpet, which, true enough, slid along with her.

"You can give a nice hop here, at any rate," cried Aunt Gerty, catching her round the waist, and waltzing all over the room, till both their picture hats fell off, and hung down their backs by the pins. "Ask me and all the boys, and give a nice sit-down supper, and do us as well as the old villain will allow you."

She was quite happy. That is just like an actress! Ariadne and I danced too, and the cats mewed loudly for strangeness. Cats hate newness of any kind, and they weren't easy till I got some newspaper, crackled it, and let them sit on it, and then they were all right. Then Mother and Aunt Gerty rang the queer-shaped bell, as if it would sting them, and got up some coals which Mother had had the forethought to order in, and lit a modest little fire in a great cave with brass images in front of it under the kind of copper hood. It wouldn't draw at first, being used to logs, and when it smoked we threw water on it, lest we dirtied the beautiful silk hangings. At last we fetched Elizabeth Cawthorne.

"Hout!" she said. "I'd like to see the fire that's going to get the better of me!"

She made it burn, sulkily, and Ariadne and I went to a shop we knew of round the corner, and bought tea and sugar and condensed milk, to make ourselves tea with the spirit-lamp Aunt Gerty had brought. We had no butter or bread, only biscuits luckily, so we couldn't stain the Cinque Cento chairs, whose gold trimmings were simply peeling off them. Sit on them we dared not, they would have let us down on the floor for a certainty. Mother and Aunt Gerty had a high old time blaming Lady Scilly for all her foolish arrangements, and then we all went down to the so-called kitchen to see how Elizabeth Cawthorne was getting on there. She was in a rage, but trying to pass it off, like a good soul as she is.

"Well, I never! Here's a gold handle to my coal-cellar door! I shall have to wipe my lily hands before I dare use it. And a fine lady of a dresser that I shall be shy to set a plain dish on. Beetles here, do you ask, woman?" (To Kate.) "They'd be ashamed to show their faces in such a smart place as this, I'm thinking. And what's this couple of drucken little candlesticks for the kitchen? Our Kate'll soon rive the fond bit handles from off them, or she's not the girl I take her for!"

She banged it hard against the dresser as servants do, to make it break, but it didn't, and she looked disappointed. Mother then suggested she should unpack a favourite frying-pan she never goes anywhere without, and sent Kate out for a pound and a half of loin-chops, and cook was to fry them for our dinners.

The kitchen fire, after all, was the only one that would burn, so we ate our chops there, and sat there till bed-time. Ariadne looked like a picture, sitting at a trestle-table, and a thing like a torch burning at the back of her head. She was thoroughly disgusted, and got quite cross, and so did Elizabeth, as the evening went on. She hated trestles, and flambeaus, and dark Rembrandtish corners, and couldn't lay her hand on her things nohow, so that when we all went up to bed, Mother said to her—

"Good-night, Elizabeth. You have been a bit upset, haven't you? I wonder we have managed to get through the day without a row!"

"So do I, ma'am," said the cook. "Heaps of times I'd have given you warning for twopence, but you never gave me ought to lay hold on."

A horrid wind sprang up and moaned us off to sleep. I thought once or twice of George out on the Mediterranean on a tippity yacht, and didn't quite want him to get drowned, though he had made us live in such an uncomfortable house. I had tried to colonize a little, and put up a photograph of Mother done at Ramsgate in a blue frame, to make me feel more at home. Ariadne had hung up all her necklaces on a row of nails. She has forty. There is one made of dried marrowfat peas, that she nibbles when she is nervous, and another of horse's jesses, or whatever you call them, sewn on red velvet. We have a bed each, costing fourteen-and-six. They are apt to shut up with you in them. There is no carpet in our room, and there are not to be any. We are to be hardy. Nothing rouses one like a touch of cold floor in the mornings, and cools one on hot nights better than the same. Our water-jug too is an odd shape. I tilted all the water out of it on to the floor the first time I tried to use it. It must be French, it is so small. I shall not wash my hands very often in the days to come, I fancy.

Ariadne began to get reconciled to our room when she had made up her mind it was like the bower of a mediæval chatelaine, or like Princess Ursula's bedroom in Carpaccio, but I prefer Early Victorian, and cried myself to sleep.

Next morning Ben come along; he had stayed all night at the Hitchings', in Corinth Road. Jessie Hitchings likes Ben best of the family. She may marry him, when he is grown up, if she likes. He has birth, but no education, so that will make them even. The only glimmering of hope I see for Ben is that in this house there seems to be no bedroom for him, unless it is a room at the top with all the water tanks in it, which makes me think perhaps George is going to send him to school? For the present we have arranged him a bed in the butler's pantry. Ben says perhaps George means him to be butler, as he has laid it down as a rule that only women servants are to be used in Cinque Cento House. They look so much nicer than men, George says; he likes a houseful of waving cap-ribbons. Mother thinks she can work a house best on one servant, and better still on none. George doesn't mind her having any amount of boys from the Home near here, but that doesn't suit Mother. She says one boy isn't much good, that two boys is only one and a half, and that three boys is no boy at all. I suppose they get playing together? Ariadne and I would, in their place, I know, and human nature is the same, even in a Home, though I can't call ours quite that.

CHAPTER VI

GEORGE makes a point of refusing to be interviewed. He hates it, unless it is for one of the best papers. Then he says that it is a sheer kindness, and that a successful man has no right to refuse some poor devil or other the chance of making an honest pound or two. So he suffers him gladly. He even is good enough to work on the thing a little in the proof: just to give the poor fellow a lift, and prevent him making a fool of himself and getting his facts all wrong. In the end George writes the whole thing entirely from beginning to end, and makes the man a present of a complete magazine article, and a very fine one too!

"I have been generous," he tells us. "I have offered myself up as a burnt sacrifice. I have given myself all, without reservation. I have nothing extenuated, everything set down in malice. I have owned to strange sins that I never committed, to idiosyncrasies that took me all my time to invent, and all to bump out an article by some one else. I have been butchered to make a journalistic holiday!"

This is all very nice and self-sacrificing of George, but this particular interview read very well when it came out, and made George seem a very interesting sort of man with some quaint habits, not half so funny as his real ones, though, and I think the interviewer might just as well have given those.

So, when I got a chance of telling the truth, I did, meaning to act for the best, and give Papa a good show and save him the trouble of telling it all himself, but nobody gave me credit for my good intentions, and kind heart.

In the first place, how dared I put myself forward and offer to see George's visitors! But the young man asked for me—at least, when he was told that George was out, he said might he see one of the young ladies? Of course I don't suppose that would have occurred to him, only I was leaning over the new aluminium bannisters, and caught his eye. Then an idea seemed to come into his head. The look of disappointment that had come over him when he was told that George was out changed to a little happy perky look, as if he had just thought of something amusing. He crooked his little finger at me as I slid down the bannister, and said would I do? and would he come in? Kate is a cheeky girl, but even the cook admits that Kate is not a patch upon me. Kate evidently didn't think it quite right, but she slunk away into the back premises, and left me to deal with the young man.

He handed me a card. I thought that very polite of him, and "*Mr. Frederick Cook*," and Representative of *The Bittern* down in the corner, explained it all to me. We take in about a hundred rags, and that's the name of one of them. It's called *The Bittern* because it booms people, so George says.

"I suppose you have come to interview my Father," I said. "I'm sorry, but he is out. Did you have an appointment?"

"No, I didn't," said the young man right out.

I liked his nice bold way of speaking; he was the least shy young man I ever met.

"I don't believe in appointments. The subject is conscious, primed, braced up, ready with a series of cards, so to speak, which he wishes to force on the patient public—a collection of least characteristic facts which he would like dragged into prominence. It is as if a man should go to the dentist with his mind made up as to the number of teeth that he is to have pulled out, a decision which should always rest with any dentist who respects himself."

He went running on like that, not a bit shy, or anything, and amused me very much.

"But then the worst of that is, you've got no appointment with George, and he is not here to have his teeth pulled out."

I really so far wasn't quite sure if he was an interviewer or a dentist, but I kept calm.

"All the better, my dear young lady, that is if you are willing to aid and abet me a little. Then we shall have a thundering good interview, I can promise you. You see, in my theory of interviewing, the actual collaboration of the patient—shall we call him?—is unnecessary. Indeed, it is more in the nature of an impediment. My method, which of course I have very few opportunities of practising, is to seek out his nearest and dearest, those who have the privilege—or annoyance—of seeing him at all hours, at all seasons, unawares. If a painter, 'tis the wife of his brush that I would question; if an author, the partner of his pen—do you take me?"

Yes, I "took" him, and as George had called me a cockatrice—a very favourite term of abuse with him—only that morning, and remembering how she swaggers about being George's Egeria, I said, "You'll have to go to Lady Scilly for that!"

"Quite so!" he said very naturally. "Your distinguished parent dedicated his last book to her, did he not? Did you approve, may I ask?"

"No," I said. "People should always dedicate all their works to their wife, whether they love her or not, that's what I think!"

"Quite so," he said again. "I see we agree famously, and between us we shall concoct a splendid interview. But now, if you would be so very good, and happen to have a small portion of leisure at your disposal——"

"I'll do what I can for you," I said, delighted at his nice polite way of putting things. "I'll take you round the house, shall I? Have you a Kodak with you? Would you like to take a snapshot at George's typewriter?"

"Certainly, if she is pretty," said the silly man, and I explained that Miss Mander was out, and that it was the machine I meant. He said one machine was very like another, but that if he might see the study, where so many beautiful thoughts had taken shape? He said it quite gravely, but I felt he was laughing in his jacket all the time.

"We'll take it all *seriam*!" I said, not wishing him to have all the fine words. "And we will begin at the beginning—I mean the atrium."

He had a little pocket-book in his hand, and he said, as I led the way through the hall, "You won't mind my writing things down as they occur to me?"

"Not at all!" I said. "If you will let me look at what you have written. I see you have put a lot already."

He laughed and handed me his book, and I read—

"*Through dusky suites, lit by stained glass windows, whose dim cloistral light, falling on lurid hangings and gorgeous masses of Titianesque drapery, and antique ebon panelling, irresistibly suggest the languorous mysteries of a mediæval palace....* Do you think your father will like this style?"

"You have made it rather stuffy—piled it on a good deal, the drapery and hangings, I mean!" I said. "Now that I know the sort of thing you write, I shan't want to read any more."

"I thought you wouldn't," he said, taking it back. "I'll read it to you. '*Behind this arras might lurk Benvenuto and his dagger*——'"

"Not Ben's dagger, but Papa's bicycle."

"We'll leave it there and keep it out of the interview," he said. "It would spoil the unity of the effect. '*On, on, through softly-carpeted ante-rooms where the footstep softer falls, than petals of blown roses on the grass....*'"

"I hate poetry!" I said. "And we mayn't walk on that part of the carpet for fear of blurring the Magellanic clouds in the pattern. Do you know anything about Magellanic clouds in carpets?"

"No, I confess I have never trod them before," he said, becoming all at once respectful to me. I expect he lives in a garret, and has no carpet at all, and I thought I would be good to him, and help him to bump out his article, and not cram him, but tell him where things really came from. So I drew his attention particularly to the aluminium eagle, and the pinchbeck serpent George picked up in Wardour Street. I left out George's famous yarn about the sack of our ancestral Palace in Turin in the fifteenth century, when the Veros were finally disseminated or dissipated, whichever it is. I don't believe it myself, but George always accounts for his swarthy complexion by his Italian grandmother. Aunt Gerty says it is all his grandmother, or in other words, all liver!

We went down-stairs into the study, which is the largest room in the house.

"Your father has realized the wish of the Psalmist," said *The Bittern* man. "*Set my feet in a large room!*"

"He likes to have room to spread himself," I said, "and to swing cats—books in, I mean."

"So your father uses missiles in the fury of composition?"

"Sometimes; but oftenest he swears, and that saves the books. He mostly swears. Look here!"

I had just found a piece of paper in Miss Mander's handwriting, and on it was written, "Selections from the nervous vocabulary of Mr. Vero-Taylor during the last hour."

The Bittern man looked at them, and, "By Jove! these are corkers!" he said. Then I thought perhaps I ought not to have let him see them. There was Drayton, the ironmonger's bill lying about too, and I saw him raise his eyebrows at the last item, "*To one chased brass handle for coal-cellar door.*"

"That's what I call being thorough!" said *The Bittern* man. "I'm thorough myself. See this interview when it is done!"

He was thorough. He looked at everything, and particularly asked to see the pen George uses. "Or perhaps he uses a stylograph?" he asked.

"Mercy, no!" I screamed out. "He would have an indigestion! This is his pen—at least, it is this week's pen. George is wasteful of pens; he eats one a week."

"Very interesting!" said he. "Most authors have a fetish, but I never heard of their eating their fetish before. This will make a nice fat paragraph. Come on!"

You see what friends we had become! We went into the dining-room, and I showed him the dresser, with all the blue china on, and the Turkey carpet spread on it, instead of a white one—that was how they had it in the Middle Ages. He sympathized with me about how uncomfortable Mediæval was, and if it wasn't for the honour and glory of it, how much we preferred Early Victoria, when the drawers draw, and the mirrors reflect—there's not one looking-glass in the house that poor Ariadne can see herself in when she's dressing to go out to a party—or chairs that will bear sitting on. Why, there are four in one room that we are forbidden to sit upon on pain of sudden death!

"Very hard lines!" said *The Bittern* man. "I confess that this point of view had not occurred to me. I shall give prominence to it in my article. Art, like the car of some fanatical Juggernaut, crushing its votaries——"

"Yes," I said. "Mother draped a flower-pot once, and sneaked Ariadne's photograph into a plush frame. You should have heard George! 'To think that any wife of his—' 'Cæsar's wife must be above suspicion!' And as for Ariadne, he had rather see her dead at his feet than folded in blue plush."

"Capital!" said *The Bittern* man. "All good grist for the interview! And now, will you show me the famous metal stairs of which I have heard so much? There are no penalties attached to that, I trust?"

"Except that we are not allowed to go up them—Ariadne and me—without taking our boots off first, for fear of scratching the polish. We have to strip our feet in the housemaid's pantry, and carry them up in our hands. That's rather a bore, you will admit!"

"And your father? Does he bow to his own decrees?"

"Oh, no!" I said. "Papa is the exception that proves the rule."

"Capital!" again remarked *The Bittern* man. "I am getting to know all about the great Mr. Vero-Taylor in the fierce light that beats upon the domestic hearth! But, by the way," he said, with a little crooked look at me, "it is usual—shall I say something about Mrs. Vero-Taylor? People generally like an allusion—just a hint of feminine presence—say the mistress of the house flitting about, tending her ferns, or what not?"

"You must put her in the kitchen, then," I said, "tending her servants. Would you like to see her?"

"I should not like to disturb her," he said politely. "Will you describe her for me?"

"Oh, mother's nice and thin—a good figure—I should hate to have one of those feather-beddy mothers, don't you know? But I don't really think you need describe her. I don't think she cares about being in the interview, thank you, but you may say that my sister Ariadne is ravishingly beautiful, if you like?"

"And what about you, Miss——?" he asked, looking at me.

"Tempe Vero-Taylor," I said. "But whatever you do, don't put me in! George would have a fit! He won't much like your mentioning Ariadne, but I don't see why she shouldn't have a show, if I can give her one."

"Very well," he said. "Your ladyship shall be obeyed. Now I really think I have got enough, unless——" I saw his eyes straying up-stairs.

"There's nothing much to see up those stairs, except George's bedroom, and I daren't take you in there. It is quite commonplace, too; not like the rest of the house, but very, *very* comfortable."

"Oho! Your father reminds me of the man who plays Othello, and doesn't trouble to black more than his face and arms," said *The Bittern* man. "And *your* rooms?"

"Oh, our rooms are cupboards. Bowers, George calls them, and says we have more room to keep our clothes in than the lady of a mediæval castle would have. Now that's all, and——"

The truth was, I wanted him to go before George came home, for I thought it might be awkward for me if I were found entertaining a newspaper man. George might have preferred to do his own interview, who knows? This reflection only just occurred to me, as all reflections do, too late. *The Bittern* man was very quick, however, and understood me. He thanked me very much, far more than he need, for on reflection I did not see how he was going to make an interview out of all the scrappy things I had told him, and I said so. He assured me I need be under no uneasiness on that score, that this particular interview would be unique of its kind, and would gain him great credit with his editor, and increase the circulation of the paper. If it had nothing else, he said, it would at least have a *succès de scandale*, at least I think that is what he said, for I don't understand French very well. While he was making all those pretty speeches we stood in the hall, and I heard the little grating noise in the lock that meant that George was fitting his key in, and oh, how I just longed to run away! But I didn't. George opened the door, and came in and shook off his big fur coat. Then he saw *The Bittern* man and came forward, and *The Bittern* man came forward too, with his funny little smile on his face that somehow reminds me of the Pied Piper we used to read of when we were little.

"I came from *The Bittern*," he said, and George nodded, to show he knew what for. "To ask you to grant me the favour of an interview——"

"I am sorry I happened to be out!" began George, and then I knew, by the sound of his voice, that *The Bittern* was a *good* paper. "But if it is not too late, I shall be happy——"

"No need, no need to trouble you now, my dear sir," the interviewer said, waving his hand a little. "I came, and I go not empty away, but with the material of a dozen articles of sovereign interest in my pocket. You left an admirable *locum tenens* in the person of your daughter here, who kindly consented to be my cicerone and relieved me of the necessity of troubling *you*. You will doubtless be relieved also. I shall have the pleasure of sending you a proof to-morrow. Good-day!"

And before George could say what he wanted to say, Mr. Cook had opened the door for himself and had gone. I said he had plenty of cheek. George said so, too, and a great deal worse. I was black and blue for a week, and *The Bittern* man never sent a proof after all, so when the article came out—"*Interviewing, New Style. A Talk with Miss Tempe Vero-Taylor,*"—I got some more. That is the first and last time I was ever interviewed. George has peculiar theories about interviewing, I see, and I shall not interfere with them in future. I should think Mr. Frederick Cook would get on, making tools of honest children to serve his ambition like that. George didn't punish him, of course, he is a power on a paper; while I am but a child in the nursery.

CHAPTER VII

I WONDER if other families have got tame countesses, who come bothering and interfering in their affairs? I don't mind our having a house-warming party at all, but I do hate that it should be to please Lady Scilly.

"A party! A party!" she said to George, clasping her hands in her silly way. "My party on the table!" like the woman in the play of *Ibsen*. "Ask all the dear, amusing literary people that I adore. And I'll bring a large contingent of smart people, if I may, to meet them. Please, *please*!"

I don't know what a contingent is, but I fancy it's something disagreeable. Lady Scilly is George's friend, not Mother's. She has only called on Mother once, and that was in the old house, and then Mother was not receiving as they call it, so she has never even seen the mistress of the house where she is going to give the party. Christina Mander, George's secretary, says that is quite the new way of doing things, and she has been about a great deal, and ought to know.

Miss Mander is a lady. She is very thin, one of those lath-and-plaster women, you know, that seem to live to support a small waist that is their greatest beauty, but when we first knew her, she was plump and jolly-looking. We practically got her for George. Years ago, when we were quite little and had had measles, we were sent down to a sort of boarding-house at Ramsgate to an old lady, an ex-dresser in some theatre Aunt Gerty knew, and who could neither see to mend or to keep us in order, though she got thirty shillings a week for doing it. They never got us up till nine; I suppose the slavey thought sufficient for the day was the evil thereof, and tried to make the evil's day as short as possible. One morning when it was quite nine, and the sun was shining in, Ariadne and I were feeling frightfully bored, so we got up in our night-gowns, moved a wardrobe, and found a door behind it into another house. It was quite a smart house, with soft plush carpets and nicely-varnished yellow doors. We went all over it. Only the cat was awake, licking herself in the window-seat. The bedroom doors were all shut except one, and we went in and found a nice girl in bed with her gold hair all spread over the pillow. She didn't seem shocked at us, but laughed, and when we had explained, she wished us to get into the bed beside her. It had sheets trimmed with lace, and her initials, C. M., on the pillow. We did this every morning till we went away. She kept us up, afterwards sending us Christmas cards and so on, and when George advertised for a secretary to help him to sub-edit *Wild Oats*, she answered it, among the thousand others, and we remembered her name and made George engage her.

She had been to Girton, and to a journalistic school, and Mr. D'Auban's dancing academy, and to Klondike—where all her hair got cut off, so that she hasn't enough to spread over the pillow now—and behind the scenes at a music-hall, and a month on the stage, and edited a paper once and wrote a novel. All before she was thirty! At every new arrangement for amusement she made her people opposed her, and prayed for her in church. But she always got her own way in the end. Her mother, Mrs. Stephen Cadwallis Mander, came here to sniff about when George first took Christina on. She is a woman of the world, tortoise-shell *pince-nez* and all, but she took to Mother at first sight, and talked to her quite naturally about this "new move of dear Christina's."

She spoke in a neat, sighing voice, and told us that Christina had developed early, and was so different to her other children; she kept on saying the name of George's new magazine, as if it shocked her very much.

"*Wild Oats!* Such a crude name! Though I suppose she must sow them somewhere, and best, perhaps, in the pages of a magazine. You'll look after her, won't you? Is there any danger"—she looked towards the study-door"—of her falling in love with her employer?" She laughed carelessly.

"Not the slightest!" said Mother, laughing too. "She will have her eyes opened, that's all, to the seamy side of artistic life."

"My daughter is so absurdly curious about that wretched seamy side. After all, it's only the side that the workers leave the knots on, they must be somewhere, just as plates must be washed up in a scullery. But we don't need to go in and gloat on the horrid sight!"

"I quite agree with you," said Mother. "Only if one happens to be the scullery-maid——"

Aunt Gerty came in just then and took her part in the conversation. I was glad to see she was dressed more quietly than usual.

"And," said Mrs. Mander, "she buys everything that comes out, especially badly-executed magazines that talk about the fore-front of progress and look just as if they were produced in the dark ages. I know that she came to your husband entirely because she wanted to help to edit his magazine—*Wild Oats*. Is not that its name? From what Chris says, it sounds so *very* advanced!"

"Oh, very," said Aunt Gerty. "But it won't live!"

"You don't say so?" Mrs. Mander put up her *pince-nez* and looked at Aunt Gerty, whom she already didn't like.

"None of my brother-in-law's things do!" Aunt Gerty went on calmly. "He is a prize wrecker—of women and magazines!"

Mrs. Mander looked startled, and Mother tried to change the conversation.

"Oh, he's a law unto himself, my brother-in-law is," went on Aunt Gerty. "But I don't think he'll convert Miss Mander to his views."

"I hope not," said Mrs. Mander, "for I notice that if you make a law unto yourself, you generally have to make a society unto yourself too! At least as far as women are concerned."

"People will always let you go your own way," said Mother; "but the point is, will they come with you—join with you in a pleasant walk?"

"Well," said Mrs. Mander, "my daughter is the most headstrong of young women. I can't control her, or you may be sure I should not have allowed her to undertake this post of secretary to Mr. Vero-Taylor."

"I gathered as much," said Mother, not offended a bit. "But I will look after her well!" She does; she gives her cod-liver oil every day to make her fat, and breakfast in bed once a week.

Christina says Lady Scilly is a female Mecænas! Ben says she a minx. Ben hates her, because she makes a fool of George, and he says Ariadne is a cad to accept her old dresses and wear them, and go out with her, but then, what is Ariadne to do? She likes to go to parties, and Mother won't go anywhere, she is quite obstinate about that. I must say that George doesn't try to persuade her much. You see, he isn't used to having a wife, socially speaking, after going about as a bachelor all those years!

George agreed to have a party here, to please Lady Scilly, but Christina is quite sure that the idea had occurred to him already, for why should he build a house for purposes of advertisement, and then hide it under a bushel? A successful party is more good than fifty interviews, so she says, and sells an edition. She knows a great deal about geniuses. She says the hermit-plan would not suit George. I asked her what the hermit-plan was. She said she had known an artist, who took a lovely old house in the suburbs of London, and lived there, and never went out; anybody who cared must come out to see him, and then it was not so easy, for his Sundays were only for a select few—very selected. He only gave tea and bread-and-butter—very little butter—and no table-cloth—plain living, and high prices, for his pictures cost a lot, though he pretended he did not care if he sold them or not; in fact, it cut him to the heart to see any of them go out into the great cold brutal world, and he never exhibited in exhibitions, but in an empty room in his own house. He said, in fun, I suppose, that if the Academy were to elect him to be an R.A., he should put the matter into the hands of his solicitors. The end of that man was, she said, that he did become a Royal Academician, quite against his will, and princes and princesses of the blood used to come and have tea with him, without a table-cloth. But that would not do for George, for he isn't at all hermit-like, and he can make epigrams! They say that is his *forte*. I hate them myself, I think they are rude, and only a clever way of hurting people's feelings so that they can't complain, but then, of course, the family gets them in the rough; epigrams, like charity, begin at home.

George began to talk a great deal about the duty of entertaining. He said a man owed it to his century. And his party must be something out of the common run; it must be individual and exceptional. He thought he would give a party like the ones they gave in the Middle Ages. Judging from what he said, I think that it must have been very uncomfortable, and very expensive, for to be really grand you had to have cygnets and peacocks to eat. People stood about round the sides of the room, or sat on the floor or on coffers, and before the evening was half over the smoke from the flambeaux made it impossible for them to see each other's faces! That didn't suit Ariadne at all, and she snubbed the idea as much as she could.

Luckily, George changed his mind, and then it was to be a supper, still Mediæval, at six o'clock. We should have had to eat with our fingers, because only the carver has a fork, and he sometimes lends it, but it can't go all round. That's the reason we have finger-bowls now, and little bits of bread beside our plates instead of big bits of brown to eat off. And when you were done, did you eat the plate? As far as I can see, everybody handed everybody they loved nice pieces off their own trenchers and drank out of the same glasses, so the fewer persons that loved one the better I should have liked it. You should have seen Mother's face when the middle-aged menu was explained to her! She said she would do what she could, but how was she going to put the grocers' and the butchers' shops back a century?

The first course, George explained, was quite easy—it was little bits of toast with honey and hypocras.

"Perhaps they will know what that is at the Stores?" Mother said, meaning to be funny. "There's a very civil young man there might help me?"

"Next course, smoked eels," went on George. "Any soup you like, only it must be flavoured with verjuice. That is the third course. Then you have venison, rabbits, pigeons, fricasseed beans, river crabs, sorrel, oranges, capers in vinegar——"

"It will relieve us for ever of the burden of entertaining for ever and ever, that's one good thing!" Mother said, "for nobody will care to try that *menu* twice!"

"It would look well in the papers, though," George said. "What do you say to barbecued pig?"

But Mother would have nothing to say to barbecued pig, and George and Lady Scilly finally settled that it was to be a masked ball, costume not obligatory, but masks and dominos imperative, with a cold collation at twelve o'clock, and all the guests to unmask then.

The date was chosen to please her, and it was changed three times, but at last it was fixed, and George got some cards printed that he had designed himself. They were quite white and plain, but with a knowing red splotch in one corner, which signified George's passionate Italian nature. I was in the study when the first dozens of packets came, with Miss Mander, and she undid them. Secretaries always take the right to open everything!

"My Goodness!" she said.

"Isn't it right?" I asked, getting hold of it, but when I had looked at it I was no wiser, for I couldn't see what was wrong. There it was, written out very nicely, "*Mr. Vero-Taylor At Home. Wednesday the twenty-first,*" and the address in the corner, and all those rules about the dominos, and that was all.

"Oh, dear darling Christina," I begged, deadly curious, "do tell me what is wrong with that? I cannot guess."

"It's just as well, perhaps," she said. "Preserve your sublime ignorance, my dear child, as long as you can."

And not another word could I get out of her! I suppose she calls that being loyal to her employer.

I told Ben, and he said he knew, and what was more, he would go one better. He got hold of one of the cards, and altered it. And then it was *Mr. Vero-Taylor and Lady Scilly At Home*! I think that was absurd, for though Lady Scilly meddles in all our affairs, she doesn't quite live here yet! and Mother does, and what's more, Mother never goes out at all except to take a servant's character, or scold the butcher, or something of the sort, so she is really the one at home! Christina took it from him, and looked at it, and I'll swear I saw her smile before she tore it up. So Ben had me there, for he still wouldn't tell me what was wrong with the first card.

We began to write in the names of the people. It took us a whole morning, Ben, Ariadne, Miss Mander and I. I offered to help, and really, though I write rather badly, I can spell better than any of them, but I don't believe they valued my help very much, and only gave me a card now and then to keep me quiet. There were six young men that Ariadne wanted asked—six, no less, if you please—and she's only been out six months! And she kept trying to force them on George, same as you do cards in a card trick! But he didn't take any notice, and kept walking up and down the room mentioning the names of all sorts of absurd people that nobody wanted, except himself. It was really going to be a very smart party; there were to be detectives and reporters, and what more can you have than that? All the countesses and dukes and so on were to come, of course, but I must say I had thought that George knew a great many more of them; he managed to scratch up so few, considering all the talk there had been about it. I kept saying, "Oh, do give me a Countess to ask. You give me all the plain people to do."

Somehow or other, George did not seem to be pleased, and he sent us all away after fifty had been written.

Next day, he told us that he had thought it all out, and he was going to do an original thing, and instead of sending out cards for his party, he was going to announce it in the pages of *The Bittern*, and that all his friends, reading it, must consider themselves bidden. Mother said how should she know how many to prepare for? I suppose the answer to that depends on the number of friends George has got, and whether they know that he considers them his friends. For think how awkward to assume that you were a friend and had a place laid for you, and then to come and find that you were only an acquaintance. I suggested that the real friends should have a hot sit-down supper, with wine, while the acquaintances should only go to a buffet and have cold pressed beef and lemonade. There should be a password, *Hot with*, and *cold without*, and they roared when I told them this, but I didn't see why. Then the party would really be of some use, for after it people would know where they were! But how about the newspaper people? They couldn't call themselves friends, or even acquaintances, so they wouldn't be able to come at all, and what would George do then? I said all this, which seems to me very sensible, but no one noticed it. And the detectives! They have to be paid for coming, surely, and I'd rather see them than any of the others. "If they don't come the party will be spoilt for me," I said to Christina.

"It will be all right," she said, and Ariadne was quite pleased, for of course, this way, her six young men can come, a dozen if they like.

Ariadne and I had costumes. I was the little Duke of Gandia, that brother of Cæsar Borgia that he killed, and Ariadne had the dress of Beatrice Cenci with a sort of bath-towel wound round her head. The funny thing is that she looks far younger than me in it, quite a little girl, while I look like a big boy. My legs are very long. George has a monk's costume, one of the Fratelli dei Morti, and it is much the same sort of looking thing as a domino. Nobody would ever know him, and he looks very nice.

I am told that at masques you have to speak a squeaky voice or alter it somehow. George will have to, because he has a very peculiar voice, that anybody would know a mile off; people call it resonant, nervous, bell-like—I call it cracked. It is one of his chief fascinations, but he will have to do without it for once, and rely on the others.

The study was to be the ball-room, only George preferred to leave signs of literary occupation in the shape of his desk, which he just shoved away on one side, with the proofs of his new novel left negligently lying on it. We sprinkled copies of his last but one about the house, in moderation; it was rather fun—I felt as if I were planting bulbs. George likes these sort of little attentions, and I knew I was not to be put off by his finding one, as he did, and scolding me and telling me to put it on the fire.

CHAPTER VIII

ABOUT nine they all began to arrive, and by ten o'clock the house was overflowing. Ben was a capital commissionaire in a District Messenger's costume he had borrowed, with George's consent, and I do believe he enjoyed himself most of anybody. Of course at first all he had to do was to stand at the door and show people in, but he hoped that later in the evening he should have to chuck somebody out. It was likely, he thought, for all the literary world of London would be sure to be at our party. I'm sorry to say that Ben was wrong there, or else the literary people didn't come, for those that did come were as quiet as lambs. There were detectives, several of them, and although I looked very particularly at their boots, which I have always been told is the way to spot a detective, I saw nothing at all out of the common. There was a man with a cloven hoof, but then he was meant for the devil. He was masked of course, but the devil needs no domino. And *I* knew all the time that it was the little man who interviewed me once instead of George for *The Bittern*, and got me into such a row, and very devilish of him it was, and I had no butter to my bread for a week because of him. How I was supposed to know that George hated the truth instead of loving it, I can't see, only *The Bittern* man knew well enough, I expect! Never, *never* again will I interfere between a man and his interviewer!

There were hosts of newspaper people there; I heard two of them discussing us, sitting in the high-backed

Medici seat. I managed to get jammed in behind, "powerless to move," as they say in the novels, even if I had wanted to. People *are* careless. I heard heaps of conversations, anyhow, people even said things to each other across me, without stopping to think whether or no I wasn't one of the family. I suppose because they were masked, they felt anonymous, as if it didn't matter what they said, and it needn't count afterwards.

The man I listened to was *The Bittern* man, dressed as the devil. The woman's domino was all shot with queer faint colours, and, if any colour, sulphur colour. She was scented too, a nice odd scent. *The Bittern* man seemed to know her.

"I cannot be mistaken; am I not talking to the most dangerous woman in London?"

The woman seemed quite complimented, and smiled under her mask.

"Not quite, but very nearly," she said. "I am a gas. Give me a name!"

"I will call you Mrs. Sulphuretta Hydrogen. How does that suit you?"

"Is it a noxious gas?" she said, "for, honestly, I never am spiteful! I only speak of things as I find them, and one must send up bright copy, or one wouldn't be taken on. I tell the truth——"

"Nothing extenuate, everything set down in malice!" said he. "The devil and *The Bittern* are much obliged to you. It is the honest truth that makes his work so easy for him. We are of a trade in more senses than one. Now tell me, can't we exchange celebrities? I'll give you my names, and you shall give me yours. I suppose all the world is here to-night?"

"All the world—and somebody else's wife!" she said quickly, and the devil rubbed his hands. "But that is the rub—we can't know who they all are till twelve o'clock, and my idea is that a good many of them will decamp before they are forced to reveal themselves. Least seen, soonest mended."

"Then we shall have to invent them!" he said. "The very form of invitation must lead to a good deal of promiscuity. Can you tell me which is Lady Scilly? She at least is sure to be here."

"Naturally! Wasn't it she who discovered George Vero-Taylor and made him the fashion, you know?"

"Do you suppose he was particularly obliged to her for digging his family out as well?"

"You naughty man! But it was a most extraordinary thing, wasn't it? Delightful, and not too scandalous to use. For the man is really quite harmless, only a frantic *poseur* and——"

"Ah, yes, and posed in London Society for ten years as an unmarried man! Suppose some nice girl had gone and fallen in love with him?"

"Ah, but he was careful, as careful as a good *parti* has to be in the London season. He lent them his books, and guanoed their minds thoroughly, but he always sheered off when they showed signs of taking him seriously."

"Chose married women to flirt with, for preference? What does the wife say?"

"The wife? So there is a wife! But no one has ever seen her. Perpetual hay-fever, or something of the sort."

"That is what Vero-Taylor gives out."

"Oh, I don't really think there is anything in—with Lady Scilly, I mean. He is too selfish—they are both too selfish. Those sort of women are like the Leaning Tower, they lean but never fall. It is an alliance of interest, so to speak. He introduces the literary element into her parties, and writes her novel for her, and in return she flatters him and takes his daughter out. Poor girl, she would be quite pretty, if she were properly dressed, but the mediæval superstition, you know—she has to dress like a Monna Somebody or other, so as to advertise his books. I believe she did refuse to have her hair shaved off her forehead *à la Rimini*, but she mostly has to comply——"

"Well, I never heard of a man using his daughter as a sandwich-man before. Which is she?"

Mrs. Sulphuretta Hydrogen pointed out Ariadne, whose bath-towel was tumbling all over her eyes.

"She looks half-starved!" said *The Bittern* man.

"My dear man," said Sulphuretta Hydrogen, "don't you know that they have a crank about meals, and refuse to have them regularly? I am told that they have a kind of buttery-hatch—a cold pie always cut in the cupboard, and they go and put their heads in and eat a bit when so disposed."

"Well, they are free, at any rate—free from the trammels of custom——"

"Oh yes, they are free, but so very sallow!"

I was getting pretty much out of patience at having so many lies told about my family, and I was just going to contradict that about the buttery and the poking our heads into a cupboard, when the fat woman that they had said was Mother, but whom I was sure was not, strode up to Mrs. Sulphuretta Hydrogen, and said—

"Begging your pardon for contradicting you, Madam, but I am in a position to state that that is not so. Miss Ariadne is thin because she chooses to be, and thinks it becoming, but I can assure you that she eats her three meals a day hearty, and Mr. Taylor isn't far behind-hand, though he is yellow!"

And then she swooped away, and I knew that it was Elizabeth Cawthorne! But where on earth had she got a domino and leave to come to the ball?

I thought I would go and look after Ariadne, who I saw could manage to make eyes out of the holes of a mask. But I suppose where there's a will there's a way. She was doing it all right, and the young men seemed to like it. Though I don't believe young men marry the girls who make eyes at them best, and as Ariadne's one object is to marry and get out of this house and have me to stay with her, I think she is going the wrong way to work. I went to her, and I asked her where Mother was.

"I am sure I don't know," she said crossly.

"I'll tell you where Elizabeth Cawthorne is," I said. "She is in the party—in the room!"

"Well, I can't help that!" said Ariadne, tossing her head. "Mother ought to look after her better."

I was sorry for poor Mother, because nobody seemed to mind about her in her own house, and even her own daughter didn't seem to care whether she was in the room or not. As for George, he was looking all over for Lady Scilly, and at last he thought he had got her, but it wasn't, for I thought I knew a little join in the hem of the domino—I seemed to remember having helped to hem it. They needn't say that eyes can't look bright in a mask, for this woman's did. She went up to George, and she didn't speak in a squeaky voice at all, but in French, not the kind of French she teaches me, but a thick, deep sort, right down her throat.

"*Eh, bien, beau masque!*" was what she said. "I know you, but you do not know me!"

"I know you by your eyes," he said. "Eyes like the sea——"

Now, Lady Scilly's eyes are quite common, it is only the work round them that makes them tell, and that would be hidden by the mask. One saw that George was talking without thinking.

"Eyes without their context mean nothing!" she said, and then I knew the woman was Christina, for that was the very thing she had once said to Ariadne to tease her. She evidently thinks it good enough to say twice.

"Come!" she said to George. "Speak to me, say anything to me that the hour and the mood permit. I want to hear how a poet makes love!"

"Madame!" said George, bowing. I think he was a little shocked, but after all, if he will give a masked ball, what can he expect? Only I had no idea that Christina could have done it so well!

"Come," she said again, tapping her foot to show that she had grown impatient. "Come, a madrigal—a *ballade*, in any kind of china!"

I fancy it was then that George began to suspect that it wasn't Lady Scilly. She couldn't have managed that about ballads and lyrics.

He asked her if she would lift up the lace of her mask a little—just a little.

"No, no, I dare not!" she cried out. "There is a hobgoblin called Ben in the room—a sort of lubber fiend who loves to play pranks on people. Why on earth don't you send that boy to school?"

I could not help giggling. George looked cross, for this was personal, and he took the first chance of leaving the mask's side. There wasn't a buzz of talk in the room, no, not at all, for everybody was trying so hard to say something clever and appropriate, that they mostly didn't say anything, but mooned about, trying to look as if they were enjoying themselves hugely, and secretly bored to death all the time. The only time people are really gay, I observe, is at a funeral, or at *Every man*, or somewhere where they particularly shouldn't be jolly.

I was thinking sadly about my dear Mother, and wondering where she was, when I ran against a Frenchman, a real Frenchman, and he asked me where was the mistress of the house, and that showed me that other people thought about her too; I didn't answer for a moment, and he went on in a kind of dreamy voice—

"I was brought here to see an English interior——"

"Well," I said. "It's inside four walls, isn't it?"

"*Mon Dieu, mademoiselle,*" said he, "I had made to myself another idea of *le home Anglais*—the fireside—the *maîtresse de la maison* with her keys depending from her girdle—the children—the sacred children, standing round her—*bébé* crowing——"

"There isn't any baby!" I said, "and a good thing too! But this is a party, don't you see, and we are all playing the fool, and we shall be sensible to-morrow, and if you will excuse me, I am one of the sacred children, and I am just looking for my mother's knee to go and stand against."

He made way for me with a "*Permettez, mademoiselle!*" and I went, thinking I would go and ask Ben at the door if he knew where she was. Ben didn't know, but he said that a woman who was standing near the door, letting the cool night-wind blow in under her mask and telling people how she enjoyed it, was Lady Scilly. She was standing almost in the street, with a man, who was George. There are tall bushes near our door, rather pretty at night, though they belong to the next-door gardens. Ben didn't know till I told him; he is the stupid child that doesn't know its own father. He told me what they had been saying. She had begun by asking him if he approved of women wearing ospreys? There's a silly thing to ask, for what could he say but that he didn't, being a poet? Then she made a face, prettyish, out of habit, forgetting that it couldn't be seen under her mask, and whined,

"Oh, I'm so sorry, it is the least wicked thing I do!"

"For beautiful women—I assume you are a beautiful woman, for purposes of dialogue," George said; "there is no law of humanity. Go on. Pluck your red pleasure from the teeth of pain." ...

"Yes, I am very wicked," she said. "My impulses are cruel. Sometimes, do you know, I am almost afraid of myself."

"As I am—as we all are," said George.

"Why, am I so very terrible? What do I do to you? Speak to me. Why are you so guarded, so unenterprising?"

She cast a stage glance round. It was very funny, but George knew that Ben was the commissionaire and Lady Scilly didn't, so she couldn't think why George was so stiff. In fact, if George had only known it, he was bi-chaperoned—if that is the way to put it—for there was me too. Ben and I enjoyed it hugely, but I don't think George did, because he could not quite make a fool of himself before Ben. Besides, it was draughty out there, and George takes cold easily. He kept trying to get her to come in, and she pretended to be babyish and wouldn't. She said she had never been out in the open street at midnight in her life before, and she thoroughly enjoyed it; that it was a Romeo and Juliet night, or some rot of that sort, and that she might never have such an opportunity again. But poor George felt he could not play Romeo, because of Ben, and there was nothing to climb, except a lamp-post that led to nothing, since Juliet was standing in the gutter below it.

George looked at his watch, and said, "In ten minutes they will give the signal for the removal of masks. Had you not better——?"

"I shall leave the party," she said. "I shall walk straight home! It will spoil all the effect of this enchanted night, if we have to meet again in the glare of——"

"The lights are shaded," George put in.

"I alluded to the glare of publicity!" she said. "I shall ask this commissionaire," she said, "to call my carriage——"

"Better not," said George hastily, "for you would have to give him your name,—your name which I know. For my sake—won't you slip back into the ball-room and submit to the ordeal, as I know it is, of unmasking like the rest? Believe me it is best."

"It is my host commands, is it not?" she said slyly, to show him that she had known it was he all the time, and ran past him, in a skittish way. As if he hadn't known all the time that she knew that he knew that she knew who he was! Grown-up people do waste so much time in pretending.

Well, I thought if masks were going to be removed, I had better take up a respectable-looking position at once, say, beside Miss Mander, which seemed suitable, and I went in. Then I saw Lady Scilly again, and wanted so to know what she was up to. She was stealing out of the room, and the devil was going with her. He was *The Bittern* man, of course, only I didn't know she knew him. They were talking very earnestly.

"You know the way?" she was asking him.

"I know the house, like the inside of a glove," he said, and indeed he did, for hadn't I taken him all over it, the day he interviewed me instead of George, and there was a row? I think he is mischievous, rather like Puck was, in *Midsummer Night's Dream*, so I thought I would stick to them. Lady Scilly wanted to go into an empty room to take off her mask and domino. That I could quite understand, as she had behaved so badly in both. *The Bittern* man offered to show her the way to George's sanctum.

"You see, you can go where you like in a show-house—or ought to be able to. It is public property, the property of the press, at any rate."

"The press is too much with us, soon and late," said she, laughing.

"Ah, but confess, my lady, you can't do without us!" said this awful young man—though I suppose he has to be cheeky, so as to get his nose in everywhere in the interest of his paper. "You suffer us gladly."

"I don't suffer at all—I shouldn't allow you to make me suffer," said she, not understanding him. Smart women never do understand things out of the Bible.

I followed them; my excuse was, that I wanted to see they didn't steal the spoons. They made the coolest remarks as they went up-stairs.

"I have never been beyond the First Floor in this House of Awe," said *The Bittern* man.

"Haven't you? It seems to get more and more comfortable and less eccentric as one goes up," said Lady Scilly.

"Art is only skin-deep," said *The Bittern* man. "Just look at that bed, which seems to me to have come from nothing more dangerously subversive or artistic than Staple's…. Come, lay down your mask and domino, and let us go down again, and wait about in the back precincts till we hear our host give the word for unmasking."

So they marched out of George's bedroom, for that was where they had got to—and as no one ever need see that, he has it quite comfortable, and modern—and sneaked down-stairs by a different way. I followed them. Soon they got quite lost and were heading straight for the kitchen. I wondered if Elizabeth had taken off her domino, and gone back to her work, for though the supper was all sent in from a shop, there would be sure to be something for her to do.

These two marched straight in, and I after them, and found themselves in a blaze of light and an empty kitchen—for the moment only, for one heard all the men stumping along from the dining-room on the other side, and the scullery-maid rinsing something in the scullery. Just as Lady Scilly and *The Bittern* man burst in, Mother was standing alone, in a checked apron, before the kitchen-dresser, and turned right round and looked at them. She looked dignified and cold, in spite of the kitchen fire, which had caught her face on one side.

Lady Scilly and *The Bittern* man took no notice of her, but walked about looking at things.

"And so this is the Poet's kitchen!" Lady Scilly said, rather scornfully. "How his pots shine!"

"Very comfortable indeed!" said Mr. Frederick Cook. He seemed to despise George. Then he continued, laughing under his mask—"It's no end of a privilege to see the humble objects that minister to the Poet's use. This is his soup-ladle, and——"

Mother made a little step forward and finished Mr. Cook's sentence for him.

"And this is his dresser, and this is his boiler, that is his cat—and I'm his wife!"

Lady Scilly skooted, Mr. Cook stayed behind and did a little bit of polite. He isn't a bad sort, and Mother rather liked him after that, and he began to come here.

CHAPTER IX

SMART women like having a fluffy dog or a child to drive with them in the afternoons. Lady Scilly hasn't got either of her own, so she is always borrowing me, and sending for me to lunch and drive. She seldom asks Ariadne, because Ariadne is out and nearer her own age—too near. That's what I tell Ariadne, when she is jealous, and makes me a scene about it, and it is true. If it were not for the honour and glory of the thing, I don't care so very much about it myself, Lady Scilly's motor is always getting into trouble, because it is so highly bred, I suppose. We run into something live—or else the kerb—most times we are out, and it's extremely agitating, though I must say she never screams, though once she fainted after it was all over. It is a mark of breeding to get into scrapes, but not make a fuss. We have all heard about it, she is just as much before the public as my father, though in a different way. I read an interview with her in *The Bittern* the other day (she had to start some Cottage Homes at Ealing to get herself into that!), and it said that hers was one of the oldest names in England, and that she was the daughter of a hundred Earls. Now I call that nonsense, for how could she be? There isn't room for a hundred Earls since the Heptarchy, unless they were all at the same time, and that is not likely.

Lord Scilly is very well born too, he's the eldest son of the Earl of Fowey. The Earl keeps him very tight. So they have to get along with expectations and a title, till the old man dies, and Lady Scilly wishes he would, but

Lord Scilly doesn't, because he's not quite a beast. He is very nice, and rather fond of Lady Scilly, though he is always scolding her. That is the expectations, they spoil the temper, I fancy. I have heard that he doesn't think it dignified, the way she goes on, lowering herself and turning his house into a menagerie. He doesn't understand why she pets authors and publishers. The authors help her to write novels, and the publishers publish them for love and ninety pounds. George is writing one for her now, and he goes to her place nearly every morning to see about it. Lord Scilly doesn't mind in the least her collaborating with George and the others, it keeps her out of mischief; but I expect he would be down upon her at once if she were to collaborate with one of her own class, that would be different.

I shall be glad when the book is finished, for Elizabeth Cawthorne, who tells me everything, doesn't think so much collaborating is quite what is due to Mother, and that if she were the mistress, "blessed if she'd let herself be put upon by a countess."

Elizabeth says Lady Scilly is a daisy—that's what her name means, Paquerette. That's what she tells me to call her. I am proud to call a grown-up person by her Christian name, and a titled lady too, and it makes Ariadne jealous, which does her good, and keeps her down. Paquerette treats Ariadne on quite another footing, any one can see she is not nearly so intimate with her as she is with me. I go there at all times and seasons, and I accept no benefits from her. I won't. If she gives me things, I take them and give them to Ariadne. So I feel I may say and think what I like of her, while amusing myself with her, and listening to all the silly things she says. The funny thing is, I am always trying to be grown-up, and she is always trying to be childish.

The other day when I got to Curzon Street about twelve—Lady Scilly had sent a messenger for me—she was still in bed in the loveliest pale-blue tea-jacket, down to where the bed-clothes came up to, and she was writing her letters in pencil on a writing-board, trying to squeeze a few words in round a great sprawling gilt monogram that took up nearly all the paper. There were three French books on the bed, they had covers with ladies with red mouths and all their hair down, and *La Femme Polype* was the name of one, and *Madame Belle-et-m'aime* another. Lady Scilly says she always gets up all her history and philosophy in French if possible, so as to improve her grasp of the language. There was also on the pillow a box of cigarettes, and a great bunch of lilies, that made me feel sleepy. There are daisies worked all over the curtains and the counterpane, and great bunches of them painted on the mirrors hanging head downwards, and about three sets of silver-topped brush things spread out on the dressing-table. As for photographs, I never saw so many in my life! There are about a dozen cabinets with "To darling, from Kitty London," and as many more with "Best love, yours cordially, Gladys Margate," and I have given up trying to count the ones of actresses! Then the men! There is one of the poet with the bumpy forehead, and wrinkly trousers, who wrote *The Sorrows of the Amethyst*, and one of the K.C. who wrote *Duchesses in the Divorce Court*—the Ollendorff man I call him; and one of the men who did the Gaiety play called *The Up-and-Down Girl*, which Lady Scilly acted in the provinces once, for a charity, till Lord Scilly stopped her. There he is in his volunteer uniform looking like a lamb. I do like Lord Scilly, and I think he's put upon. So I am as nice to him as I can be when I see him, which isn't often. He never comes into her room where I principally am. There's a desk in one corner, where she writes her little notes—I don't suppose she ever wrote a real letter in her life, her handwriting is so big it would burst the post-bag—and there are two sorts of racks on it, one to hold her bills that she hasn't paid, and that's got printed on it in gold "*Oh Horrors!*" and another with those she has paid with "*Thank Heaven!*" on it, though that one is mostly empty. She never hardly pays bills, she says it is waste of tissue, and bad form, but sends something on account, and that I think is a very good way, for however broke you are, you must go on ordering dresses, else the dressmaker would close your account, and if you only go on long enough, the chances are you'll die first and leave a nice little bill behind you, that, being dead, you can't be expected to pay!

I hate kissing people in bed, I nearly always tumble over them; and also, if they are writing, I can't help seeing what it is, and then if it is "*Dearests*" and "*Darlings*" I do feel awkward. But to-day when she had said "How do you do?" she handed me the writing-board.

"Write for me, dear," she said, "to the most odious woman in London. And the most insolent, and the most unwashed! Insolent! Yes, positively she dared to play Lady Ildegonde in *The Devey Devastator* at a *matinée* at Camberwell yesterday, in perfect dreams of dresses— stood by the management of course—and nails like a coal-heaver's. Now don't you think, that as the part of Lady Ildegonde was admittedly written round my personality, with my entire consent, that it is an outrage for Irene Lauderdale to dress the part better than I can afford to do! I shall not forgive her. Now you write. '*Dear thing!*' Don't be surprised, I can't afford to quarrel with her, unfortunately! '*You were wonderful yesterday! I know what's what, and believe me that's it!*' I mean the dresses, but she will think I mean her playing! That is what we call diplomacy. Don't say any more. Short, and spiteful. Now seal it. I will see that Mrs. Ptomaine guys Lauderdale in Romeo. Tommy will do anything for me, and *The Bittern* will do anything for her. We will go and see her this very afternoon. I must get up, I suppose. Ring for Miller, dear. Oh, good heavens! how bored I am!"

She threw one of the French novels (they were library books, so it didn't matter) across the room, and it fell into the wash-basin, and then she seemed to feel better.

"I wish I could do without Miller!" she said. "Old Miller hates me, and I loathe her. But she will never leave me. Too good 'perks' for that. She always folds up my frocks as if she knew they would belong to her one day. So they will! I can't afford to quarrel with a woman who can do my hair carelessly, with a single hair-pin. What am I going to wear to-day, Miller?"

"Well," said Mrs. Miller (she's Scotch, and she is rather stingy of "ladyships"), "there's your blue that come home last week. It seems a pity to leave it aside just yet."

"You mean you can do without it a little longer, eh, Miller? No, I can't put that on, it's too big for me since massage. I simply swim in it."

"Then there is the grey *panne*."

"Oh, that dam-panne, as I call it. No, it makes me look like my own maid. No offence to you, Miller."

"I don't intend to take any, my lady," said Miller, pursing up her lips. "What about your black with sequins?"

"Yes, let's have the vicious sequins. It will go with the child's hair. You see, I dress to you, my dear."

But I knew it was only that she likes things to go nicely together, just as she chooses her horses to be a pair.

Then she sat down and did her face, very neatly; it is about the only thing she does really well. She put red on her lips, and white on her nose, and black on her eyes, till she looked like a Siamese doll I once had before I licked the paint off. I paid particular attention, for I shall do it when I am grown-up, that is if I am able to afford it—the best paints—and I am told that stands you in about four hundred a year.

Her hair is the very newest gold shade, the one they have in Paris—rather purplish—it will be blue next season, I dare say! It is just a little bit dark down by the roots, which is pretty, I think, and looks so very natural. All the time Miller was dressing it, she worked away at the front with the stick of her comb, pulling little bits out, and putting them back, and staring into a hand-glass as anxiously as if her life depended on it, while Miller patiently gummed some little tendrils of hair down on her forehead.

"Child, child," she said to me. "Do you know what makes me sigh?"

"Indigestion?" I asked, quite on the chance, but she said it wasn't, that she never had had it, it was only because she felt so terribly, so diabolically, so preternaturally ugly.

"Oh no, you look sweet!" I said. I really thought so, but Miller grinned.

"You are delightful!" Lady Scilly said. "And you can have that boa you are fiddling with, if you like. Tulle is death to me! Makes me meretricious; and, child, when your time comes, don't ever—ever—have anything to do with massage! It grows on one so! One can't leave it off, and it has to be always with one, like the poor. I have actually to subsidize a masseuse to live round the corner, and she cheeks me all the time. Oh, *la, la!*"

I know about massage. I massed Ariadne once, according to a system we read of in a book. I've seldom had such a chance at her. I pinched her black and blue, and she kept saying, "Go on! Harder! Harder!" but as it didn't seem to agree with her afterwards, I didn't do it again. But I took the boa to give Ariadne, I have no use for such things myself.

When Lady Scilly was ready she said—"We won't lunch in, we will go to Prince's and have a *filet*. Scilly's in a bad temper because of bills. Well, bills must come,— and I may go, I suppose. There's no reason one shouldn't keep out of their way."

She stuck a hat on with twenty feathers in it, and we went down, and she told the butler to call a hansom now, and tell the carriage to fetch us at three o'clock.

The butler said, "Very well, my lady. Your ladyship has a lunch-party of ten!" all in the same voice.

"So I have! Oh, Parker, what a fool I am!" and she flopped into a hall seat.

"Yes, my lady," Parker said, quite politely, closing the hall-door again. He has known her from a child, so he may be rude.

So we took off our hats, at least I did—she wears a hat every time she can, except in bed—and went into the library where Lord Scilly was, and her cousin, a young man from the Foreign Office, Simon Hermyre, that I know.

Lord Scilly came up to her and said out loud, "You have got too much on!"

She softly dabbed her face with her handkerchief to please him, but so as not to disturb anything, and the young man from the Foreign Office laughed. He is a fifth cousin. Lady Scilly says her cousins grow like blackberries on every bush—one of the penalties of greatness.

"I've never really seen your face, Paquerette," he said, "and I do believe it would justify my wildest expectations. Still, I think you are right not to make it too cheap. Who's coming? Smart people, or one of your Bohemian crowds?"

"You'll see," she said. "Mrs. Ptomaine, for one."

"Dear Tommy!" said he. "I love her.... Desist, O wasp!" he said to one that had come in by the window and was bothering him. "This is a precursor of Tommy."

"Tommy's all right, so long as she hasn't got her knife into you. She favours you, Simon. You are to take her in, and distract her, and see that she doesn't make eyes at my tame millionaire."

"Oh, Mr. Pawky!" said Simon. "Is he coming? You should put me opposite, so that I could intercept the glances. And why mayn't Tommy have a bit of him? She's terribly thin!"

"Because he isn't a very big millionaire—only half a one—and there's only just enough for me. So you know what you have got to do. You may flirt wildly with Tommy, if nothing else will do. Let me see, who else is coming? Oh, Marston, the actor, a nice boy, gives me boxes, and mortally afraid of Lauderdale—and some odd fill-ups. Just think, I nearly went out to lunch with this child, and forgot you all. I should like to have seen all your faces!"

Then all these people came, and Lady Scilly put me on one side of the millionaire and herself on the other. He looked very mild and indigestible, and as if millionairing didn't agree with him. He could only drink hot water and eat dry toast. He made a little "How-Are-You-My-Pretty-Dear" conversation with me, but he attended most to Lady Scilly, of course. She was telling him all about Miss Lauderdale, and *Lady Ildegonde* and the dresses, and discussing Society, as it is now.

"Titles! Why, my dear man, no one cares a fig for birth now-a-days. No, the only thing we care for is culture, and the only thing we can't forgive is for people to bore us!"

I wondered where the poor millionaire came in, for he can't culture, while he certainly does bore, but I suppose Lady Scilly wouldn't waste her time for nothing, and perhaps there is some other attraction Society takes count of that she didn't mention?

"I'll go anywhere and everywhere to be amused," she went on. "I'd go to Gatti's Music Hall under the Arches—only music halls are a bit stale now! I'd go to a prize-fight in a sewer—anything to get some colour into my life!"

"Paint the town red, wouldn't you!" muttered Lord Scilly.

"That is the way we all are," Lady Scilly went on. "Look at Kitty London! She is going to marry a perfect darling of an acrobat, who can play billiards on his own back!"

"Cheap culture that!" said Lord Scilly, and I don't know what he meant, but I knew he meant to be nasty; but the millionaire went on sipping his hot water, and enjoyed having a countess talk like that to him, and stood her any amount of dinners at the Paxton for it, I dare say. They say he runs it?

He was well protected, but still I could not help thinking that Mrs. Ptomaine on the other side of the table, not even opposite, seemed to have her eye on him, one of them at any rate, Simon couldn't manage to distract both. I didn't like her. She came to our ball in a mask, and flirted with Mr. Frederick Cook. I quite saw why Simon Hermyre compared her to a wasp. She looked as if she sat up too late and drank too much tea, and I was sure that though they were very smart, her petticoats were all muddy at the bottom. She called Lady Scilly "Darling!" across the table every now and then to show how intimate she was. Lady Scilly never cares or notices. It is one of her charms. The actor was on her other side. I saw Lord Scilly stare at his eighteen rings and his nice painted face, as if he were a new arrival. But there is some excuse for him, he was just up—he said so—and I dare say he was too tired to wash the paint off when he got home this morning. Besides that, he is acting Juliet to Miss Lauderdale's Romeo—that is the way they do it now. I wish I had seen Shakespeare when men acted men's parts and women did women, but I was born too late for that.

When we got up from lunch, Mrs. Ptomaine cleverly caught her dress in a leg of her chair, and she wouldn't let the actor disengage it, but waited till the millionaire came past her seat and had a feeble try at it. She smiled at him very gratefully for tearing a large bit of the flounce off in getting it out, but after all, it made an introduction, and she can have a new piece of common lace put in. Afterwards in the drawing-room she had quite a nice chat with him, before Lady Scilly sent somebody to break it up, as she did, after five minutes.

At four o'clock they all went and we took our drive after all. Lady Scilly never pays calls—only the bourgeois do—but we went to see Mrs. Ptomaine.

"I hadn't a word with Tommy to-day," Lady Scilly said, "and I had several little things to arrange with her. I can't sleep till I have put a spoke in Lauderdale's wheel. Poor Tommy! What a fright she looked to-day! But she is not a bad sort, is Tommy, and devoted to me!"

"What does she do?" I asked.

"Oh, she works the press for me. She has command of half-a-dozen papers. Goodness knows how, for I am sure no editor would ever care for her to make love to him! She is useful, you see, she describes my dresses free. I don't care for that myself, naturally, but the dressmakers do, if their names are given, and then they don't worry so with their bills. And she interviewed me once, and I gave Kitty London such a lesson—things I wanted conveyed to her, you know, and could not quite say myself! It is rather a good idea to conduct one's quarrels through the press, isn't it? Here we are at Tommy's flat! Up at the very, very top! The vulture in its eyrie—is it the vulture that has an eyrie? I know it has a ragged neck with cheap fur round it! Up we go! No lift! One oughtn't to visit with flats without a lift! You ring!"

I rang, and Mrs. Ptomaine herself opened the door.

"So soon, darling! Delightful!" she said. She didn't look very pleased to see us, I thought, but she was "in to tea," I could see, for there were three kinds of little tea-cakes and a yellow cake made with egg-powder.

"I wanted to prime you about your critique of *Lady Ildegonde*, you know. Now, Tommy, it is understood, Lauderdale is to be snubbed and punished for her impertinence in daring to act *me*, in Camille's dresses."

"Darling, quite so! Of course. I had it nearly written. Dearest, you don't trust your Tommy."

"Not so much darling dear, now, if you don't mind," said Lady Scilly. "We are alone, and this child doesn't need impressing. It fidgets me."

"All right, sweetheart—I beg your pardon," said Mrs. Ptomaine, quite obligingly; but talk of fidgeting, she herself was in a terrible state. "Is it too early for tea?"

"Too late you mean, Tommy. What is the matter with you? Have you got a headache?"

"Three distinct headaches," said poor Tommy. "Did three first nights last night, and got a separate headache for each."

"How interesting!" said Lady Scilly. "I mean I am very sorry. Is there nothing I can do?"

"No, no, nothing. I have experience of these. Nothing but complete rest will do any good. If I could just lie down and darken the room and think of nothing for an hour."

Lady Scilly got up to go after such a plain hint as that, and we were just opening the door when it opened itself and let in the millionaire!

Mrs. Ptomaine made the best of it. She got up to receive him with a very pained smile on the side of her face next Lady Scilly, and said to her in an undertone, "No chance for me, you see! This man will want his tea. *Must* you go?"

Lady Scilly hadn't even said she must go, but she did go, and p.d.q. as my brother Ben says. What was more, she said "Good-bye, Mrs. Ptomaine," in a tone that must have peeled the skin off poor Tommy's nose. No more "dears" and "darlings"! To the millionaire she said, "So we meet again?" and from the way she said that polite thing, I should say he would have serious doubts as to whether he would ever be invited to drink toast-and-water in her house any more.

"There are as good millionaires in South Africa as ever came out of it," she said to me, going down-stairs. "Poor old Pawky! One woman after another exploits the dear old thing. They are kind to him, *pour le bon motif!* He did say to me in a first introduction, 'Hev' you any bills?' But I put it down to his South African manners and his idea of breaking the ice and making conversation. Tommy will fleece him. I hope she'll get him to give her a new carpet!"

I know that Mr. Pawky gave Lady Scilly her box at the Opera, but then it was on consideration of her allowing him to sit in it with her now and then. Thus she gives a *quid pro quo*, which poor Tommy can't do, having nothing marketable about her, not even a title.

If he values Lady Scilly's kindness he is a fool to run after Tommy so obviously. But that is what I have noticed about these rich people; they seem to lose their heads, let themselves go cheap every now and then. Tommy is so ugly—she never looked nice in her life except when she was Mrs. Sulphuretta Hydrogen, at our party, and wore a mask and flirted with Mr. Frederick Cook—that he must be demented, or jealous of Frederick Cook, perhaps?

She has an organ, I mean a paper she's on, and I suppose she can write Mr. Pawky up. Still I think he has made a bad exchange, for Mrs. Ptomaine won't last. They change the staffs of those papers in the night, and any morning Mr. Frederick Cook may walk down to the office and find a new man sitting at his desk, and the same with Mrs. Ptomaine,—where there's a way (of making a little) there's a minx to take it! so she often says.

Lady Scilly can't lose her title except to change it for another and a nicer.

CHAPTER X

IT is a very odd thing that with a father a novelist, who can sell ten thousand copies of a book, you can't get any sort of useful advice on the subject he has made peculiarly his own. Ariadne would much sooner consult the cook about such things. And it is not nice to ask advice from a person who can oblige you to follow it! George can't in fairness advise as an author and command as a father, so the result is that Ariadne makes blunders at all these parties she goes to now. Poor girl, she only has me to consult. I say it is a mistake the moment you enter a room to fix your eyes on the man you want to dance with you, or even to ask him for a dance as Ariadne did once. She said she thought he was too shy to ask her, though he did know her a little, and she wanted to see if he danced as beautifully as he looked. A man shy! It takes a shy girl like Ariadne to imagine that! For Ariadne is both shy and superstitious. She gets that from Lady Scilly and Lady Scilly's aunt, the Countess of Plyndyn. A very fat old lady with a corresponding hand, that when she holds it out to a fortune-teller, it is like counting the creases in a feather-bed. She makes them take count of every crease though, and begs them to invent a fate for her.

"Haven't I got a future like other people?" she whines, and then the poor paid fortune-teller, in a great hurry, sows a crop of initials in her hand, and she is not more than pleased, and takes it as a right to have three husbands, although she is already seventy.

Lady Scilly never thinks of having an afternoon-party now without at least two fortune-tellers in different parts of the house. You see people waiting in little lumps at the doors; in a little more, and they would be tying their handkerchiefs to the handles, just as you do to bathing-machines, to say who has the right to go in first. They go in shyly, just like people who have made a stumble in the street, looking silly, and they come out looking humble, like people who have been having their hair washed. The fortune-teller doesn't tell women the very serious things, for instance, that they are going to die themselves, though she tells them when their husbands are. They always tell Ariadne what sort of coloured man she is going to marry, but as there are only two sorts of coloured men, fair and dark, it is sure to come right sometimes. The last time the woman said, "Fair—verging on red!" and as Ariadne doesn't know any man who has anything like red hair except Mr. Aix, whom she doesn't care for, she frowned and said, "Are you quite sure?" The woman changed it to dark, almost black, in a great hurry, and Ariadne was pleased, for it is a safer colour. Ariadne wears a piece of wood let into a bracelet that Lady Scilly gave her, just the same as she wears herself, and touches it whenever she thinks misfortune is in the air, or when she is afraid of making a fool of herself more than usual. She took me out to gather May dew in Kensington Gardens, and very smutty it was. She always counts cherry-stones, and once at the Islingtons' lunch when it came badly, she actually swallowed Never!

Now, in Lady Scilly's set, they call her "The girl that swallowed Never," and it seems to amuse them. Anything amuses them, especially a nickname. I myself wonder Ariadne did not have appendicitis, or at least that apple-tree growing out of her ear they used to tell us of when we were children. At luncheon parties now, they make a joke of refusing to help her to greengage, cherry, or plum-tart, in fact to anything countable, and Ariadne doesn't seem to see that it is plain to them all that she is anxious to be married, which, though it is true, sounds unpleasant, at any rate for the men. She is wild to be married, and to go away and leave this house and have a house of her own that she can ask me to come and stay at, and Miss Mander. I think it is a very good wish, only why make it public? Nor she needn't let every one know that George only gives her fifteen pounds a year to dress like a lady on. It is cheaper to dress like an artist or a Bohemian, or in character, and so she does. We don't have any dressmaker, we hardly know the feel of one even. Mother and Ariadne make their own clothes, and Mother never going out, is able to give Ariadne a little extra off her own allowance. I don't know how much that is. She will never tell.

Mother has all the taste that Aunt Gerty hasn't got. It is odd, how taste skips one in a family! Aunt Gerty is like a very smart rag-doll, dressed in odds and ends to show the fashion on a small scale. And fashion after all is only a matter of "bulge." You bulge in a different place every year, and if you can only bulge a little earlier, or leave off bulging in any particular place sooner than other people, well, you may consider you are a well-dressed woman!

Ariadne makes money doing his reviews for George. He gives her sixpence a head, when he remembers to. Dozens of books come in to our house every week, from *The Bittern*, and for *Wild Oats*. George is "Pease Blossom" on *The Bittern*. We don't need to subscribe to a library, we live in a book-shop practically, for they are all sold in Booksellers' Row afterwards. George takes the important ones, of course, and gives the smaller fry to Ariadne to do. She is his understudy. When they are ready George writes hers up, and Christina types them, and it all goes in together. He once reviewed a batch of bad ones under the heading of *Darnel*, and people thought him clever but malicious.

Papa doesn't know it, but Ariadne has an understudy too. She lets the novels out to me, and gives me twopence a head. I must say that she has no idea of beating one down. I read them as carefully as I have time for—it depends on how many Ariadne gives me—and then when she is doing her hair, I sit beside her, and tell her the plots. The more improper ones she keeps to herself, but I read those for pleasure, not work, so it's all right.

Ariadne knows about a dozen useful phrases that she didn't invent, but found ready made. "Up to the level of this author's reputation" is one; "marks a distinct advance," "breezy," "strong, or convincing," and the opposites, "unconvincing," "weak," "morbid," "effete," are useful ones. She uses all these turn and turn about, and always mentions "a fine sense of atmosphere" if she honestly can.

She has great fun sometimes, when she meets the authors in society. She flirts with them till they get confidential, and tell her about their books, and how totally they have been misunderstood by the press, and what a crassly ignorant set reviewers are! They explain to her that not one of the whole d——d crew has the slightest sense of responsibility, especially The *Bittern*, which has got the most God-forsaken staff that ever paper went to the devil with! Ariadne is amused at all this and gives them another chance of conversation, and then they go on to quote her own words to her!

Once, though, she got caught, and George very nearly took all the reviewing away from her, for he had to stand the racket himself, of course. She had actually said at the end of the review that it was a pity Mr. —— I forget the author's name—did not relieve our anxiety as to the perpetrator of the hellish crime, which to the very end he allowed to remain shrouded in obscurity. Well, as a matter of fact, there was a hanging scene and dying confession in the last chapter but one, but Ariadne unfortunately burnt that before she had got to it. She was using the novel as a screen to keep the draught off the flame for heating her tongs, and so she never read that part, and had to make up her own end. The editor of The *Bittern* had to acknowledge the error and apologize in a footnote, because the author threatened a libel action. Ariadne doesn't care about meeting that man in society!

It is fairer at any rate for Ariadne to review books than George, because she doesn't write them. People who write books shouldn't have the right to say what they think of other people's; it is like a mother listening to tales in the nursery, and putting one child in the corner to please another. I once went into the study and saw George walking up and down, and throwing light bits of furniture about.

"D—m the fellow! He's stolen the babe unborn of an excellent plot of mine, and mauled it and ruined it, beyond recognition!"

It was no use my putting in my word, and saying, "Well, then, George, you can use it again." He went on fuming and fussing, loudly dictating a regular corker of a review.

"I'll let him have it! Go on, please, Miss Mander. '*The signal ineptitude of this author's*——'"

I am sure that was going to be a very unpleasant review to read, though I never saw it in print.

Ariadne is sentimental, and doesn't care for realistic novels at all, which is a pity, as George's greatest friend, and the person who comes oftenest to this house, is a realist, and wrote a novel called *The Laundress*. He lived in Shoreditch in a tenement dwelling for a whole year to learn how to write it from the laundresses themselves,— he went to tea with a different laundress every afternoon? The one he wrote about had three diamond rings and three husbands to match. He himself wore flannel shirts then, not nice frock-coats such as he has now, but the flannel shirts weren't because he was poor, but so as not to frighten the laundresses by looking too smart. Then the book came out, and there was a great fuss about it, and it was published at sixpence, and our cook bought it, and it lies on the kitchen-table beside the cookery-book.

That is the reason Mr. Aix, being a realist, makes more money than Papa, who is an idealist. You see, Duchesses and Countesses want to hear all about laundresses, just as much as cooks do, but though Duchesses and Countesses are interested in mediæval knights and maidens, cooks—nor yet laundresses— aren't.

"The suburbs do not appreciate me as they do you, old man!" he says sometimes. "If I was proper, they wouldn't even look at me!"

"Ay! the suburbs?" George says dreamily; "the kind, the mild, the tenderly trustful suburbs. I manipulate them freely. I have taught Peckham Rye and Clapham that there are stranger things in Pall Mall and Piccadilly than are dreamt of in their simple philosophy——"

"You have tickled the Philistines, not smitten them!" says Mr. Aix.

"I have shocked them—they love being shocked! I have startled them—that does them good. I have puzzled them—not altogether unpleasantly. I have inured them to Dukes and familiarized them with Duchesses, as the butcher hardens his pony to a motor-car. I reduce to a common, romantic denominator——"

"You are like those useful earthworms of *le père* Darwin, bringing up soil and interweaving strata," said Mr. Aix wearily.

George accepted the worm reluctantly, and went on. "Yes, I dominate the lower strata, they dote on any topsy-turvy upper-class gospel I chose at the moment to formulate for their crass benefit. Miss Mander, did you ever envisage Peckham?"

"I lived there and sold matches once," said she, "and, moreover, I've kept a Home for distressed female-authors in the Isle of Dogs."

"Is there anything you haven't done?" said Mr. Aix, quite jealous of a woman interfering in his own line. He always makes a point of living among his raw material. When he was writing *The Serio-Comic*, in order to get the serious atmosphere—which I should have thought gin would have done for well enough—he went every night of his life to some music hall or other, and went behind and talked to them, and fastened their frocks at the back for them, and put in hair-pins when they stuck out just as they were going on. Then he stood them drinks, and didn't preach for his life, for if he had, the serio-comics wouldn't have told him anything or shown him the secret of their inner life. He had to pretend that he thought them and their life all that was perfect. Christina calls this novel "The Sweetmeat in the Gutter," and loves it, though George says it is as broad as it's long, and that ladies shouldn't read it. But Christina has been to Klondike and seen the seamy side, so it doesn't matter. *I* have read *The Serio-Comic*, and I can't see anything wrong. There's more seriousness than fun in it. Miss Deucie Dulcimer's real name is Frances Raggles, and she's the mother of five in the course of three hundred and fifty pages, and there's a brandy-and-soda in every chapter.

Mr. Aix is forty, but he looks like a boy. He has a snub soft nose like Lady Scilly's pug, with wrinkles on the bridge of it. He wears spectacles because of his weak eyes, and he always says "Quite so," as if he were good-natured enough to agree with Providence in everything. He is the opposite of George, who is proud to be considered cat-like. Perhaps that is why they are friends. If Mr. Aix were a dog, he would knock over everything with his tail. He has no tact. He never drinks anything but water, and does calisthenics before breakfast with an exerciser on a door. He is the kind of man who would put stops in a telegram—so very punctilious. His eyes are wall, and look different ways, and Aunt Gerty says that once at a dance he asked two girls for the same polka, and they both accepted, because he looked at them both at the same time.

He is about the only person who doesn't think Ariadne pretty, so Ariadne naturally dislikes him. She can't help it. If we didn't let her think she was pretty, she would have jaundice, or something lingering of that sort. She snubs Mr. Aix, but somehow he won't consider himself snubbed. It comes of having no sense of decency, as the reviews say of him. Christina chaffs him, and teases him about his next novel, and asks him if it is to be called *The Dustman* or *The General*, and what the *locale* is to be, the scullery or the collecting-places just outside London?

I have an idea that it will be called *The Seamstress*, for he has lately taken to coming up into the little entresol on the stairs where we sit and stitch, and make our frocks, and asking us to teach him to sew. He puts out a hand like a sheaf of bananas, Ariadne fits a needle into one of them, and he cobbles away quite painstakingly for an hour.

Once he came up when Ariadne was awfully tired, and could hardly keep her eyes open, as she always is after a dance.

"I have often wondered," he began, "what must be the sensations of a young girl on entering on her kingdom of the ball-room. Is she dazzled, is she obfuscated by the twinkling repetition of the lights? are her senses stunned or stimulated by the ponderous beat of the time, relentless under its top-dressing of melody, like despair underlying frivolity? Is she——?"

He would have gone on for ever if I had not interrupted—

"I can tell you. She's thinking all the time, 'Is there a hair-pin sticking out? Is the tip of my nose shiny? Is my dress too short in front, and is it properly fastened at the back, and what does Mr. —— it depends which Mister is there that evening—think of it all?"

"Don't, Tempe!" said Ariadne.

"No, no, Miss Tempe, go on, I beg of you. Go on being indiscreet. Tell me some more things about women."

"Do you know why women always sit on one side when they are alone in a hansom?"

"No, I have no idea. Some charmingly morbid reason, I suppose?"

"Oh, you can call it morbid, if you like," I said. "It is only because there happens to be a looking-glass there."

George and Mr. Aix have different publishers, but the same literary agent. A publisher once took them both to the top of a high hill in Surrey and tempted them—to sell him the rights of every novel they did for ten years, and be kept in luxury by him. But they both shook their heads and said, "You must go to Middleman!" Then he took them to a London restaurant and made them drunk, and still they shook their heads and sent him to Middleman, who makes all their bargains for them, but he can't control all the reviews.

One morning Mr. Aix came in to see George, with a blue press-cutting in his hand; I was in the study then, as it happened, and I did not go. George never minds our hearing everything, he says it is too much of an effort to be a hero to one's typewriter, or one's daughter.

"I am in a rage!" Mr. Aix said, and so I suppose he was, though he looked more like a white gooseberry than ever. "Just let me get hold of this fellow they have got on *The Bittern*, and see if I don't wring his neck for him!"

George didn't say anything, and so I asked—somebody had to—"What has *The Bittern* man done, please?"

"Done! He has dammed me with faint praise, that's all! I'd have the fellow know that I'm read in every pothouse, every kitchen in England! Here, George, take it, and read it, the infamous thing!"

George read it—at least he ran his eyes over it. He didn't seem to want to see it particularly, and gave it back as if it bit him, saying—

"Well, my dear fellow, you must take the rough with the smooth—one can always learn something from criticism, or so I find!"

"What the devil do you suppose I am to learn from an incompetent paste-and-scissors understrapper like that? He wants a good hiding, that's what he wants, and I for one would have no objection to giving it him!"

"Well, it wasn't me wrote it, Mr. Aix," I said, "nor Ariadne!" He isn't supposed to know that George farms out his reviews.

Mr. Aix laughed, and left off being cross. The odd thing was, that it had only just missed being Ariadne or me, for the book certainly came in for review. Most likely George wrote it, or else why didn't he trouble to read it, when it was given him to read? It looks as if he were growing a little tiny bit of a conscience, for he knows he ought to have said to *The Bittern* editor, "Avaunt! Don't tempt an author to review his friend's book, when he knows he cannot speak well of it for so many reasons!" That is my idea of literary morality.

CHAPTER XI

GEORGE came back from his yachting tour with the Scillys very brown and cheerful, having collected enough sunshine for a new book, and Christina is typing it at his dictation.

George is a cranky dictator, and it takes her all her time to keep in touch with him. I have watched her at it. Sometimes he stops and can't for the life of him find the right word, and I can tell by her eyes that she knows it, and is too polite to give it him; just the way one longs to help out a stutterer. But I have seen her put the word down out of her own head long before George has shouted it at her, as he does in the end. She picks and chooses, too, a little, for George is a tidy swearer, as the cabman said. I suppose he learned it in the high society he goes among! He does it all the time he is composing; it relieves the tension, he says, and she doesn't mind. She manages him. George pretends he knows he is being managed, which shows that he doesn't really think he is. I asked her once why she didn't marry, but she said the profession of typewriting was not so binding as the other, for you could get down off your high stool if you wanted.

Christina always says rude things about epigrams and marriage. She is not very old, only thirty; but she says she has outgrown them both. Of course in this house epigrams are the same as bread-and-butter, hers and ours, for George pays her a good salary for typing those that he makes ready for print. As for epigrams, she says she can make them herself, and here are some I found written out in her handwriting on a china memorandum tablet. I expect she keeps a separate tablet for her remarks on Marriage.

1. Man cannot live by epigram alone.

2. Epigrams are like the paper-streamers they fling out of the boxes at a *bal masqué* at the Opera. They flat fall immediately afterwards.

3. An epigram is like the deadly Upas Tree, and blights everything in the shape of conversation that grows near it.

4. Reverse an epigram and you get a platitude.

5. The savage, sour, and friendless epigram. The last sounds to me all wrong, for it has no verb. But I give it as I find it.

George's new novel is to be called *The Senior Epigrammatist*, and the scene is laid in the Smart Sea Islands.

"Our well-known blend," said Mr. Aix, "of opaline sea and crystal epigram knocks the public every time! But mark me, Christina dear, this sunlight soap won't wash clothes. It isn't for home consumption. It gladdens publishers' offices, but leaves the domestic hearth cold. The fires of passion——"

"Don't talk to me of passion," said Christina. "I just detest the word. Passion is piggish! It's a perfect disgrace to have primitive instincts, and I wouldn't be seen dead with a temperament, in these days."

She was putting a new ribbon into her typewriter and trying it. She typed something like this—

Christina x x x Ball x x C.B. x x (——) C. Ball B B——

"Who is Ball?" said Mr. Aix anxiously.

Christina answered as if she meant to bite his head off.

"A man who never made an epigram in his life, and stands six foot six in his shoes."

"The noble savage, eh? Well, well, I wish him luck!"

I knew who Ball was; it is Peter Ball, and Christina likes him. She hasn't said or typed anything against marriage since she knew him.

It was at a concert that some friends of hers gave in Queen's Gate, that she first met him. I was with her, and we all sat in rows on rout seats, that skidded and flew off like shirt-buttons across the room whenever you got up suddenly. Peter Ball sat next us, and his legs were long, though his feet were small. He had a golden beard, which I hate, and so, I thought, did Christina. She had always said there was one thing she would not marry, and that was a beard.

He wished out loud that he hadn't got let in for the sitting-down seats, so that he could not make a clean bolt of it when he had had enough of Miss Squallini. There was not any Miss of that name on the programme, so though he said loud, no one could be offended. A Maddle. Xeres told us quite slyly, lifting her eyebrows up and down, that "she knew a bank!" as if she had got up early like the worm, and found it all by herself. After that, one of the spare hostesses came wandering by and introduced him to us. He began to talk to Christina without looking at her, and gradually he forgot his legs and put one under the rout seat in front of him and lifted it up without thinking. The lady on it looked round indignantly and Christina smiled. After that he talked to us all through the programme though people shoo'd him, and then he stopped for a little and apologized, and went on again.

"I don't often turn up at this sort of function, do you?" he asked Christina.

"No, I do not," she replied, "I have too much to do as a general thing."

"And stay at home and do it," said he; "you're wise."

"I have to!" said Christina. "Oh," she sighed, "I am so dreadfully hot."

It was June.

"Why do you wear that bag?" he said, meaning her motor tulle veil, which was absurdly thick and made her look as if she had small-pox. But every one else apparently had a different form of the same disease, shown by a different size in spots. She said so, and that she wore a veil like every one else.

"Get out of it, can't you, and let me take care of it for you, and that boa thing you have got round your neck."

She took it off, and the boa, and gave them to him.

"I am afraid you will drop the boa, and let the veil work under the seat," she said in a fright, as he nipped them both in one great hand. So he pinned them, boa, veil, and all, to his grey speckled trousers with her hatpin, and sat all through the rest of the concert, looking at the bunch at his knee. I never saw a man like that before, he didn't seem at all like the people who come to Cinque Cento House. I didn't seem to see him there, and I rather thought I should like to. Why, he would make George straighten his back!

"I say," he said presently, "do you like gramophones?"

"I love them," said Christina, and I knew it was a lie.

"My people have a perfectly splendid one!" said he, and his whole face lighted up. "I wish you could hear it."

Christina wished she could, and he said—

"Oh, then, we will manage it somehow."

When the concert was over he didn't bolt as he had said he wanted to, but gave us ices, Christina one, me two, and then Christina put the bag on again.

"If you were in my motor in that thing in a shower you'd get drowned," said he. "Why, it would *hold* the water. I should like to drive you in my motor all the same. I say, can't I call on you?"

Christina told him very nicely that she was private secretary to the author, Mr. George Vero-Taylor, and hadn't much time for herself. She seemed to say that this made a call impossible.

"Ah, I see! Live in, do you? Well, I'll call there, drop my pasteboard, all straight and formal, you know, and then there can be no objection to my giving you a spin in the motor. Right you are! Sinky Cento House. What a rum name! Suggests drains! Never mind, I'll be there, and then when I've made the acquaintance of your chaperon, she'll allow you to come to tea with my mater, and make the acquaintance of the gramophone. My mater's too old to go out. It's a ripper, the gramophone, I mean, like some other people I am thinking of!"

"What a breezy man!" said Christina, on the way home. "He reminds me of The Northman I used to draw at South Kensington. I broke him, and had to pay seven-and-six for him." Then she began to think—I believe it was about Peter Ball. He *was* handsome, for he had blue eyes and a little short, straight nose like the Sovereigns in Madame Tussaud's.

"Isn't he exactly like Harold of England?" I said to Christina. "I hope George won't snub him when he comes to see you?"

"He won't come," said she; "but if he did he wouldn't know he was being snubbed."

"No, he would say to George, 'Keep your snubs for a man of your own size.' But, Christina dear, I always *thought* you hated both marriage and gramophones."

"I am not so sure about gramophones," said she. "Perhaps a very big one——?"

"A six-footer, like Mr. Peter Ball, eh?"

She was quite moody and absent in the 'bus going home, and wouldn't go on top to please me. Then I accidentally stuck my umbrella in over the top of her shoe as I walked beside her, and then she was too cross to speak at all. I respected her mood. That is why I am beloved in the home circle. But I have my own ideas, and they keep me amused.

I was unfortunately out of the way when Mr. Peter Ball did call, three days later. Mother and Christina were in, and Ariadne, who gave me a true account of it all. She says the first thing he said to Christina was, "I hope you don't think I have been too precipitate?" I suppose he meant in calling? He stared about him a good deal at first, and she thought that George's queer furniture made him feel shy, and that he thought the ivory figure of Buddha quite indecent. She was sure he didn't admire her (Ariadne), but only Christina, because Christina is a "tailor-made" girl, that men like. Mother made the tea very strong that afternoon, so as to make him feel at home, and then after all he didn't touch tea. She kindly offered him a brandy-and-soda and he declined that, but I expect it was only because it would have seemed disrespectful to Christina. All men are alike, and prone to a b. and s. if they can get it without disgrace. Mother was sure that he had fallen head-over-ears in love with Christina, and she with him at the very first sight. She told me so, and said she meant to help it on.

"It is because Christina is so used to seeing George every day," said I. "Peter Ball is very different, isn't he?"

Mother said that there was no accounting for tastes, and that for her part she considered George's type was the nicest. But whatever we did, she said, we were not to chaff Christina about it, and put her off a very good match. A girl of Christina's sort never took kindly to chaff, and though she should be sorry to lose Christina as a secretary to George, it being impossible to tell what sort of minx he might engage in her place, she for one wouldn't like any personal consideration whatever to interfere with Christina's establishment in life. Peter Ball is a landed gentry. He is M.F.H. in the county of Northumberland to the Rattenraw Hunt, and a capital shot and first-rate angler. When his old mother dies he will be richer, but he is a good son, and often stays with her in Leinster Gardens where he has asked me and Christina to go to tea next week.

I promised not to chaff, but if she had only known, it would have taken a steam-crane to put Christina off that particular thing. She talked lots about Peter. He was the "finest specimen of humanity she had ever come across!" "Such a contrast to the little anæmic, effete, ambisextrous (I hope I have got it right?) creatures that haunt Cinque Cento House, who are all trying to get more out of their heads than is in them!" "Greek in his simplicity, a sort of mixture of John Bull and Antinöus!" I say, just wait till you see his mother; nice men's mothers are sometimes sad eye-openers, and Peter Ball is always talking about his. Also it is quite on the cards that she may not like Christina, and then I am sure he will never propose to her. He is an admirable son. I believe he keeps a gramophone just to attract the girls he admires into his mother's cave, and give her the opportunity of looking over them, and making up her mind if they are fit to be her Peter's wife or no.

When the eventful day came, Christina was on thorns. She didn't know how to dress. She finally left off the chiffon bag and wore a fringe-net, and her best-cut "tailor-made," and took out her ear-rings lest they should damn her in his mother's eyes. Then at exactly five minutes to four we rang the bell in 1000 Leinster Square.

A proud butler opened the door. George will only let us have maids, although he could afford ten butlers.

The house was beautiful, and not a bit like ours. "Early Victorian," Christina whispered me. She was dreadfully nervous, and made me too. I dropped my umbrella in the rack with such a clatter that she blushed and scolded me. Then a palm-leaf tickled my head as I went by, and I begged its pardon, thinking some one behind was trying to attract my attention. We were taken into a big room with pedestal things in gold and stucco set down at intervals, and a clock with a bare pendulum which looks simply undressed to me, and a bronze Father Time with his sickle lying lazily across the top. On another clock there was a gilt man in a gilt cart whipping up two gilt horses. The carpet had large bouquets of roses on it, and I thought what a good game it would be to pretend they were islands and hop across from one to the other. I began, but she stopped me. In a corner was the gramophone, like a great brass ear put out to hear what you were saying. It was playing when we went in, like an old man with a wheeze, and in came Peter Ball looking as if he had just got out of a bath, and said, "How-do-you-do! it is playing 'Coppelia.'" Then it played "Valse Bleue" and "Casey at the Wake," and "Casey as Doctor," and "When other Lips," and then Peter Ball said his mother was ready.

Into another room we went, full of Berlin wool-work chairs, and screens of Potiphar and his wife, and the curtains were of green rep with ropes of silk to tie them back and gilt festoons to hide their beginnings, and an old old lady in a big arm-chair and a lace cap with nodding bugles was in a corner, just like another and older bit of furniture.

We were introduced; she was very deaf and very blind, and I am not sure she didn't think I was the girl Peter wanted to marry. However that might be, she seemed pleased with us, and we talked of her son and the house. Christina, who used to say she preferred a Chéret poster to a Titian, and plain deal to mahogany, admired everything freely. The rosewood wheelbarrow with silver fittings given to Peter Ball's father when he laid a first stone somewhere, she said was superb and so graceful; the picture of old Mrs. Ball by Ingres in a poke bonnet and short waist she said was far superior to anything by Burne Jones.

"Who is Burne Jones?" said the old lady, and Christina denied Burne Jones cheerfully. I thought of my favourite piece of poetry—

"See, ye Ladies that are coy,
What the mighty Love can do!"

Then we had tea (the cake in a silver basket on a fringed mat, if you please!), and after we had talked a little more, we said good-bye, and Peter took us out. He had rushed out of the room just five minutes before, when the first symptoms of leave-taking manifested themselves, and we saw why, when we passed out through the first room where the gramophone was. It played us out with "The Wedding March," surely a graceful thought of Peter Ball's!

"He's very nice, but what a pity he hasn't got taste!" I said as we came away. You see, I am used to Cinque Cento House, and I have always been told that there is only one taste, and that ours is it.

"Taste!" Christina mooned, as we got into a 'bus. "There's so much of it about, isn't there? On my word, it will soon be quite *chic* to be vulgar."

It was not difficult to tell which way the wind was blowing after that. It was about this time that Mr. Aix found Christina typing her own name and Peter's on a sheet of III Imperial. He hadn't even set eyes on Peter Ball then, but he did a few days later, when Peter Ball came to tea, holding his grey kid gloves in his hand. George, luckily, was out again, really out, not pretending to be in his study, and Mr. Aix it was who opened the front-door for Peter when he went away at seven.

"A man!" he said, when he came back to us all in the winter garden, and Christina was just going out— escaping to her own room to think over Peter Ball, I dare say—and she said as she passed him—

"I could hug you for saying that, Mr. Aix."

"No, you couldn't," said he. "I am popularly supposed to be repellent. A lady said I was like a white stick of celery grown in a dark cellar. Another, of music-hall celebrity, compared me to a blasted pipe-stem. I do not look for success with your sex. It was kind of you to think of it, though."

Peter Ball meant business, or else we could not have all spoken of it so openly. George was awfully cross at the idea of having to find a new secretary. Lady Scilly said she thought he could do better than Christina, who was too forward (and too pretty). She tried very hard to flirt with Peter herself, but perhaps Peter thought *he* could do better, and wouldn't. She looked into his face and said, "You great big beauty!" She told him "high" stories, as Christina and I call them, and he wouldn't laugh. She asked him right out why he wouldn't, and he answered equally right out, "Because I disapprove of all jesting with regard to the relations of the sexes!"

Lady Scilly looked disgusted, and left him severely alone, as he meant her to.

For weeks after this he was like a full pail of water one is afraid to carry without spilling. At last he slopped over, and asked Christina to be his wife. I wasn't in the room, of course, but Christina was nice and told us afterwards. He went on his knees, she says, and I believe her, because I found a cushion on the floor immediately after, before the housemaid had tidied the room, and I think he had managed to put it under his knees without her seeing. Our floor is bony.

"The very moment," she said, "he had got me to say yes, he jumped up and rushed out without his hat, to send a telegram to his mother with the good news!"

She thought this so nice of him and so flattering, as showing that he hadn't made quite sure of her. For though we all knew she meant to take him, he was not supposed to be aware of it. Considering that Christina is grown up, she ought to be able to make a man think exactly what she wishes him to think about her. Such power comes, or should come, with advancing years, and is one of its compensations. Ariadne, of course, isn't old enough to have left off being quite transparent, and regrets it deeply in some of her poetry.

Christina was married to Peter Ball almost directly, and Ariadne and I were her bridesmaids. Mrs. Mander gave us our dresses and hats. They were quite fashionable; she would have no nonsense or necklaces. Ariadne looked smart and like other people, for once. She didn't look so pretty, but it is a mistake to want to go about the streets looking like a picture. Prettiness isn't everything, and the really smartest people would disdain to look simply ready for an artist to paint them.

Simon Hermyre, Lady Scilly's best friend, was Peter Ball's best man. He had met Ariadne at the Scillys', but at Christina's wedding he said that he should not have known her again. He began to take some notice of her. She at once asked him to call, and it was a great mistake, for he never did. It is awkward for Ariadne, I admit, for Mother not going out, and George being perfectly useless as a father, she has to do all her own asking.

That can't be helped, but Ariadne is always hasty and strikes while the iron is too hot. Simon Hermyre did *rather* like her, but he wasn't quite sure that he actually wanted to take her on, and all that that means—and whether he liked her enough to risk making Lady Scilly angry about it, as of course she would be. At all events he didn't come—his chief kept him in till six o'clock every day, or some excuse of that sort. As if a man couldn't always manage a call if he wanted to, even if he were third secretary to some one in the planet Mars!

CHAPTER XII

WE never used to go away for more than a week every summer to Brighton or Herne Bay, but now that we live in the heart of the town, as of course St. John's Wood is, it has been decided that we want a whole month at the sea. This year Mother and Aunt Gerty chose Whitby in Yorkshire. It is convenient for Aunt Gerty—something about a company that she is thinking of joining in the autumn. George didn't care where we went, as he isn't to be with us. He just forks out the money as Mother asks for it; he trusts her implicitly not to waste it, and to do things as cheap as they can be done and yet decently, because after all we *are* his family, and everybody knows that now.

I sometimes think he would come with us himself, if Aunt Gerty wasn't so much about.

Ariadne and Aunt Gerty haven't got an ounce of country fibre in them. They get at loggerheads with the country at once. The mildest cows chase them, they manage to nearly drown themselves in the tiniest ditches, the quietest old pony rears if they drive him. If they pick a mushroom it is sure to be a toadstool; if they bite into a pear there's a wasp inside it; if they take hold of a village baby they are sure to drop it. They haven't country good manners, they leave gates open, they trample down grass, they entice dogs away, they startle geese and set hens running, and offend everybody all round.

So they weren't particularly happy in the first rooms we took, at a farm just out of Whitby. There was one stuffy little best parlour, sealed up like a bottle of medecine, and one mouldy geranium looking as if it couldn't help it on the window-sill, and the "Seven Deadly Sins" in chromo on the walls, and Rebecca at a well of Berlin wools over the mantelpiece. They covered the family Bible with an antimacassar, and Aunt Gerty's theatrical photos without which she never travels, and suppressed the frosty ornament in a glass case of one of Mrs. Wilson's wedding-cakes. Mrs. Wilson married early, she says, and I say she married often, for there are three of them! It *was* uncomfortable. Mother didn't complain, Aunt Gerty did. She had nowhere to hang up her dresses; they were all getting spoilt; she couldn't see to do her hair in the wretched little scrap of looking-glass, and the room was so small that she twice set fire to her bed-curtains, curling her hair, which she did twenty times a day, for there was always wind or rain or something. The walls were so thin that she could hear every word Mr. and Mrs. Wilson said to each other in the next room, quarrelling and arranging the bill and so on. She couldn't sleep with the window shut, and all sorts of horrid buggy things came in if you left it open. It was so dreadfully lonely here, and she had never "seen so much land" in her life.

Aunt Gerty has been on tour often enough to get used to uncomfortable lodgings, lodgings not chosen by herself, very likely, and her luggage all fetched away the day before she leaves by the baggage man! But it is in a town, and that makes all the difference. Give her a strip of mirror in the door of her wardrobe, and a gas-jet ready to set fire to her window-curtains, and a row of shops outside to cheer her up, and she won't think of grumbling.

The landlady didn't consider us a particularly good "let." I used to hear her in bed in the mornings explaining to Mr. Wilson, who is a railway porter, how glad she would be to be "shot" of us if it wasn't for the money. "Ay, lass!" he would answer, and then I used to hear him turning over in bed and going to sleep again.

"They're better to keep a week than a fortnight!" she used to say. "What with their late dinners and breakfasts in bed, and their black coffee, and all sitting down for an hour o' mornings polishing up them ondacent brown boots—they darsen't trust the help, no, not since she went and rubbed them with lard—poor girl, she meant well,—and she fit to rive her legs off answering the parlour bell every minute! Well, the sooner I see their backs, the better pleased I shall be!"

We took the hint and gave up the rooms, and got some nicer ones in town on the quay. Aunt Gerty left off bothering Mother to have late dinner and strong coffee, and we lived on herrings and cream cheeses, the cheapest things in Whitby. I mean the herrings. When they have a good catch, they sell them at a halfpenny each on the quay-side, or slap their children with them, or shy them at strangers. Anything to keep the market up!

Mrs. Bennison, our new landlady, isn't a Whitby woman, but her husband is, and owns a boat, and takes Ben out sailing, and tries to make a man of him. We hardly ever see him, so we know he is happy. Mother and Aunt Gerty sit one on each side of the bow window the greater part of the day, and make blouses, and read at the same time. George would throw their books into the harbour if he caught them in their hands; they are the sort he disapproves of. I won't say who the authors of these are, as being a literary man's daughter it might give offence, but they are by women mostly. George vetoes women's books too, for they are generally bad, and if they are good, they have no business to be.

Just now, George isn't here to object, he is at Homburg, doing a cure. He always gets brain fag towards the end of the season like his other friends. It seems to me the smartest illness to have, except appendicitis. The moment Goodwood is over, they all troop off to Germany or Switzerland and pay pounds to some doctor who only makes them leave off eating and drinking too much, and go to bed a little before daylight. It is kill and then cure with the smart set, every year. George does what is right and usual—bathes in champagne at Wiesbaden, and drinks the water rotten eggs have been boiled in at Homburg. He does it in good company, to take the taste away. Mr. Aix drew us a picture of George and a Duchess walking up and down a parade, with a glass tube connected with a tumbler, in their mouths, talking about emulating "The Life of the Busy Bee" as they went along.

About the middle of August we heard he had come
back to England and was paying his usual round of visits
to Barefront, and Baddeley and Fylingdales Tower.
Nearly all these places have real battlements and ghosts.
Fylingdales Tower is near here. Mother and I and Aunt
Gerty joined a cheap trip to it, the other day, and were
taken all over the house for a shilling. I don't even believe
The Family was away, but stowed away *pro tem.* and
staring at us through some chink and loathing us. I did
manage to persuade Aunt Gerty not to throw away her
sandwich paper in the grate of the fire-place of the room
where Edward the Third had slept on his way to
Alnwick, but kindly keep it till we were got into the
Park. But she was very irreverent all the same, and
insisted on setting her hat straight in the glass of Queen
Elizabeth's portrait, and that was the only picture she
looked at at all. I don't care for pictures much. I like the
house, which is old and grey and bleached, as if it never
got a good night's sleep. Too many spirits to break its
rest. I don't believe in ghosts really, but I often wonder
what are the white things one sees? I don't see so many as
I did when I was quite a child. Aunt Gerty shivered and
went Brr! She hated it all, she is so very modern. She
admitted that she only went with us because she had
hoped George might be actually staying there, and would
see his own sister-in-law among the trippers and get a
nasty jar. Mother is a lady, and knew quite well that he
wasn't there, or else she would not have let Aunt Gerty
go, or gone herself, even *incog.* George *had* been there
recently, though, for the black-satin housekeeper said so,
and that she read his books herself when she had time, or

a headache. "He's quite a pet of her ladyship's," she told Aunt Gerty, who had spotted one of George's books on a table and asked questions. She was dying to tell the old thing that we were relations of the great Mr. Vero-Taylor, but dursn't, for Mother's eye was on her. Mother looked as pleased as Punch though, and gazed at the chairs (behind plush railings) that her husband had sat on, and at the portrait in Greek dress, by Sir Alma Tadema, of the lady who "made a pet of him."

George had written from Homburg once or twice to me, and I used to read his letters out to Mother, who naturally wanted to hear his news. She was a little annoyed because he didn't mention if he was wearing the thicker vests as the weather was getting chilly, and begged me to ask him to be explicit in my next, but I did not, because it might have shamed him in the eyes of his countesses if he left the letter about, as of course he would. George respects the sanctity of private communication so much, that he never tore up a letter in his life; the housemaid collects them when she is doing his room, and brings them to Mother, who hasn't time to read them, any more than the housemaid has.

The third week in August George wrote to me, and told me to engage him rooms in Fylingdales Crescent on the East Cliff. You might have knocked me down with a feather!

Mother was hurt at George's having written to me, not her, on such a pure matter of business, until I explained that he merely did it to please the child! One doesn't mind making oneself out a baby to avoid hurting a mother's feelings. I don't know if Mother quite accepted this explanation, but she said no more about it, and told Mr. Aix the good news. He is in lodgings here, to be near us—Aunt Gerty thinks it is to be near her, and he lets her think anything she likes. He looks forward to George's coming with great interest, and says he will look like some rare exotic on the beach, such as a humming-bird or a gazelle. Aunt Gerty at once got hold of the visitors' list.

"Let's see which of his little lot is coming to Whitby?" she said, and hunted carefully through three columns till she found that Adelaide Countess of Fylingdales, Mr. Sidney Robinson, nurse baby and suite, were at the Fylingdales Hotel, on the East Cliff. Lord Fylingdales, her eldest son, is the widower of a Gaiety girl who actually died after she had been a Countess a year, poor dear! Aunt Gerty knew her. He is Lord of the Manor here, and his portrait is all over the place.

"Old Adelaide's a shocking frump, Lucy; you needn't distress yourself about her!" said Aunt Gerty consolingly to Mother.

"I am not distressing myself about her, Gertrude," replied my Mother, and she didn't look at all distressed in her neat short blue serge seaside dress, and shady hat. She looked ten.

"I know her son," Aunt Gerty went on. "A fish without a backbone. I very nearly had the privilege of leading him astray myself. It is Irene Lauderdale now, I hear."

"I wish you'd stow your theatrical recollections, Gerty," said Mother. "Come, Tempe, get your things on, we will go and take rooms for your father and my husband."

"Brava!" said Mr. Aix. "Capital accent there."

"Oh, you go along!" said Mother, and we went off at once and engaged George's rooms. We got very nice large ones, with dark green outside shutters to the windows, and took a great deal of trouble to explain George's little ways to them, for their sake as well as his. Ben will valet him. Mother told the people that he is bringing his man, who will, however, sleep out. George never gets up till twelve, French fashion.

Poor Ben, he may as well make himself useful, for he certainly isn't ornamental just now. He can't speak, he can only croak, and though he isn't very big, he seems to have the power of burrowing inside himself and bringing up a great voice like a steam-roller. He is not a manly man, yet, but he certainly is a boily boy. He has got some spots on his face that he thinks much bigger than they really are, and he keeps them and himself out of sight as much as possible. He says just now he doesn't care at all what he does, he doesn't even mind playing servant for a bit, if George would like it. Mother tells him he is a good boy and the comfort of her life, and that if she can manage it, she will get him sent to college after this, only he had better please the mammon of unrighteousness all he can. So he means to be a good valet to the Mammon.

The Fylingdales Hotel is in the best part of the town, on the East Cliff, and they dine late there every evening, and don't pull the blinds down, and the townspeople walk backwards and forwards, and watch the people dining at seven-thirty, dressed in their nudity. I think evening dress looks quite wrong at the seaside. Aunt Gerty and Mother put on a different blouse every evening, and look nice and cosy and comfortable, though George does say sarcastic things about the tyranny of the blouse, and the way Aunt Gerty will call it Blowse. I wash my face, that is all the dressing *I* do. Ben puts on an old smoker of George's, and flattens out his hair to support the character of being the only gentleman of the party, unless Mr. Aix is there to supper, and the less said about Mr. Aix's clothes the better.

Ben makes boats all day, when he isn't in one, and Ariadne makes poetry. Her one idea, having come to the sea for her health, is to avoid it, and seek the rather scrubby sort of woods which is all you can expect at the seaside. So every afternoon nearly we take a donkey to Ruswarp or to Cock Mill, and "ride and tie." We used to pick out a very smart donkey, but a very naughty one. He was called Bishop Beck, perhaps for that reason, and he went slow,—that was to be expected, but when he stopped quite still and wouldn't move for an hour or more in the middle of Cock Mill Wood, long, long after one had stopped beating him (for he looked at us and made us feel ridiculous), Ariadne said she would rather do without adventitious aid of this kind, for it interfered with her afflatus.

She walks up and down in the wood paths, finding rhymes, which seems the hardest part of poetry.

"Dreams—streams—gleams—" she goes on.

"Breams?" I suggest.

"Not a poetical image!"

"It isn't an image, it is a fish."

"It won't do. Am I writing this poem or are you?"

I don't argue. It doesn't really matter much how Ariadne's poems turn out. Being Papa's daughter she is sure to find a hearty reception for her initial volume of verse.

We used to stay out till what Ariadne called Dryad time. She thought she saw white figures hiding behind the trees in the dusk. Little pellets made of nuts and acorns and dead leaves, and so on, used to fall on us out of the thickets, and Ariadne said it was the Dryads pelting us. She thinks trees are alive, and that one of the reasons you hear ghosts in all old houses, is the wood creaking because in the night it remembers it was once a tree. I prefer to believe in ordinary solid ghosts instead of rational explanations like that. But still Ariadne's funny ideas make a walk quite interesting. Of course we never talk of such things at home, among materialists and realists like Aunt Gerty and Mother and George. George makes plenty of use of birds in his books, but he once came home from a visit to St. John's College at Cambridge, and told us that he had been kept awake all night by a beastly nightingale under his window. Now I have never heard this much-vaunted bird, but I am sure, from Matthew Arnold's poem where he calls it Eugenia, it must be a heavenly sound, quite worth while being kept awake by.

Ariadne and I stay out very late till it is getting dark, hoping to hear it, in Cock Mill Wood, and then we go home and race through supper, and then go out again, on the quays and piers this time. We don't know or care what George and his friends are doing, up above us, in the smart hotel on the cliff. What I should just love would be for some of them and George to come down for a walk in the dark and perhaps meet us, and for George to say, "Who are those little wandering vagabonds flitting about like bats? Why doesn't their father or mother keep them at home in the evenings?" It would be so nice, and Arabian Nightish!

At very high tides, we stay out very late, and take a shawl, and sit on a capstan and tuck it round us, and listen for a certain noise we love. It is when the water gets into a little corner in the heap of stones by the Scotch Head, and gets sucked in among them somehow, and then we hear a sort of sob that is better than any ghost. Ariadne and I put our heads under the shawl when we hear it, but not quite, so as to prevent us hearing properly.

The harbour smells at low water, and the town children yell and scream, and it isn't poetical then. So Ariadne and I like to go away on the Scaur and put our fingers in anemones' mouths, and pop seaweed purses, and pretend we are lovers cut off by the tide, as they are in novels. In the afternoons when the harbour is full we sit on the mound above the Khyber Pass, and watch the water filling up the hole between the opposite cliff and the cliff ladder. It is all quite quiet then. We don't hear any town cries, for the children that make the noise are turned out of their playground, and their mothers out of their good drying-ground, and the boats begin to go out of the harbour in a long, soft, slow procession—

And the stately ships go on
To their haven under the hill.

I am sure Tennyson meant Whitby when he wrote that.

One night we could not sleep because the woman next door had had her "man" drowned, and cried and moaned for hours. He was a fisherman, and we had seen his boat go out third in the row the day before. He is supposed to have fallen overboard in the night? Next day, Mother went in and gave her five shillings and she stopped crying.

Mr. Aix had a try to paint the view in front of our windows. At least he said there was no such thing in nature as a "view," and left out the Church and the Abbey, because they "conventionalized" things so. He belongs, he said, to the Impressionist School, if any. He got quite excited about his drawing, and at last went and borrowed a station truck to sit on; it raised him a little. One day a chance lady sat down on one of the handles, and over he went. It served him right for leaving out the two best things in Whitby.

When George came, Ariadne and I used to take turns to go and lunch with him at his breakfast, where we had French cookery. There were leathery omelets that bounced up like the stick in the boys' game when you touched the end of them with a spoon, and fillets that you wouldn't have condescended to have for a pillow, but still, it was French.

We were dressed nicely and took our clean gloves in our hands, and George wasn't ashamed of us, and introduced us to his friends. Lady Fylingdales' Mr. Sidney Robinson said I was like George—that I had his nose. I went to bed that night with a clothes-peg out of the yard on it, to improve its shape. But the old lady was half blind, and all made of manner. I also saw the Lord

Aunt Gerty might have led astray, and he hadn't a manner of any sort, and his nose wanted to run away with his chin.

George had no fault whatever to find with the arrangements Mother had made for his comfort, and he told her so, the first time he saw her, in Baxter Gate, coming out of the Post Office. The first place George flies to in a town is the Post Office, to send telegrams. He corresponds entirely by telegram with some people; he says it is paying five-pence more for the privilege of saying less. We had been shopping. George spotted us, and Mother thought he had rather not be recognized, but he was good that day and he actually left Mr. Sidney Robinson—a commoner, married to a countess, and that exactly describes him, Aunt Gerty says—to say a word to his own wife. It was market day, and we had bought several things in the Hall across the water. A pound of blackberries and a cream cheese, and a chicken and a cabbage, each from a different old woman with a covered basket. Mother had a net and I a basket to put them in. I was glad that George did not offer to "relieve" us of them, like the young men Aunt Gerty picks up here; but he stopped and talked to us quite nicely for a long time. He and Mother seemed to have a great deal to say to each other, and the basket-handle began to cut my arm in half. Also it was a very hot day. George had on a white linen suit, and a straw hat from Panama. He looked quite cool, and like Lohengrin or the Baker's man. Mother didn't. She looked hot. I touched her elbow, not so much because of my arm that ached, but because she looked like that, nor did I think it looks well to stand talking in the street to gentlemen, even if it is your own husband.

"Well, George," she said, taking my hint at once, "we must be going on. The butter is melting and the chicken grilling and the cabbage wilting while I stand here talking to you."

"Charming!" said George, but he wasn't thinking of us, but of Mr. Robinson, who was champing a few yards away. We said "Good-bye" without shaking hands. George, I think, might have lifted his hat. I have read of fine gentlemen who lifted their hat to an apple-woman, let alone their wife and child.

George and his friend walked off together. I suppose the Robinson man was too well-bred to ask George who his lady-friend was, as any of Aunt Gerty's men would do, but he certainly stared a good deal. Of course he knows who we are, everybody in Whitby does, I should think, and they most likely conclude that it is less unkindness than the eccentricity of genius. If you haven't got that blasted thing called genius, I suppose you can bear to live in the same house with your wife!

We walked slowly home with our purchases. Mother had a headache all dinner, and lay down in the afternoon.

"I met your father, Ben," she said at supper. "His boots want a little attention."

"I don't believe," said Ben crossly, "that any one ever had a more tiresome man to valet. He will wear his clothes all wrong, and then is always ragging and jawing at a fellow because they don't look nice."

"Hush, Ben, he is your father."

"Hah, I was forgetting!" said Ben, and gave one of his great laughs, as if you were breaking up coal, or something. Ben is now so changeable and nervous that you never know where to have him. He is growing up all wrong, but what can you expect of a boy brought up by women? He never sees a boy of his own position, though I know that in London he has some low companions he daren't bring to the house. The Hitchings are his only respectable friends, but they live such a long way off now. Jessie Hitchings is devoted to Ben, but she is only a girl like Ariadne and me. Mr. Hitchings told mother, years ago, that the boy was being ruined, and Mother cried and said she knew it, but could do nothing, for his father was by way of educating him at home till something could be settled. Snaps of Latin, and snacks of Greek, that is all George gives the poor boy when he has a moment, and that is never.

This is the only grievance Mother has, although Aunt Gerty is always trying to persuade her she has several, and putting her back up. Mother ends by getting cross with her.

"For goodness' sake, you Job's comforter, you, leave off your eternal girding at George. Can't you see, that as long as a man has his career to establish—his way to make——"

"His blessed thoroughfare is made long ago, or ought to be. That is what I can't get over——"

"You aren't asked to get over it. It is not your funeral, it is mine, so shut up. A man like George, who is dependant on the public favour, needs to be most absurdly particular, and careful what he does lest he injure his prestige. Look at yourself! You know very well in your own profession how very damaging it is for an actor to be married; that if an actress marries her manager, he has to pay dear for it in the receipts. She had better not figure as his wife in the bills, if she wants him to get on. You can't eat your cake—I mean your title—and have it. No, it's bound to be Miss Gertrude Jennynge on the bills, even if it is Mrs. What-do-you-call-it in the lodgings, with a ring on her finger, and every right to call herself a married woman. The public don't care for spliced idols. An artist has to stand clear, and preserve his individuality, such as it is!"

"And run straight all the time. I'll give George credit for that. But there, whatever's the good of it to you? A man can make a woman pretty fairly miserable, even if he is stone-faithful to her. It's then it seems all wrong somehow, and doesn't give her a chance of paying him in his own coin!"

I think Aunt Gerty is the reason why George fights so shy of his family. He hates her style, and yet he can hardly forbid Mother seeing as much as she likes of her own sister. The trail of the stage is over us all. Not that I see anything a bit wicked about the stage myself! I have never noticed anything at all wrong, and actors and actresses are the kindest people in the world! But there is a queer, worn, threadbare, rough, second-rate feeling about them. Off the stage—and I have never seen them on—they are tired and slouchy and easy-going. Aunt Gerty is most good-tempered and will do anything to help a pal, and takes things as they come; those are her good points. But she talks such a lot about herself, and never opens a book that isn't a novel, and wears cheap muslins and beaded slippers in the street, and lots of chains that seem to be always getting caught on men's buttons. She calls men "fellows." She is always going to play Juliet at one of the London houses. Meantime she puts up with provincial companies. She makes the best of it, and she tells us she is going to play Nerissa in the Bacon Company, as if she had got engaged for a parlourmaid in a good house, and discusses Ariel as if Ariel were a tweeny or up-and-down girl between the sky and the earth, and Puck a smart clever Buttons. She speaks of her nice legs as a workman might of his bag of tools. She can sing and dance, when she isn't asked to act. She has cut all her hair short to make it easier for wigs. Her great extravagance is in wigs. She calls them "sliding roofs" for convenience in talking about them in trains and omnibuses. When she did wear her own hair she dyed it, so I like the wigs better, as there's no deception.

If Mother was ever an actress, which I don't somehow believe, though Jessie Hitchings said once that she had heard people say so, it has all been knocked out of her. She dresses very well, always in simpler things than Aunt Gerty. She left off her waist years ago, to please George, and now that it is the fashion not to have one, she is in the right box—I mean stays. Her hair is brown, and she mayn't frizzle it, so it is soft and pretty like a baby's. She generally wears black, over lovely white frilled petticoats that she gets up herself to keep the bills down. She has such little hands that she can pick her gloves out of the five-and-a-half boxes at sales, which are always much reduced. So few people have small hands. She may not wear high heels, and that is a grief to her, as she isn't very tall, but hers are very pretty feet, and she can dance.

George doesn't know that she can dance. I do. Once Mr. Aix asked her to dance for him when I was in the room. Aunt Gerty played on the tin-kettle piano. Mother danced a cake-walk, which I thought very ugly, and then a queer step that a friend had taught her when she was a child. In one part of it she was dancing on her hands and her feet at the same time. It was the queerest thing, and she left her dress down for that and it lay in swirls about the carpet. Mr. Aix said it was the dance that Salome must have danced before Herod, and he quite understood John the Baptist, and where did she get it? But Mother wouldn't tell him. She said it was a memory of her stormy youth in the East End.

Mr. Aix said that she could make her fortune doing it as a turn at a Society music hall, as it would be something quite new and decadent. That is just what Society wants—the slight, morbid flavour! Then Mother put on her short skirt and did the ordinary vulgar kind of dance they teach now, and I liked it best. She was everywhere at once, smart and spreading out in all directions, like spun glass on a Christmas card. Her eyes danced too. Ben said he couldn't have believed she was his mother!

Then Aunt Gerty performed, and she is professional. But it was not the same thing. Aunt Gerty's legs are thick, and compared with Mother's like forced asparagus to the little pretty, thin, field-grown kind. Mother's dancing was emphatically dramatic, Mr. Aix said.

I asked him if Mother could act, and he answered, "My dear child, your mother can do anything she has a mind to."

"Then why doesn't she have a mind?" I at once said, forgetting how it would upset our household and George if she were to go on the stage. Mother naturally remembers this, and stays domestic out of virtue.

"I wish you would write a play for me, Mr. Aix," said Aunt Gerty, "and I would get a millionaire to run it. I wonder, now, what one could do with Mr. Bowser?"

She went off in a brown study, and Mr. Aix said rudely, "I will write a play for Lucy sooner," looking at Mother, who was sitting fanning herself with her pocket-handkerchief. "She has got the stuff in her, I do believe. Gad! What a chance! What a lever! What a facer—!"

And he dropped off into a brown study too! Mother went and mended Ben's blazer.

Mr. Aix isn't staying with us, we have no room in our house; he has a room over the coast-guard's wife, but he comes in to us for his meals. I don't believe George realizes this, or he would tell him he is throwing himself away, and losing a good chance of advertising his books. Mr. Aix's books seem to go without advertising, more than George's do—I suppose it is because they are so improper.

At any rate, he prefers to throw in his lot with us. One day we were all having a picnic-tea at Cock Mill. The party consisted of Mother, me and Ariadne, Aunt Gerty and Mr. Aix, and an actor friend of hers and his wife, who was acting for a week at the Saloon Theatre. Mr. Bowser, whom Aunt Gerty wants either to marry or get a theatre out of, was with us too. They call him the King of Whitby, because he owns so many plots in it, and is going to stand for it in the brewing interest next election. We had secured the nicest table, the one nearest the stream, and had just tucked our legs neatly under it, when a carriage drove up. Aunt Gerty and the King of

Whitby were at that moment in the old woman's cottage who gives us the hot water, toasting tea-cakes.

The Fylingdales' party got out of that carriage, and George got slowly down off the box. They trooped into the enclosure, and Mr. Sidney Robinson, trying to be funny, asked the old woman if she could see her way to giving them some tea.

"Here o' puppose, Sir!" said she, as of course she is. She pointed out the table that was left and that led them past us.

If Aunt Gerty had been there with Mr. Bowser she would certainly have claimed George as a relation and said something awkward, but she was luckily toasting tea-cakes, and had perhaps not even seen them. I saw George just look at Mother, and I saw her smile a very little, and make him a sign that he was to go right past us, and not speak or seem to know us before. Of course Mr. Aix never spoils any one's game, not even George's. So he went on talking hard to the actor's wife, though I saw his lip curl. I, of course, never need be given a cue twice, so I kicked Mother hard under the table for sympathy, but preserved a calm superior.

Aunt Gerty and Mr. Bowser came out with plates full of tea-cakes they had cooked, and I didn't know if it was the fire or Mr. Bowser had made Aunt Gerty's cheeks so red—I hoped the latter for her sake. They had no idea of what had happened while they had been toasting and flirting, it appeared from their manners, which were bad. Aunt Gerty always puts an extra polish on hers when George is present, and even Mr. Bowser would have added a frill or so to suit the aristocracy.

Our party was very gay. Actors all can make you laugh if they can do nothing else, and our shrieks of laughter must have made the other party quite envious, for they were as quiet as a mouse and as dull as the stream all overshadowed with nut-bushes and alders that grew over it just there.

Suddenly George got up, and left them, and came over to us, and Aunt Gerty swallowed her tea the wrong way round, and had to have her shoulder thumped.

George took no notice of her, but put his hand on Mr. Aix's shoulder and said something to him in a low voice.

"Not if I know it!" Mr. Aix answered, quite violently, adding, "Many thanks, old fellow, I am happier where I am."

George looked awfully put out. Of course I knew what he wanted. Those smart people up at the other table had expressed a wish to see Mr. Aix. He is a successful though painfully realistic novelist, and George had told them he was actually sitting at the next table, and had promised to bring him over to them to be introduced. In his disappointment, he glared at us all, especially the actor, who didn't care a brass farthing for George's displeasure, and went on eating tea-cake *ad nauseam*.

"Oh, all right!" said George, to cover his vexation, "if you prefer to bury yourself in a——"

"Easy all!" Mr. Aix said. "Leave everybody to enjoy themselves in their own way. And we are depriving your delightful friends of——"

George had turned and gone back to his delightful friends long before Mr. Aix had finished his sentence, and Aunt Gerty patted the poor man on the back till he wriggled.

"Loyal fellow!" she said several times. She had got well on to it now, and she started a fit of giggles that lasted all the rest of the time we were there. It didn't matter much, for we were all quite drunk on weak tea and laughter.

But we turned as silent as mice as the Fylingdales' party, having had enough of their dull tea, streamed past us, and got into their carriage, and rolled away. George was not with them. I dare say he had got over the hedge and gone round to meet the break by the road, not wanting to walk past our party again, and to avoid unpleasantness. I supposed he had paid for the tea; but no, this grand party forgot to do that, so that in the end

Mr. Aix paid for their refreshment for the old woman's sake that she should not suffer.

When they had gone, we felt relieved; but it sobered us somehow. Aunt Gerty and the gentlemen smoked quietly, and we were so still that we could hear the little beck bubbling over the loose stones beside us. Then Aunt Gerty was persuaded to recite something, and she did "Loraine, Loraine, Loree!" in a shy, modest voice. You see these were all her real bosses, and she valued their approval, and the actor's wife is considered very stiff in the profession. She herself sang "The banks of Allan Water" very sadly and solidly, and Aunt Gerty cried. To cheer us all up again the actor—rather a famous one, Mr. D—L——, did one of his humorous recitations out of his London repertory for us, so that we nearly died with laughing, and Aunt Gerty dried her tears, and whispered to me that trying to laugh like a lady was so painful that she longed to take a short cut out of her stays.

CHAPTER XIII

LADY SCILLY came to Whitby and took a big house in St. Hilda's Terrace.

"They can't be parted long, poor things!" Aunt Gerty said, and Mother hushed her. She brought her great friend Miss Irene Lauderdale with her, for a good blow, before she went to America.

Then all the shops came out with portraits of Irene, in "smalls" as Dick Turpin, and Irene as "The Pumpeydore," and Irene as Greek Slave, and Irene in Venus. They had her on picture postcards too in all the principal stationers' windows. I should have thought she would have been ashamed to walk down the street, hung with her own likeness like a row of looking-glasses that reflected her. But these very languid—what Aunt Gerty calls "la-di-dah" sort of people—can stand anything, so long as it's public.

When she wasn't dressed up as Turpin or Pompadour or Venus, she was just a tall, thin, and ragged-looking woman. She had red lips that stuck out a long, long way, and crinkly red hair, and large eyes like two gig-lamps coming at you down the street. She generally had a dog with her, and its lead kept getting twisted round the wheels of carts, and round my father's legs as he walked along Skinner Street beside her. He wouldn't have stood that from any one but a popular favourite.

I was walking along behind them a few days after she came, with Aunt Gerty. They stopped at Truelove's and looked at the picture-postcards. She became very serious all at once.

"I must go in and procure Myself!" she said to George, sniggling. In they went, and Aunt Gerty and I walked in after them. Mrs. Truelove's shop and library are very dark. As for the morality of it, we had as good a right to buy picture-postcards as they, and, as I had ascertained from other rencounters of this kind, George knows very well how to ignore his family when needful for his policy. I do not resent it, for one never knows how a daughter's presence may interfere with a father's plans and arrangements, and I am sure I don't want to injure his sales!

Irene turned over all the cards, including the Venus set, and did not approve of them, especially of the ones where she is turning away her face altogether.

"The blighted idiot!" she said, meaning I suppose the photographer, "has completely missed my beautiful Botticelli back! The effect is decidedly meretricious. I am a very good woman. Ah, these are better!"

She had got hold of some of herself in a spoon bonnet and long jacket, and she sang out loud, while Aunt Gerty's open mouth betrayed her shock at her audacity—

"Oh, I'm Contrition Eliza,
And she's Salvation Jane.
We once were wrong, we now are right,
We'll never go wrong again."

"I can't quite promise that, alas! My friends won't let me. I will send Salvation Jane to Lord R——y, a very dear old friend of mine. A dozen dozen, please; isn't that a gross? Oh, what a naughty word! Will you pay, Mr. Vero-Taylor?"

"Good business!" said my Aunt. "Let me see? How much has she rooked him?"

"Please don't ask me to do sums," said I. "Besides, George has a perfect right to do as he pleases with his own money!"

George paid cheerfully, and then asked for some cards with cats on them.

"Whatever do you want them for?" asked Irene. (He never lets me say whatever.)

"To send to my children."

"Ah, yes, your sweet children! Where are they?" she asked.

"In the nursery," was George's answer, as if he cared whether we were in the copper or the stockpot! It saved him from having to say Whitby, however.

"And now," she said, "do me a great kindness. Buy me your last great book."

"There ought to be some of my work here," George replied gravely, and made a move in our direction, where Mrs. Truelove was. Mrs. Truelove sings in the choir at the Church upon the Hill, and so loud she would bring the roof off nearly, but in her own shop she is as mild as a lamb. George asked her for *Dewlaps* (of which the heroine is a Tuscan cow), and *The Pretty Lady*, of which Lady Scilly is the heroine, and *The Light that was on Land and Sea*, and *Simple Simon*, of which the hero really was a pieman, only an Italian one. Poor Mrs. Truelove looked blank.

"I am afraid, Sir, we do not stock them, but I can order——"

George interrupted her. "Such is Fame! I have no doubt, *Belle Irene*, that if you were to ask for any one of Aix's books—*The Dustman*, or *The Laundress*, or *Slackbaked!* you would be offered a plethora of them."

Irene took her cue. "But," she drawled, "it is extraordinary! Impossible! Inconceivable! Books like yours, that rejoice the thirsty soul, that refrigerate the arid body, that bring God's great gift of sunshine down into our too gloomy grey homes! I always say this, dear, dear Mr. Vero-Taylor, that you, of all men, have caught the secret of imprisoning the jolly sunbeams. Every page of yours is instinct with light——"

It sounded like an advertisement of some new kind of soap. Aunt Gerty didn't like it at all, and in a rage with George she put out her hand suddenly and spilt a vase of flowers in water.

"Brute!" she said, and the assistant who mopped up the water kept saying, "Not at all!" not thinking Aunt Gerty meant the gentleman who had just left the shop in haste, but as apologizing for her own stupidity in upsetting the water.

"Who was that lady?" I asked Aunt Gerty as we went home, though I knew well enough.

"Izzie Lawder, a lady! I remember her—well, perhaps I hadn't better say what I remember her! She and I—she had got on a bit ahead of me even then—played together at the 'Lane' in 'Devil Darling!' ten years ago. She has got on since. Everybody to give her a leg up! You know the sort—dyed hair and interest! She soon left nice honest me behind."

"Hadn't you the interest, Aunt Gerty?" I knew she had the other thing.

"Don't be impertinent, Miss. Let us get home and tell Lucy. Won't she be electrified!"

But Mother wasn't a bit electrified.

"All in the way of business, my dear girl!" she said to Aunt Gerty, who chattered about Irene all the rest of that day. "Do subside about my wrongs, if you don't mind. I dare say he wants to get her to play lead in the drama he is writing with Lady Scilly, and that is why he is so civil to her."

"Another ill-bred amateur! What will they make of it?" snorted Aunt Gerty.

"Irene Lauderdale is Lady Scilly's best friend."

"Best enemy, you mean. However, it is the same thing. These unnatural friendships between Society women and actresses sicken me! Always in each other's pockets! It is a bad advertisement for them both, and there she was, plastering George up with compliments about his books, that I don't believe she has ever read a single one of. Sunshine indeed! He may well put sunshine into his novels; he has taken pretty good care to take it all out of one poor woman's life!"

"I am perfectly happy, Gertrude. I look happy, I am sure."

"You sham it."

"That is the next best thing to being it."

"A wretched skim-milk substitute! You are a right good sort, Lucy, and have got a husband that doesn't come within a hundred miles of appreciating you."

"Yes, he does, and at my true value, I suspect. I am good for what I do; I know my place and I fill it. I should only hamper George if I insisted on sharing his life and knowing his friends. I am too low for some of them, I admit; but I am too high for Irene Lauderdale. I wouldn't condescend to have anything to do with her. I despise and scorn her!" said Mother quite loudly for her, and suddenly too, as she began so mild.

I thought what a good actress she would have made. I believe Aunt Gerty thought so too, for she screamed out, "Bravo, Luce!" Mother burst into tears. I don't think it is nice for a daughter to see a mother's tears, so I left the room and went into the back room where Ben was messing at something as boys will. I told him on no account whatever to go into the front room to Mother till half-an-hour had elapsed. I thought that was enough law to give her. Ben naturally asked why, and hit me over the head, not hard—Ben is a gentleman and always tempers the blow to the shy sister, but still I preferred taking a whack to giving Mother away.

A few days after that Mother went up to Fylingdales Crescent to see George on business, and found him in bed with a bad cold. You see these Society people, who are only getting their amusement cheap out of George, don't understand the constitution of their toy, and he doesn't like to let them see that he is only a mortal author, and that it is death to him to be without his hat for a minute or his coat for half-an-hour. He has got a very sensitive mucous membrane and catches cold in no time. I sometimes think it is the opposite of Faith-healing with him—George *believes* himself into his colds. He says that the sensitive mucous is the invariable concomitant of the artistic temperament, which he has. Mr. Aix says he hasn't that, what he has is the biliolymphatic one, and that makes George very angry. However this may be, the tiniest bit of swagger costs him a cold in the head, and that is what he has now. He had already altered his will and begun to talk of flying to the South to be extinguished there gently, when Mother came to him.

"My dear boy, no!" Mother said, and George groaned as he always does when she calls him boy, but invalids can't be choosers of phrases. "You aren't going to die just yet." She went on, kindly banging his pillows about—"I shall have to stay here with you a little, though, I fancy, to look after you. I shouldn't wonder if they didn't make objections in the house. There will be a bit of a fuss."

"Who will make a fuss, Mother?" I asked, "and why should they?"

"Don't ask questions about what you don't understand," Mother said sharply, though what else really should I ask questions about? "Run home and tell your Aunt that I am going to get a room here for a night or two, and that she is to send my things, just what I'll want for a couple of nights."

"Night-gown and toothbrush," said I. As I left George put out his hand to Mother and said quite nicely—

"You are very good to me, dear. And can you really stay and soothe the sick man's pillow?"

Mother sat down and put the blanket in its proper place, not grazing his cheek, and gave him a drink, and read to him out of Anatole France. She kept saying, "I *know* they'll think I am not respectable."

The thought seemed to amuse her very much, and George too, and I left them, and went home and gave Aunt Gerty her directions. Aunt Gerty chuckled as Mother had said she would, and said—

"This will clear up George's ideas a little! Nothing like an ugly illness for letting a man know who his true friends are! Looks lovely, don't he? Is its blessed poet's nose a good deal swollen?"

I said no, George looked very nice in bed, a mixture of the Pope and Napoleon combined. I left her and went back to Mother with her things. George by that time was arranged. He had a silk handkerchief tied over his forehead. He said he did that to keep his brain from being too active, like the British workman girds his loins with a belt before he begins to dig. He looked very happy and quite stupid. I took our cat Robert the Devil up with me and put him on George's chest to soothe him. It did, and he played with my hair.

"I am an angel when I am ill," he said; "don't you find me so? Strong natures like mine——"

Mother then came in with a great bunch of roses,— seaside roses always look coarse, I think—and a lot of cards.

"Lord and Lady Scilly and Lady Fylingdales and Mr. Sidney Robinson and Lord John Daman have called to inquire, and Miss Irene Lauderdale has left these flowers for you, George. Look at them and be done with it, for I don't mean to have them left messing about in my sickroom, exhausting the air. Tempe can take them home when you have smelt them, though I don't suppose you can smell anything just now."

She put them to his nose and he smelt. Irene's card was on the top. It had a monogram in one corner—a gold skull and crossbones. I never heard of people having their monogram on their visiting-card before, but one lives and learns.

"I don't, of course, expect you to admire The Lauderdale as a woman," George said. "But what, as a dramatic authority, do you think of her as an actress?"

"I consider that dear old Ger could do quite as well if she had one half her chances," Mother said eagerly.

"No doubt, no doubt! The cleverness lies in laying hold of the chances! Irene has a genius for advertisement."

"Look after the 'ads,'" said my Mother, "and the acts will take care of themselves."

"Good!" said George, "I should like to have said that myself."

"I dare say you will, George," said Mother quite nicely, "when once I get you well again."

I do think Mother is rather fond of George: she got him cured in less than a week, but she didn't let him out once during that time, and had him all to herself. It was great fun, seeing all his friends wandering about Whitby bored to death because Vero-Taylor was confined to the house. They used to get hold of me and Ariadne, and ask us how long they were going to be deprived of the pleasure of his society? They knew who we were by this time and made pets of us, as much as we would let them. I was too proud, but Ariadne's decision was complicated by a hopeless attachment she had started. "Love is enough!" she used to say, "and I *must* go to Saltergate with the Scillys, for Simon is going!"

CHAPTER XIV

THE young man that Ariadne loves is a more than friend of Lady Scilly, and I knew him first. He was there that day I lunched for the first time. On rice-pudding, I remember. Ariadne hardly knew him till we came here, though they had both taken part in Christina's wedding. He had just noticed her then; for once she was well turned out. On the strength of that notice she asked him to call, and he didn't; he would call now if she asked him, but we don't want him coming to the house on the quay, for we couldn't insulate Aunt Gerty.

He stays with Lady Scilly in the house she has taken in St. Hilda's Terrace. Irene Lauderdale is there. He hates Irene, and contrives never to be in her company more than he can help! That's one to us.

His own family lives up in the dales, Pickering way. George stayed there once, when Lady Hermyre was alive, and builds a sort of little recitation on what he observed in his friend's house. Whatever isn't ormolu is buhl. There are six Portland vases along the cornice of the house containing the ashes of the family. Portraits of stiff horses and squat owners all the way up-stairs. Everything, including the butler, excessively *collet monté*, excepting the portraits of the ladies of the family, frowning ascetically over their own bodices *décolleté à outrance*. Sir Frederick is one of the most prominent racing men of Yorkshire, and the stables are model, but the house isn't. Prayers, bed at ten, no bridge, and early breakfast, and prayers again. I don't think George will ever be asked again, but I don't wonder Lady Scilly was able to get hold of Simon. *She* doesn't frown over her *décolleté* bodices, and she is amusing in her silly way. Simon hangs round like one of those young fox-hound puppies "at walk" that one sees in the villages, and Lord Scilly looks after his future and got him into the Foreign Office. I believe, though, Lord Scilly twigs about Ariadne caring for him, that Lady Scilly doesn't, or else she would not let him out so freely. She would be like most teachers and insist on her pupil's finishing his term. A wise woman would not have brought Irene Lauderdale down here, to preoccupy her. It will take her all her time to keep Simon away from Ariadne, if once I give my mind to it. I do. Ariadne and Simon don't make appointments, but they keep them. I am generally there, but I don't count. There is the Geological Museum on the Quay, which is never used for anything but casual appointments, and the old Library, where they have all the three-volume people, Mrs. Gaskell and Miss Jewsbury and Mrs. Oliphant. Ariadne and I read three a day regularly. We sometimes meet Simon on the quay, when we are carrying a whole hodful, and Ariadne won't let him carry them for her, she doesn't like him to know that she is reading all about Love.

Simon doesn't really want to find out. He never wants very much anything. He never fights any point. That is what I like about him, and hate about Bohemians. They never glide or slip over things, they always scrape and drag and insist. But people who have got their roots in the country, as Simon has, are simple and not fussy and have no fads. I wonder what Simon thinks of George? It is the last thing he would tell me or Ariadne. He likes Mr. Aix, rather, but he would not, perhaps, if he had read any of his novels? Mr. Aix makes him laugh, and I like to hear his nice little curly laugh. If only Simon's eyes were bigger, he really would be very handsome. Ariadne's, however, are big enough for two.

This is the first time she has ever been in love, she says, and it hurts—women. It doesn't hurt a man who loves in vain, only clears up his ideas a little, and shows him the kind of girl he really does want when the first choice refuses him. A refusal from first choice only sends him straight off with his heart in his mouth to second choice, who is waiting for the chance of him. I am sure that is the way most marriages are made—hearts on the rebound. The first girl is a true benefactor to her species, and gets her fun and her practice into the bargain. Ariadne has now reduced this to a system, from novels. In refusing, you must remember to hope after you have said that it can never be, that you will at least always be friends. With regard to accepting, she thinks and I think, that the nicest way is to hide your burning face on the lapel of his coat and say nothing, and then when you come up again the rough stuff of his coat has made you blush, a thing neither Ariadne nor I have ever been able to manage for ourselves.

Novels tell you all sorts of things, for instance, when and what to resent, otherwise you might say thank you!

for what is really an affront. Out on the Cliff Walk the other day, it came on to rain, and a man offered to lend Ariadne his umbrella, and see her to her own door. A harmless, nay useful proposal. But my sister knew—from novels—that that sort of thing leads to all sorts of wickedness, and that she must unconditionally, absolutely refuse. She was broken-hearted at having to sacrifice her best hat, but bravely bowed and refused his offer, and went off in the rain, feeling his disappointed eyes right through the back of her head, and hearing the plop-plop of the rain-drops on the crown of her hat all the way home. But she had behaved well. That was her consolation.

Aunt Gerty took that man on afterwards—she met him turning out of the reading-room at the saloon, and he offered the very same umbrella! Aunt Gerty accepted it, and hopes to accept the owner too some day, for it was Mr. Bowser.

Ariadne goes the wrong way to work. Her one idea when she gets on at all with any man—and she does get on with Simon, that is certain—is to collar him, to curtail his liberty, and give him as many opportunities of being alone with her as she can. She says it is an universal feminine instinct. Very well, if she chooses to be guided by this wretched feminine instinct, she will muff the whole thing. She should let the idea of being alone with her come from him, lead him on to propose it, and manage it himself, and then—squash it!

Men are very easily put off or frightened; a racehorse isn't in it with them. To feel at ease, they must be made to think that it is all quite casual, that nobody has arranged anything, and that as for themselves, though there is no harm in them, no one particularly wants them. If they can get it into their heads that they won't be conspicuous by their absence, they buck up immediately, and want to be in your pocket. When one is at a theatre, one is quite comforted by the sight of Extra Exit stuck up here and there, although I dare say if you came to thump at those doors in despair you would find it no go!

So when Ariadne makes a face at me to leave her, I don't see it. I sit tight, wherever we are, knowing that young men adore being chaperoned. And at parties, if you notice, the one woman they never throw a word to is the woman they adore, and mean to secure. They want to marry her, not talk to her. The casual Society girl will do for that. Ariadne sometimes comes back from a party quite disconsolate, because so-and-so hasn't said a word more than was strictly necessary for politeness to her.

"Excelsior!" I said. "I do really believe he is thinking of it."

Simon always seems to have plenty of pocket-money, and gives to beggars in the street. Yet his eyes are little, and Cook always said that that goes with meanness. Anyway they are very bright, like an animal that you come on suddenly in a clump of green in a wood, perhaps I mean a hare? He always sees jokes first, and looks up and laughs. He is very keen on hunting, and singing, but his father snubs him, and says he doesn't ride as straight as Almeria, and has no more voice than an old cock-sparrow. He would see better to ride if he wasn't short-sighted, anyway. I don't believe he ever reads, except Mr. Sponge's Tour and Mr. Jorrocks' something or other, and books in the Badminton Library. He knows a little history, about St. Hilda and the Abbey, and I shouldn't be surprised to hear that he thought she was some sort of ancestress of his, and that Cædmon was a stable-boy about his Aunt Fylingdales' estate.

I feel quite like a mother to him, and Ariadne loves him passionately, and is leaving off eating for his sake. Not on purpose exactly, but because she is so worried about him. He is awfully nice to her, but he never gets any nicer. He is nice to anybody; it is only because Ariadne is the only girl in the set here about his own age, that it seems as if it would be neat and right that he should fall in love with her. I am not quite sure that Simon can fall in love, it is the dull men who do that best, not the universal favourites. But if Simon has any love latent, I am anxious to get it all for Ariadne.

She hates herrings now, and doesn't care for cream. She lives principally on jam-tarts and cheese-cakes. It is the proper thing to go about eleven in the morning to that shop on the quay and eat tarts and cheese-cakes standing, and watch people pass, and the bridge opening and shutting to let tall funnels go through. Ariadne sometimes has to wade through half-a-dozen tarts before Simon and Lady Scilly and the dogs and the rest of them come round the corner of Flowergate, and surely it is a pity to spoil your complexion for the sake of any young man in the world? No digestion could stand the way Ariadne treats hers for long. She plays it very low down on her constitution generally. She won't go to bed till awfully late, but sits by the window telling her sorrow to the sea and the stars, and writing poems to the harbour-bar, that never moans that I know of. Luckily, as yet, it doesn't show in her face that she has been burning the midnight oil, or candles. She burns three short fours a night sometimes that she buys herself. She has made three pounds altogether by writing poems that Mr. Aix puts in an American paper for her. She doesn't let Simon know that she publishes, for it would discredit her in his eyes. He says there's no harm in girls scribbling if they like, but he is jolly well glad his sister doesn't.

Simon is proud of his sister Almeria, and thinks her a "splendid girl." She lives at their place with her widowed father, eight miles inland, and only comes to Whitby when rough weather and wrecks are expected. Then every one walks up and down the pier, and hopes that a hapless barque will come drifting to their very feet. I don't mean we actually want there to be a wreck, but if it has to be, it may as well be where one can see it. For Ariadne has a tender heart, and when Aunt Gerty put the loaf upside down on the trencher the other day, Ariadne at once kindly put it on its right end again, for a loaf upside down always betokens a wreck, and she knows all the superstitions there are.

The two piers here are so awkwardly placed that in rough weather the poor boats can't always clear them. So it is a regular party on the pier when the South Cone is hoisted at the coastguard-station. Irene Lauderdale wears a little shawl over her head like a factory girl. It can't blow away, she says. She has been photographed like that, with Lord Fylingdales. They say she is going to marry him, and do what Aunt Gerty refused to do.

I don't know if they are a very united family, but certainly his sisters chaperon him most carefully, and have taken care to be great friends with Irene, so as to have an excuse for being always with her. Lord Fylingdales never gets a chance of seeing her alone. Dear Emily (Lady Fenton) and dear Louisa (Mrs. Hugh Gore) are devoted to dear Irene, and she thinks it is because she is so nice, so good form, not because she is so nasty. They perfectly loathe and detest her. I heard Lady Fenton abusing her to some one, talking in the same breath of Almeria Hermyre as "one of us." The sisters would prefer Lord Fylingdales to marry his cousin Almeria, of course, but her get-up is simply appalling. She wears plain skirts and pea-shooter caps, and no fringe. George says she has the most uncompromising forehead he ever saw—a *front candide* with a vengeance! I should think she soaps it well every morning, it looks like that.

Her father is about as queer as an old family can make him. I wish some one would tell me why if you came in with the Conqueror you are generally queer, or without a chin? Why do you always marry your near relations? Do you get queerer as you go on? No one ever answers these questions. Sir Frederick Hermyre has acres of stubbly chin, true, but he takes it out in queerness. He always wears white duck trousers, like the pictures of Wellington, whom he is rather like. He says "what is the good of being a gentleman if you can't wear a shabby coat?" and does wear it. His house at Highsam is a show house, only they don't show it. They are too careless, and too untidy, and too mean in the shape of housekeepers. One day some Whitby tourists went over to Saltergate in a break, and strolled up his drive to look at the Jacobean Front, and met Sir Frederick, as shabby as usual; he had been working in a stone quarry he has there, I believe.

"Did you wish to see me?" he asked the front tourist politely.

"Thanks, old cock, any extra charge?" said the tourist. It was of course all the fault of those old trousers and linen coat, and I have heard that Sir Frederick was not so very angry, and stood the man a glass of beer. He is a Liberal in spite of owning land. Simon is a Conservative. Eldest sons are always different politics to their fathers. We never see the old man hardly except on these stormy pier parties, and then he stalks up and down the pier with his daughter among us all, and though he isn't exactly rude to anybody, he never seems to hear or care to hear what anybody is saying. Blood tells. Lady Scilly has given him up in disgust long ago; he simply answered her straight as long as he could, and when he didn't understand her, he just shook his head and grinned and turned away.

Simon stood by, looking rather like a little whipped dog. He is awfully afraid of his father, who isn't proud of him, but of Almeria, who he says has got all the brains of the family, and ought to have been the boy.

Simon tried introducing Ariadne to Almeria, but Ariadne's fringe proved an insuperable barrier. As for Ariadne, Almeria's naked forehead made her feel quite shy, she said, such a double-bedded kind of forehead as that needed covering. I said, all the same, she was an idiot not to make friends with Simon's sister, for he had obviously a great respect for the girl's opinion. She might have plenty of sense in spite of her bald forehead and clumpers of boots! But it was no use, they stood glaring at each other like two Highland cattle, while Simon was trying to invent a mutual bond between them.

"My sister writes a little," he said.

"Only for nothing in the Parish Magazine," said Almeria, witheringly.

—"And goes about," he went on, "with a hammer collecting——"

"Bedlamites and Amorites," said I, to make them laugh.

They didn't laugh, and Simon continued—

"And pebbling and mossing and growing sea anemones in basins."

Then I got excited, and as Ariadne stood mum, I supported the conversation.

"And isn't it funny to feel them claw your finger if you put it in their mouth—well, they are all mouth, aren't they?"

"And stomach!" said Almeria, turning away politely.

Ariadne had hardly said a word, but had left the conversation to me. But any one could see that these two never could get on. Ariadne looked as she stood on the pier, plucking at bits of hair that would get loose, just like a pale butterfly caught in the rain, while Almeria stood as fast as a capstan and as stumpy. And the abominable thing was, that Almeria was not in the least rude. She was always civil, perfectly civil—but civility is the greatest preserver of distances there is if people only knew.

Simon gave her up as far as Ariadne was concerned. He stuck to Ariadne, but did not neglect other girls or any one else for her sake, and so compromise her. He has got a lot of tact. Ariadne hasn't any, but she is gentle and easily led, and Simon is the kind of boy who is going to grow masterful, and likes a girl who gives him the chance of standing up for her and managing for her. Perhaps he is a little bit sorry for her. Not because she is so dreadfully in love with him; he isn't conceited enough to see that, or Ariadne would have shown him long ago. He is sorry for her because she gives herself away so in so many ways, looking pretty all the time. That is important, for it is no good looking pathetic, unless you look pretty as well. He chaffs her about her fluffy hats that go all limp in the salt sea-spray, and her pretty thin shoes that let the water in, and her hair that never will stay where she wants it. She has got into the way of continually arranging herself, patting a bow here, pulling her sleeves down over her wrist, and arranging her hair. "Always at work!" he says suddenly, and Ariadne's guilty hands go down like clockwork. It isn't rude, the way he says it. He looks at her kindly, not cheekily. It is that kind sort of fatherly look that I like, and that makes me think he is fond of Ariadne.

She is different from Lady Scilly, whom he is beginning slightly to detest. Sometimes he looks quite glum when she is ordering him about, but he obeys. What do married women do to men to make them their slaves as they do, and yet one can see by their eyes that they don't want to? And why are the women themselves the last to see that the servant wants to give notice and would willingly forfeit a month's wages to be allowed to leave at once? Lady Scilly is just like a mistress who avoids going down into her own kitchen to order dinner, at a time when relations are strained, lest the cook takes the chance of giving her warning. Lady Scilly is the least bit afraid of Simon's cooling off, and just now prefers to give him his orders from a distance.

She calls Lord Scilly "Silly-Billy," and "my harmless, necessary husband." He is not dangerous, and he certainly is useful, for she really could not go about alone wearing the hats she does. She has one made of a whole parrot, and a coat made of leopard skins. I like Lord Scilly. He is rather fat, and knows it. He has a hoarse sort of voice, and yet I don't think he drinks much. Perhaps it is the open-air life that he leads among horses and dogs and grooms; at Summer Meetings and Doncaster, and so on. He is well known as a fearless rider, and risks his neck with the greatest pleasure. If I were Lady Scilly, I should much prefer him to George, though not to Simon. His chest is broader than George's, and he is taller than Simon, but then she isn't married to either of those. Marriage is like the rennet you put into the junket—it turns it!

He seems quite used to the kind of wife he has got. He isn't at all anxious to change her. He hardly ever talks about her—even to me. That is manners. Even George has got that sort of manners, so that half these smart people don't realize that my father has got a wife, or ever had one! They might, if they liked, and after all, if Mother doesn't choose to know his friends, he cannot force her! She won't go out with him, though she makes no difficulties about our going. She likes us to go, as it opens our eyes and gives us chances. Her business is to see that we are clean and have nice hair not to disgrace him, and we don't, or he would soon chuck us.

Lord Scilly always insists on our being asked to the picnics and parties they give. He likes us. He takes more notice of us than she does. I think he is a very lonely man, and quite glad of a little notice and attention even from a child. He is very observant too, I don't believe much goes past his eye. He thinks of everything from the racing point of view. Once when Lady Scilly and Ariadne were both standing on either side of Simon, receiving about an equal share of his attention, or so it seemed, Lord Scilly suddenly chuckled and said—

"I back the little 'un!"

He always talks of and to Ariadne as if she were very young indeed, and it is the surest way to rile her. She never forgave Mrs. Ptomaine a notice of hers on the dresses at some Private View or other, when she alluded to Ariadne's frock as worn by "a very young girl." Lord Scilly thinks a girl ought to be able to stand chaff, and is always testing her.

Ariadne had a birthday while we were at Whitby, and it fell on the day fixed for a picnic to Robin Hood's Bay. Simon sent her a present by the first post in the morning, a fan that he had written all the way to London for, in payment of some bet or other he had invented—I suppose he did not think it right to give an unmarried girl a present without some excuse like that?—and of course Mother and Aunt Gerty and I gave her something, and even George forked out a sovereign. That was all she expected, and not even that.

However, all the way driving to the picnic, Lord Scilly kept telling her that he was going to give her something as well; I was sure he was only teasing her, for there are no shops worth mentioning in Robin Hood's Bay, so I advised her to brace herself for a disappointment.

The moment he got to Robin Hood's Bay, he was off by himself, and away quite ten minutes, coming back with a showy paper parcel. At lunch he gave it her with a great deal of ceremony, so that everybody was looking. It was worse than I even had thought, a hideous china mug with "A Present for a Good Girl" on it in gilt letters. Ariadne has it now, only the servants have washed off the gilt lettering, using soda as they will. The baby was christened in it. But I am anticipating.

I had my eye on her as she untied the parcel, hoping and wondering if she would stay a lady in her great disappointment? She did. She thanked him quite formally and prettily for his charming present, though I saw her lip tremble a very little. I was awfully pleased with her, and so was Simon Hermyre, for I saw he particularly noticed her behaviour. As for the Scillys, their nasty little joke fell rather flat in consequence of Ariadne's discretion.

It was a most fearfully hot day. We all sat on the cliff in tiers, and talked about the delightful golden weather which was so oppressive and beastly that there was nothing to do but lie about and smoke. So they did. The men mopped their foreheads when they thought no one was looking, and the women used *papier poudrée* slyly in their handkerchiefs. Only Ariadne had none to use, and kept cool by sheer force of will. I was all right, being only a child.

Ariadne was sitting a little apart, with me, and she was writing a Poem to the sea, and she told me in a whisper as far as she had got—

"The patient world about their feet
Lay still, and weltered in the heat."

"What else could it do but lie still?" I said, and suddenly just then Simon got up—

"I say! I'm going to take the kids for a sail! Bring your new mug, Missy, and take your tiny sister by the hand, so that she doesn't fall and break her nose on the cliff steps."

After the mug incident I don't see how anybody could have objected, or tried to prevent Ariadne from taking the advantages of being treated as a baby, and I expect that was what Simon thought. Anyhow, Ariadne got up, and went with Simon and me as bold as any lion. It is a well-known fact that Lady Scilly can't stand the sea in small quantities like what you get in a boat, though of course she goes yachting cheerfully. None of the others were enough interested in Simon to care to move, and take any exercise in this heat. George gave her an approving little nod as she passed him.

We had a lovely sail of a whole hour's duration. We had an old boatman wearing his whiskers stiffened with tallow, who told us he had been a smuggler, and treated Ariadne and Simon as if they were an engaged couple, out for a spree, with me thrown in for a make-weight. It came on to blow a little, and got much cooler. Ariadne lost her hat, and had to borrow a red silk handkerchief of Simon's and tie a knot in it at all four corners and wear it so. She looked most proud and happy, as if she had on a crown, not a hat.

When Lady Scilly saw the latest thing in hats, she cried out, "Oh, my poor Ariadne!" and helped her to hide herself more or less in the waggonette going home. I didn't know before how becoming the cap was!

CHAPTER XV

WHEN George came, he took out a family subscription to the weekly balls at the Saloon, and we go, Ariadne and I. Mother will not and Aunt Gerty may not. Mother expressly stipulates that she shall refrain from doing as she wishes in this one particular, and as Aunt Gerty is mother's guest, she has to please her hostess. She grumbles a good deal at George's bearishness to her, in depriving her of any source of amusement in this dull place, but as a matter of fact she is very much taken up with Mr. Bowser. He was Ariadne's umbrella man. The Umbrella dodge came off with Aunt Gerty, and this unpoetical two became fast friends on the cliff-walk one rainy day. Mr. Bowser is a rich brewer, and very much mixed up with the politics of this place. He owns three blocks of lodging-houses on the Front. Of course Simon Hermyre's people won't have anything to do with him. It would be awkward if Ariadne married Simon and Bowser had previously married Ariadne's legal aunt. If Aunt Gerty does marry Mr. Bowser, then I do think George would be justified in cutting himself off from us all. To be the brother-in-law of Mr. Bowser would be the ruin of him. Well, chay Sarah, Sarah! as George says sometimes. At any rate we have no right to interfere with Aunt Gerty trying to do the best she can for herself. She is awfully kind to us and very loyal, Mother says, and she never gets a good word from George to make her anxious to please *him*. Mother gives her plenty of rope in the Bowser business, on condition she doesn't try to squeeze herself into the Saloon dancing set where George's friends go.

The dancing at the Saloon is very poor. The balls are only an excuse for going out on the Parade and watching the sea with a man. I like to watch it best myself, without a man. I like to see the whole dark sheet of water far away, and the thin white line near by that is all there is to tell one where the little waves are lying flattened out on the shore. The tide slips in so softly, minding its own business through the long evening while the idiots above galumph about and dance polkas in the great hall inside, with flags from the Crimea on the walls that flap in the draught of the North wind, and remind us constantly that we are hung over the sea.

There is a nice boy I like—he is twelve, quite young, and doesn't need conversing with. I simply take him about with me to prevent people meeting me and saying, the way they do, "What, child, all *alo-one* by yourself?" which is so irritating.

He never interferes, he trusts me, he likes me. He is the son of Sir Edward Fynes of Barsom, and they keep horses. I might say they eat horses and drink horses and sleep on horses there. Ernie wants me to like him, so he brought me a list of his father's yearlings, with their names and weights and what they fetched at the sale written out in his own hand. It interested him, so he thought it would interest me. It must have taken him hours to do, and when he put it into my hand, and ran away, what amusement do you think I could get out of this sort of thing?

Witch, ch. f. (II.B.) 2 yrs. Mr. Brooks 21 guins.

Milkmaid (h.h.) 3 yrs. " Wingate 30 guins.

Sappho (H.B. + ch.f.) Foal, 6 yrs. Lord Manham 35 guins.

And so on for a page of foolscap. Rather an odd sort of love-letter, but I saw he meant it, and didn't tease him.

Ernie and I moon about all the evening and watch the others. It is not etiquette to interfere with a lady who has her own cavalier, and that is why I annex Ernie, as Lady Scilly does Simon. We don't dance. I don't care to begin the dance racket till I am out and forced, not I, nor do I suppose the grown-ups want a couple of children getting into their legs and throwing them down. No, I watch them, and Ernie watches me.

Simon Hermyre and Lady Scilly dance half the time together. I suppose it is *de rigueur*. And when they are not dancing they are talking of money. I have heard them. I don't mind listening, for, of course, money isn't private. And I think it revolting to talk business on moonlight nights by the sea. They argue about bulls and bears and berthas, which puzzled me at first, till Ernie told me they did not mean either animals or women. Simon is not at all interested in any of them. Ernie (who is at Eton) says it is because he has nothing on, and only talks about stocks to please her.

Simon does not talk about dirty money when he is with my sister, he does not talk much about anything, and yet they seem to be enjoying themselves. Perhaps Ariadne is a rest after Lady Scilly?

One damp evening, Ariadne and he came out of the big hall together, but before she sat down in her white dress on one of the iron seats outside, Simon carefully wiped it with his handkerchief, though it hadn't been raining. Then, without thinking apparently, he put it up to his own forehead.

"Phew! I'm hot," he said. "It's a weary old world! Hope I die soon!"

Simon talks broad Yorkshire, I notice. Lady Scilly had been Simon's partner before Ariadne, and I had passed with my boy—that's what the grown-up women always call their special men!—just as Simon had taken out his nice gold-backed pocket-book with his initials in diamonds that I envy him so.

"Blow these wretched figures! They won't come!" I heard him say.

"On they come fast enough, not single spies, but in battalions," Lady Scilly had answered pettishly; "what I complain of is that they won't go! See if you can't pull me through, dear boy."

I thought it indecent of her to make poor Simon do her sums for her, on a heavenly night like this, when the tide is fully in, and all you can see through the white rails of the Esplanade is a soft creeping heap of dark water, like a pailful of ink. Simon now got up and looked down into it, and his forehead became one mass of wrinkles, like a Humphrey's iron building.

And Ariadne got up too, and looked into the water with him, but she said nothing. I know her pretty well, and that it was because she had nothing to say, and as he evidently didn't want her to say it, it didn't matter. She had put her hand on the railing, and it looked very nice and white in the moonlight somehow, quite like a novel heroine's, so she is repaid for her trouble and expense in almond paste-balls. Simon Hermyre looked at it, as I used to stand and look at a peach or an apple on the wall when I was little. He would have liked to pick it, as I would the apple or peach, and hold it tight in his own hand, I thought, but he didn't, but sighed instead and said—

"I wish I had a mother!" That wretched Ernie boy began to giggle. I nearly smothered him, for I wanted to hear what Ariadne would say.

"Do you?" she said. "I have."

Did any one ever hear anything so stupid and obvious? Yet Simon seemed to like it, for the next thing he said was—

"Why don't I know your mother? I expect she is gentle and sweet like you."

I have no doubt Ariadne would have been imbecile enough to answer Yes, not seeing the pitfall there was hidden in the words, but at that very moment George and Lady Scilly came out with a lot of other people. They came drifting along to the balustrade where we were, and Lady Scilly put her hand on Simon's shoulder very lightly, and George put his heavily on Ariadne's.

Simon whisked away his shoulder and wriggled as much as he dared. Ariadne of course could not move at all. She said afterwards she felt as if it was her own marriage-service, and that George was "giving this woman away" quite naturally. He likes to see her with Simon and shows it, it is the only time in his life that he is what they call fatherly.

Lady Scilly gave Simon two taps. "I love this thing, you know," she said to George. Then, going a little way back—"Just look at them! Isn't it idyllic? Romeo and Juliet spooning on a balcony over the sea instead of over a garden, and with a squawking gull instead of a nightingale to listen to. And I—poor I—am Romeo's deserted Rosaline. Did Rosaline take on Mercutio, I wonder, when she had had enough of Romeo?"

She glared up at George, and the moonlight caught her face the wrong way and made her look old. All the same, she would not have dared to say all this if she hadn't felt sure of Simon, and it proved that he hadn't been silly enough to make her think it worth while to be jealous of Ariadne.

"I always thought Mercutio by far the most interesting character in the piece. Come, good Mercutio! Romeo, fare—I mean flirt well!"

They turned away and left Simon grinding his little pearly teeth.

"I consider all that in *beastly* taste!" he said, whacking the rail with Ariadne's fan. Of course it broke, and Ariadne cried out like a baby when you have smashed its favourite toy.

Simon was thoroughly out of temper with all the world, Ariadne included. Lady Scilly had called him Romeo; well, he was jealous of Mercutio! Such is man— and boy! He spoke quite crossly to Ariadne.

"I'll give you a new one. I'll give you twenty new ones. Let us go in and dance—dance like the devil!"

Ernie told me a great deal about Lady Scilly after they had all gone in. He knows a lot about her, through his father, who has a place near the Scillys in Wiltshire. He says his father says that at this present moment she hasn't got a cent to call her own; what with gambling, and betting, she is fairly broke. I wish, then, she would try to borrow money off George—just once—for that would choke him off her soonest of anything, and then he would perhaps be nicer to mother?

Ariadne would not go to bed at all that night. She sat in the window, eating dried raisins, just to keep soul and body together. And all the time her affairs were progressing most favourably. She was vexed because she saw that Lady Scilly did not consider her worth being jealous of. I told her she was never nearer getting Simon than now when he was bringing a heart that Lady Scilly had bruised by sordid monetary considerations to her, to stroke and make well by her soothing ways. And Ariadne is soothing, she can do the silence dodge well. She is a regular walking rest-cure, I tell her, for those that like it.

Simon was unusually nice to her all the next week, just as I prophesied he would be. Then an untoward event happened.

There were dances at the Saloon only once a week. Next night a conjuror came to the Saloon Hall, called Dapping, and Aunt Gerty took us, paying one shilling each for us. There were worse seats, only sixpence, but there were also better, viz. the first four rows were three shillings. The Scilly party with Irene Lauderdale were in them, and on the other side, very obviously keeping themselves to themselves, there was Sir Frederick Hermyre and Almeria, and a severe woman aunt, and

Simon in attendance. The Hermyres were staying all night at the hotel, and he had to be with them for once, waiting on his father, not on Lady Scilly. It couldn't have been as amusing for him as her party, that laughed and joked, but still Simon as usual looked quite happy as he was. He would have thought it rude to look bored, and he did look so nice and clean, with his little *retroussé* nose next to his father's beak, and Almeria's large knuckle-duster of a proboscis framing them. I don't suppose Simon even knew Ariadne and I were there, for we were a long way behind, and he doesn't love Ariadne enough yet to scent her everywhere. Next us was Mr. Bowser, Aunt Getty's mash, as she calls him. I believe she had told him we were to be there. Ariadne and I were disgusted at being mixed with Bowser, and tried to make believe we were a separate party, and talked hard to ourselves all the time. Ariadne was in a white muslin she had made herself—window-curtain stuff from Equality's sale. It was pretty, but casual. She never will have patience to overcast the seams or settle which side they are to be on, definitely. She had made her hat too, of chiffon with a great trail of ivy leaves over the crown. I wished she had been dressed more soberly, considering the company we were in.

I wasn't attending very much, but presently I heard Mr. Dapping with Mr. Bowser, who as a leading citizen had gone on the stage, planning out a sort of trick. Dapping was first blindfolded, and Bowser was to go into the body of the hall and pretend to murder some one, and Dapping would tell him afterwards whom he had murdered. Dapping even went off the platform so as to be quite sure not to see, and Mr. Bowser came down the gangway in the middle, shaking his snub head about as he selected a victim—and he had actually the cheek to choose Ariadne!

He didn't ask Aunt Gerty or Ariadne either, if he might take this liberty, but just seized Ariadne by her thin muslin shoulder, and pretended to drive a knife into her back. It all happened before she had time to stop him. She wriggled, but of course they thought she was acting up. Then he sat down, quite pleased with himself, beside Aunt Gerty, and Mr. Dapping was released and his eyes unbandaged, and he came plunging down the gangway till he came to our row. He was intensely excited and puffing like a steam-engine, very disagreeable to hear.

He seized Ariadne by the same shoulder Bowser had murdered her at, and shook her, saying, "This is the victim!"

It made Ariadne horribly common, Aunt Gerty said afterwards, though she might easily have prevented it and told Bowser to hit one of his own class! Anyhow, poor Ariadne turned all the colours of the rose and the rainbow, and nearly cried for shame. She might as well have been on the stage, for she was just as public. All the Scilly party had of course turned round and were staring with all their eyes. Sir Frederick and Almeria never moved at all. Poor Simon did,—just once—and I saw his scared, disgusted face looking over his shoulder. I had never seen him look like that before. It was awful!

The conjuror went calmly on to the next trick, but poor Ariadne had been thoroughly upset. She whispered to me, "I can't stand any more of this. I believe I shall faint!"

That wasn't true, I knew, she can't faint if she tries, but still any one could see that she was feeling very uncomfortable.

I said to my aunt, "We are going, Ariadne and I. You can stay behind if you like."

And we got up and passed out amid a row of sympathetic—that was the worst of it—faces. Of course Aunt Gerty followed us out presently, and scolded Ariadne all the way home for allowing herself to be made a victim of. Ariadne never spoke, till we got in and up in our room. Then she burst out crying.

"He will never speak to me again. I know he won't. He is very proud, and I have disgraced him—disgraced him before his order!"

"You can't disgrace that until you are married to him, I suppose, and now you never will be."

"No," Ariadne said, meekly, "I am unworthy of him."

"You are very weak!" said I, "but on the whole I consider it was Aunt Gerty's fault. Brewing away like that and not attending to her charges!"

Ariadne cried and hocketed, as the cook used to say, all night, and I tried to comfort her and tell her that Simon would probably come to call next day to show that *noblesse oblige*, and that he didn't think anything of it. Of course when I remembered his face, I didn't suppose he would ever care to see a girl who had been pummelled, first by Bowser and then by Dapping, again.

All next day Ariadne would not go out. She said she could not meet the eye of Whitby. It rained luckily. Next day she still wouldn't, and as it was one of the best days we have had, I began to think that she was going too far with her remorse, and was quite cross with her.

"No one ever remembers anything that happened to some one else," I said; "and they can't see that your shoulder is black and blue under your gown."

"I feel as if I had been publicly flogged, and I had on my white muslin too," she moaned, though I don't know what she meant, that it had made a more conspicuous object, or was bad for the dress, or what.

"I know one thing," she gulped. "Aunt Gerty or no Aunt Gerty, I shall cut Mr. Bowser next time I see him— cut him dead."

"Why not? He murdered you."

I think this was Ariadne's first sorrow, and lasted quite a week. She would only go out after dark, to hide her shame from every eye. Mother encouraged her, and said she knew how she must feel. To Aunt Gerty she said several times, "Never again!" which is the most awful thing to say to any one. It meant that Aunt Gerty wasn't to be trusted with girls, and especially George's girls. Mother gave it her well.

"You should have prevented Ariadne from letting herself down like that! I shall never hear the end of it from George."

"George indeed! Why wasn't George looking after his own precious kids then? I don't think he's got any need to talk! My Lord Scilly will be having a word with him some of these days, or I shall be very much surprised!"

"You hold your wicked, lying tongue!" was all Mother said to her. Mother, somehow, hasn't the heart to be hard on Aunt Gerty.

I could have told Aunt Gerty that Lord Scilly was keeping quite calm. He can manage Lady Scilly well enough. I have heard him say so. "Paquerette knows the side her bread is buttered as well as any woman living! She is a right good sort, is Paquerette, only she likes to kick her heels a bit! She and I understand each other!"

He talks like this, as if they were like Darby and Joan, but Lady Scilly doesn't agree with him, or says she doesn't. "Scilly and I," she once said to Ariadne, "are an astigmatic couple." She meant, she explained, that they are like two eyes whose sight is different. I fancy his is the long-sighted eye.

Well, this little row was soon over as far as Mother and Aunt Gerty were concerned. George's scolding was short and sweet, Aunt Gerty said, and she couldn't possibly dislike him more than she did already. But Ariadne could not get over her disgrace for ages. She still wouldn't stir out of the house, but I went out regularly and policed Lady Scilly and Simon. Of course this contretemps to Ariadne has had the effect of throwing them into each other's arms worse than ever. They became inseparable. If Lady Scilly had only known it, Simon's being near her made her look quite old and anxious, whereas she made him look young and bored.

One morning I stood and watched them leaning over the wooden rail of the quay. Everybody leans there in the mornings, it's fashionable, and if you lean a little forward or backward you can either see or not be seen by the person who is hanging over it a few yards further on. The boats were as usual unloading their big haul of herrings, and the sleepy-eyed sailors (they have been up all night!) were sitting smoking lazily on the edges of the boats. Lady Scilly was in white linen, so awfully pure and angelic-looking that the little boys dabbed her with fish-scales as they passed her. She was talking to Simon about money earnestly, and took no notice. She was telling him that Lord Scilly likes money so much that he didn't ever like to let it out of his hands. What business of Simon Hermyre's is it, I should like to know, what Lord Scilly chooses to do with his money? Everybody seems to think Simon is going to be rich, because he is the son of Sir Frederick Hermyre, but that is no criterion. He always seems to have plenty of pocket-money, but I still think it mean of a full-grown woman to borrow money of a boy.

"Do let me have the pleasure," he kept saying, and "Do let me!" and goodness knows why, for she seemed to be in no hurry to prevent him! I suppose it is why people like Simon so much, that he always seems to be trying to do what they want in spite of themselves.

"Then that is settled, thank the Lord!" I heard him say at last. (My sailor buffer between me and her had begun to talk to a man below, and rather drowned their conversation.) "Just look at that sheet of silver on the floor of the boat—all one night's haul! Suppose it was shillings and half-crowns?"

"Yes, only suppose! And the sailors treading carelessly about in it, as you might in the train of one of my silver-embroidered dresses! It is very like a full court-train, isn't it, the one you are going to have the privilege of paying for?"

Simon said yes it was, but he didn't seem to like her quite so much as he did since she gave in and let him pay her bill. He seemed to have grown a little bit older all of a sudden, he had a sort of aged, pinched look come over his face.

Then I saw, I positively saw, the thought of my sister Ariadne come there and make him handsome and boyish again, and I wriggled past my sailor and came round behind her and said, "How do you do?"

Lady Scilly having done with Simon for the moment, left him and went to speak to Mr. Sidney Robinson and George, who had just come up from their bathe.

"How is your sister?" Simon asked me.

"Very well, thank you—at least I mean not very well——"

"I don't wonder. I was so sorry for her the other night."

"Did you loathe her? Your face looked as if you did."

"Nothing of the kind! But if I ever get a chance of doing that brute Bowser some injury I'll—— And the people she was with——? I beg your pardon, but that young lady who was in charge of you both—wasn't it her business to prevent Miss Vero-Taylor's good-nature being imposed upon?"

He meant Aunt Gerty, of course. I made up my mind in a second what was best to do for the best of all.

"Oh, *that* person," said I. "She wasn't anything to do with us. Miss Gertrude Jenynge, playing at the Saloon Theatre, I believe?"

"I think that your sister should not be allowed to go to places like that alone."

"Why, I was with her!"

"What earthly good are you, you small elf?" asked Simon seriously and kindly, smiling down at me. "I wish to goodness *my* sister——"

I know what he meant. That he wished he could persuade Almeria to take to Ariadne and boss her about. But he didn't say it. He is so prim and reserved about his family. He simply asked to be remembered to Ariadne, and that he was going to stay with some people at a place called Henderland in Northumberland.

"Henderland," said I, "that's near where Christina lives."

"Who is Christina?"

"Why, George's old secretary. She is a Mrs. Ball now. You were her best man."

"Peter Ball's! Good old Ball! So I was. Bless me. '*Have you forgotten, love, so soon—That* church *in June?*' Yes, of course I used to call her the Woman who Would—marry the good Ball, I mean. I shall be over there some time next month shooting. She gave me a general invitation."

He wouldn't say when he was likely to be at Rattenraw, it is a little way men have of defending themselves against girls like Ariadne. Now Ariadne and I had a particular invitation to go and stay with Christina for a fortnight, as it happened, and if Ariadne had been having this talk instead of me, she would have told him, and tried to pin him down to a time, but I was wiser. I said "Good-bye" quite shortly, as if I wasn't at all interested in his movements, and went home. I was a little ashamed of one thing, I had told a lie about Aunt Gerty and denied her before men, as the Scripture says. But it was not for my own sake. Fifty Aunt Gertys can't hurt me, but one can do Ariadne lots of harm and ruin her social prestige. On the way home I thought what I would do, and did it at lunch.

"Please, Aunt Gerty," I said, "if you meet me on the quays or anywhere when I am talking to Mr. Simon Hermyre, I must beg of you not to be familiar with me, for I have told him that you were no relation, and I gave him your stage name when he asked me who you were."

"Oh, did he ask?" said Aunt Gerty, jumping about. "He must have seen me somewhere. In *Trixy's Trust* perhaps? I made a hit there. Well, child, you may as well bring us together. Use my professional name, of course."

"All right," said I. I did not tell her Simon was off to-morrow. Now don't you call that eating your cake and having it!

CHAPTER XVI

WE all hoped that Mr. Bowser would find he liked Aunt Gerty well enough to wish to relieve us of her, but we evidently wished it so strongly that he did not see his way to obliging us. These things get into the air somehow, and put people off. Of course Aunt Gerty herself wished it more than anybody, and she was feeling considerably annoyed as she completed the arrangements for a rather seedy sort of autumn tour, which she would not have had to do if she could have pulled it off with the brewer. She wreaked her vexation on us, us and Mother, who was very patient, knowing what poor Aunt Gerty was feeling. But Ariadne, who was feeling very much the same way, and had to suffer in silence, resented it, and when Aunt Gerty hustled her, hustled back in spite of her broken heart.

George left for Scotland. He *says* he is going to shoot with the Scillys. I don't know why, but I have a fancy he has gone to Ben Rhydding, all alone, to cure his gout. It didn't matter. It was settled that we were to go to stay with Christina in Northumberland.

Ariadne didn't like going straight on from Whitby, because she would have preferred to get her country outfit in London; but of course the difference on fares made that impossible. It is one of the curious things about Finance, that George should make so much money, and we should still have to think of a beggarly three hundred miles or so at a penny a mile. That is what it costs third-class, as of course we go. The all-the-year-round conservatory at Cinque Cento House costs George three hundred a year alone to keep up, and the Hall of Arms (as it is written up over the door) at the back of the house must be done up every few months. It is all white (five coats!) to set off George's black velvet fencing costume and his neat legs.

George has *so* much taste. He simply lives at Christie's. He cannot help buying cabinets and chairs at a few hundred pounds apiece. He says they are realizable property. Ariadne and I would like to realize them.

The great point with Ariadne was how to dress suitably for Christina's. I said same as London, only shorter and plainer. Ariadne hankered after a proper *bonâ fide* shooting toilette. She had the sovereign George gave her for her birthday, and two pounds she had made by a poem, and another Mother gave her. She looks much best dressed quietly, nothing mannish or exact suits her, for it at once brings out the out-of-drawing-ness of her face, which is of the Burne-Jones type. She has grown to that, being trained up in it from her earliest years. All types can be acquired. In the face of this, she went out and bought a *Miriam's Home Journal*, and selected a pattern of Stylish Dress for the Moors, and got a cheap tailor in the town to make it up for her. Ye Gods, as Aunt Gerty says! I used to go with her to be fitted. It was a heart-breaking business. They took her in and let her out, kneeling about her with their mouths full of pins so that you couldn't scold them lest you gave them a shock and drove all the pins down their throat, and the little tailor kept saying, "A pleat here would be beneficial to it, Madam," or to his assistant, "Remove that fulness there!" till there wasn't a straight seam left in it, it was all bias and bulge.

Ariadne cried over the way that skirt hung for an hour when it came home. "Too much of bias hast thou, poor Ariadne," I said to her, imitating the pompous tailor; but although I chaffed her I went to him and made him take ten shillings off the bill.

I couldn't help thinking of a real country girl like Almeria Hermyre, when Ariadne put this confection on for the first time in the privateness of our bedroom. It was brown tweed turned up with "real cow" as Ben said; there is even a piece of leather stitched on to her shoulder where she is to rest her gun. Ariadne, who once pulled one leg, that I daresay he could easily spare, off a daddy-long-legs, and considered herself little better than a murderer!

Ben, who was present at this private view, did not like her in it, and told her so. He is so truthful that he never waits to be asked his opinion. So long as he didn't tease her about Simon Hermyre, it did not matter, but he is quite a gentleman, though rough. Indeed, nobody mentioned Simon, though I could not help thinking of him a good deal in connection with Ariadne's new dress. I was sure we should see him somewhere in Northumberland. It isn't as big as America, and where there is even a faint will there is generally a way. Ariadne was thinking of him when she bought a billycock hat on purpose to stick in a moorcock's wing Simon had once given her that he had shot. I did not interfere, for I thought if he saw her in it he might think some other fellow had given her a moorcock's feather; there are plenty of them about, and plenty of fools to shoot them.

I myself did not make much preparation. Just a new elastic to my hat, and new laces to my boots. How delightful it is to care for no man! How it simplifies life! All this bother about Ariadne has choked me off love for a long while to come. I don't care if it never comes my way at all. But I am only fourteen, and have not got the place in my head ready for it yet, anyway. I don't believe that Love is a woman's whole existence any more than it is a man's. We are like ships, made in water-tight compartments, so that if something goes wrong with one compartment the whole concern isn't done for. Until I am old enough to set a whole compartment aside for Love, I can be easy and watch the others wallowing. Life is one huge party to me, and the girls who are not out yet watching it through the bannisters and getting a taste of the ices now and then.

I don't study dinners at home, we have never given one in Cinque Cento House. George entertains a good deal at the Club, when he can get Lady Scilly or some one like that to play hostess and give the signal to rise for him, a thing, somehow, that no man ever seems capable of doing for himself.

Mother and Aunt Gerty saw us off for Morpeth, at Whitby station. Aunt Gerty looked far more excited than just seeing a couple of nieces off could make her, and I soon saw the reason of it, Mr. Bowser was leaving by the same train! He went first-class of course, which was annoying for Aunt Gerty, as that made him be at the other end of the train, too far off to see how prettily she kissed her nieces good-bye, and bought them *Funny Bits* and chocolate creams. We got the creams anyhow. Children often profit by their elders' foolish fancies.

Mother wouldn't even let us kiss her out of the carriage-window for fear the train started and we got dragged out, and sure enough we did go on suddenly, in that slidy, masterful way trains have. I have a particular affinity to trains. My great-grandfather built an engine and had it called after him. When he was dying, he was taken in his chair to where the Great Northern trains pass every day, and drew his last breath as the Scotch Express rattled by.

To return. I noticed that Aunt Gerty looked awfully pleased about something, and kept sticking her hip out in an engaging way she has, and I concluded that Mr. Bowser had at last spotted her and thrown her an encouraging nod, perhaps blown her a kiss, only he is perhaps not quite low enough for that? But whatever it was, it made her happy. Oh, if they only could all get the man they want *at the time* they want him, what a nice place the world would be, for children at any rate! All grown-up people's tempers come because they can't get what they want. And here was I, boxed up with one who hadn't got what she wanted, for a whole blessed day! She was simply weltering in love, if I may say so. She had a penny note-book ready to write poetry in, and meant to dream and write and cry for four hours. I had a nice improper six-penny of my Aunt Gerty's, but I scarcely hoped that Ariadne would allow me to enjoy it.

Of course not. She soon began bothering. As soon as we were properly started, she pulled up her thousand times too thick veil, badly put on—Ariadne is too simple ever to learn to put on a veil properly as other women do—and looked hard at herself in her pocket looking-glass, and sighed and settled her loose tendril and unsettled it, and pinched her cheek to massage it and restore the subcutaneous deposit the doctor had told her about. She seemed hopeless and sad, for presently she said—

"No, I am not looking beautiful to-day!"

A pretty white tear, like a pearl button, shook on her eyelashes, and I wondered how long she could keep it hanging there? I do believe she was anxious to look nice because she had an idea she might see Simon at Morpeth. But one never does see people at stations, and personally, I think that Ariadne would be far prettier if she didn't know she was pretty. It is most unkind and inconsiderate of her so-called friends to keep telling her so. It is just like our horrid lot. In Simon's set, they would die sooner than pay a girl a compliment to her face. But she has got so hardened to it that I always have to take her down gently, so as not to hurt her, same as one does with invalids.

"It doesn't matter how you look," I said, "there is nobody but porters to see you, and you don't want to mash them and distract them from their work and make them get the points all wrong. I should have thought you preferred being alone. You can write in your book. Let us do George's dodge, and stand at the window whenever we come into a station and look as repulsive as we can."

George likes to keep the carriage all to himself, and taught us what to do to secure it, the only time he ever travelled with us. We made a prominent object of Ben, very sticky with lollipops, and managed to be by ourselves all the way.

Ariadne was unwilling to do this now. She sat still in her corner and brooded, and that did just as well, for the would-be passengers looked in and saw her, and made up their minds that she was recovering from scarlet fever, or at least measles. I stood in the window, squarely, and looked ugly for two. I was interested in the country. It is quite hideous between Whitby and Morpeth. The reason is that it is an industrial centre. I began to wish that our eating (kitchen boilers) and keeping warm (coal) didn't mean so many people having to live black, and whole counties in a blanket of smoke. I don't think I approve of civilization, if this is what it comes out of?

When the train slowed down at Morpeth, I could not help calling out to Ariadne, "I told you so!" for there was Christina Ball in a muslin dress, with a soft floppy chiffon hat and no veil at all. She was sitting in a little pony-cart, with an ugly child that couldn't be hers; we saw her from the train. It was a shock to Ariadne, and she was wild to get our box into the cloak-room first and unlock it and get out one of her old dresses. But how could she dress in the waiting-room? And besides, she would be certain to muddle the next thing I told her (and so she did).

We got out of the station and into the trap. Christina had a new pony and couldn't get down—and it was arranged that our luggage was to come on by carrier, as our wicker trunk would be sure to scratch the smart new dog-cart.

Off we went, I thought, and I am sure Ariadne thought, a little too like the wind. But Ariadne wanted to appear at ease, and casual and countrified, so she pretended to take an interest in the scenery, and said to Christina, "Look at the lovely tone of that verdigris on the pond!"

The ugly child twitched her feet under the rug beside me; she said nothing, but looked it.

"Oh, the duck-weed!" said Christina, who knows Ariadne too well to be amused by anything she says. "Miss Emerson Tree here—allow me to introduce Peter's

American niece, Miss Jane Emerson Tree—calls it the 'stagnance.'"

The ugly child still didn't say anything, though "stagnance" was just as absurd a word for mildew on a pond as verdigris, and I began to be quite afraid of one who, though so young, didn't seem to want to fly out. She turned half round though, and seemed to be staring hard at the body of Ariadne's shooting dress with its patch on the left shoulder. Christina went on enlightening us about the country and telling us the sort of things we were likely to ask and make fools of ourselves about. I do believe she was afraid of our saying something specially silly before Jane Emerson Tree, and wanted to save us from ourselves.

It came at last, and Ariadne nearly toppled out of the cart. The ugly child spoke in the most strong American accent, and the way she leant upon the last syllable of the word *despise* was the nastiest thing I ever heard.

"Oh, I do just *despise* your waist!" she said to Ariadne; "I've been looking at it all the way we've come."

Christina absently took hold of her whip and then rattled it back in its socket. She then scolded Jane till I should have thought any ordinary child couldn't have gone on sitting up, but this one did, never saying a word, but pursed her mouth in till there was hardly a line to be seen. Then Christina began to tell us how dull she had found it living in the country, and how difficult to get acclimatized at first.

"But in the end, the country rubs off on one," she sighed, "and a good thing too. Oh, the mistakes I made at first! You know that Peter and I have both been staying with the dear Bishop of Guyzance."

"Oh, Christina, you *have* changed!" said I.

"I know, dear, three services on Sunday and a shilling for the offertory. So different from Newton Hall and Farm Street. As I was saying, I came back from Lale Castle the day before yesterday, post haste, to hatch some chickens——"

"I thought a hen did that?" ventured Ariadne.

"Right you are! I pretended to Peter that it was an insane desire to kiss the baby, but I was an hour in the house before I even thought of the child. The hen was due to hatch fifteen. I interviewed her every hour, much to her disgust. At last, crack!—one came out——"

"You mean chipped the shell," said Ariadne primly.

"Right again! I put it in a basket by the kitchen fire, the servants shunted it for dinner, it got cold, it died in the night. Yesterday five more happened, I popped them in the mild oven for a minute, just then some one pinched my baby—he screamed, and went on screaming like an electric-bell gone wrong. I had to go and look after him—cook made a blazing fire, do you see?—I have only saved five out of that brood."

"How very funny!" said Ariadne, who wasn't a bit amused.

I was. Christina told us of a little hen Peter had before, who had been used to be set to ducks, and who had learned to march them all down to the nearest pond. The first lot of chickens had been driven to a watery and unfamiliar death.

"Would you like to go and be photographed to-morrow?" she asked Ariadne, and Ariadne was on the *qui vive* at once. "They all think one an unnatural parent here, if one doesn't take one's brood to be perpetuated at Oldfort every year. But the trains there are so awkward for us. I am fighting the railway authorities tooth and nail, trying to persuade them to put on a slip carriage. They do it for Keiller and his marmalade, so why not for me? Say! I am on the pony's neck! I am going to put the seat back, take the reins a minute!"

Ariadne didn't of course like her giving them to me, but everybody always sees at once that I am the practical one.

When the seat was arranged she went bubbling on.

"Next week is our Harvest Festival and School feast, and Ball in the school-house. The gaieties of this Parish! I haven't had tea with myself for a whole week. I am a very hard worker, you don't know! Peter says I lie awake at nights thinking of stodgy moral books to recommend for the Village Library. I recommend some, not all, of my late patron's, your father's, works. The Vicar here is a dear old dodderer, and was so shocked when I recommended him *The Road to Rome*! It's a book of travel, you know. We have a young man here, too, quite an eligible, he told me so. He is so shy, you see, he says the wrong thing. I wonder whether you'll make anything of him? To a flirt, all things are possible."

"I am not a flirt—now," said Ariadne.

She was nearly giving the whole thing away, only the pony bolted, at least Christina said it was an attempt at bolting. "My God, pony!" she said to it, and it stopped, shocked at her swearing, I suppose.

"And there's Simon Hermyre in the neighbourhood. Henderland is not more than ten miles off."

Ariadne at once sat tight—too tight. It was almost painful, and showed in her face too.

Just as we were driving in at the gate of Rattenraw, Jane Emerson Tree spoke again, and actually about Ariadne's body.

"Any way, it's on all crooked," she said, as if she was continuing the previous discussion. Peter came out to meet us, and she was lifted down. They couldn't, I suppose, leave her sitting and just put her away in the coach-house all night. That is what I should have done, and cooled her hot blood. But I saw how it was when we got in and were having tea. She had hers "laced"—I mean brandy in it. Peter is awfully proud of her and thinks she will be a great actress and astonish the world some day. She certainly mimicked Peter to his face. I will let her know if I catch her mimicking Ariadne! Peter enjoyed it. The moment a child is really rude, people think it is going to do great things. I have noticed that. Now I would no sooner think of criticizing a grown-up person's things to her face as I would of—kissing Emerson Tree's very ugly mug, though I wouldn't tell her so, otherwise than by my reluctance to embrace her. Peter calls her "the little witch."

"The little witch," he says, "was being neglected, or thought she was, at lunch the other day, and in a trice she called out to the butler, 'I say, Holmes, old man, look alive with those potatoes, will you!' You should have seen the old boy's face!"

I did see the old boy's face. He was waiting at tea.

Christina told us stories about her all tea-time; she listened quietly as she munched buns. How when she saw the new baby she said, "Dash it all! why it's bald!" How one rainy day she was lost, and they found her with six of her village friends walking in a straight line down to the pond, barefooted and bareheaded and their mouths open, quacking, and to catch the rain-drops like ducks do. How she has done all the absurd things children do in books, such as aspinalling the cat—as if a cat ever stayed to be aspinalled!—and gunpowder into ovens, and frogs into boots, and hedgehogs into beds. (She says so, but I believe she put the clothes-brush, and Peter mistook it with his feet in the dark!) And once when a noted Socialist man had been staying there and rashly talked before her, she had given away the furniture.

"She went solemnly down the village," said Christina, "making presents of the unearned increment in the shape of things she didn't want and I did. Missing tensions of sewing-machines and valves of cycles and stray door-knobs and other bits of rolling stock—all disappeared. When it came to the spare sugar-tongs and my best silver scissors, however, I had to scold her. Oh, she'll be a great actress some day."

We listened, and I am sure no one could tell from my face how I disapproved of it all,—unless Duse the second, who, after all, was a child too, twigged how ridiculous they were making her look? Anyhow, after she had made three usual scenes and one extraordinary one because we were there, and had been noisily taken off to bed, they left off discussing her and took up a perfectly safe subject; "shoots" and who to have. Christina teases, she always did, even in the days when she used to put us head first down rabbit-holes.

"Has he a wife?" she asks, whenever Peter proposes a man.

"My dear, I haven't the slightest idea. All I know is he is a capital shot, and brings down his pheasants in good style!"

"These good shots bring down such bad wives—I mean from the house-party point of view," she says. "To look at their choice, they would always seem to have fired recklessly into the brown and got pot luck. You see I am boxed up with your friends' bad shots all day. I can't possibly make my housewifely duties last all the morning, and I object to have Jane brought down in her best frock and her worst behaviour to make sport for idle women. And she hates grown-up ladies, and has the wit to come in with segments of the Wanny Crag on her boots and her hair full of straws, so as to be sent out of the drawing-room to 'muck herself up.'"

"I don't like that phrase, Christina!"

"Don't be so aggressively pure, Peter!"

Ariadne and I have called him "Pure Peter" ever since, but he is not bad, really. It is a mercy when one's friends show a little consideration in their marriage, and one mustn't be too particular, for the world is full of bounders one might have got, and had to be civil to. Peter Ball talks about "Vickings" and keeps a chart of the weather, but except for fussy ways like that, he is quite a gentleman.

CHAPTER XVII

ARIADNE got fatter at Rattenraw, which is humiliating enough to a girl in her position. I can't say that she kept that up at all well, beyond looking sad, sometimes when she wasn't thinking, or at meals. She has to pretend to be *distraite*, for really she is very all there, and likes her dinner. Peter Ball, carving the roast red beef, holds his knife up in the air to tease her, and says to her, when she won't answer his question whether she wants some more?—"Thinking of the old 'un, what?" He doesn't know how near the truth he is, except in age. He knows nothing of Ariadne's affairs, he prefers not to know, but takes her word for it that she has a secret sorrow connected with a member of his sex.

Jane Emerson Tree doesn't take any notice of Ariadne or of me either; she is put out at not being allowed to say rude things about us. She is a free-born American citizen. Christina has made Ariadne rip the leather patch off the shoulder of the waist Jane Emerson objected to, and has lent her a common straw sailor hat, which suits her better than the billycock. A sailor hat, you see, isn't a hat, it is a tile, and so can't either become or unbecome.

Simon Hermyre might have been at Henderland, or at Lord Manham's, or at Barsom, Sir Edward Fynes' place; neither places are more than ten miles or so off; but he made no sign, nor did he answer a letter Christina wrote to him, so Ariadne was practically forced to flirt with the only other man of her own rank in the village,

besides Peter. He is the Squire of Rattenraw, and lives in
the old Hall, and plays the fiddle, and keeps only one
servant. Yet he came in before the Conquest. That is
what becomes of all our old families. He isn't old, but
very wrinkled. That comes of so frequently meeting the
wind and exposure. His corduroy velvet coat and his skin
are much of a muchness. He is shy and wild, as Peter
remarked of the grouse this year. As I said, he is all there
is, here, till Christina's "shoots" come off, and Ariadne
egged him on—the amount of egging on a shy man
takes!—to ask her, and then accepted to go out fishing
with him. She sat all the afternoon on a bank near by, in
a biting North-west wind straight down from the Wanny
Crags, that blew the egg off the sandwiches and the froth
off the ginger-beer. He asked her if she felt chilly
("Chilly!" she thought) about sixteen times, and said By
Gosh when he didn't catch anything, which was
frequent, and "What in thunder's got 'em?" alluding to
the trout, when at last in despair they packed up to go
home. Ariadne got back to tea chilled to the bone and
disappointed at the heart to find him so coarse without
being interesting. She thinks all local farmers and squires
ought to be like Mr. Heathcliff in *Wuthering Heights* and
hide a burning lava of passion under their upper crust of
cold indifference. Squire Rochester is good and dull. He
does admire Ariadne, I daresay, though I am not up in
the country signs of love, and it seems the least he could
do for a real London beauty who is good enough to sit
on a sticky and muddy bank bald of grass and full of
worm-holes, and some of them protruding disgustingly

as she said, for a whole afternoon watching him not catching fish!

He leaves vegetable marrows and nosegays as big as cabbages "for the ladies" at the back-door, because he is so shy. He squeezes all Christina's rings into her hands whenever he meets her, but these are as much signs of love for Christina as for Ariadne, and Peter Ball says Ariadne must take care and not to be like "Miss Baxter (whoever she was) who refused a gent before he asked her."

Christina thinks he *is* a bit attracted, and that it is a good thing for Ariadne to have a man to play with, in her forlorn condition, and that whatever the Squire gets, even a hopeless passion, that he will be able to get over it. She considers that men have a thicker sort of skin than women, and if they are unhappy, can turn up their shirt-sleeves and get very hot and throw it off. The Squire keeps lots of cattle and is by way of being butcher to the village. Christina buys a whole sheep of him sometimes. He has plenty of distractions, and she always takes the side of the woman—*esprit de corpse*, I think they call it. I myself think there should be the same law for men as for women, and I have a great mind to tell the Squire to save his nosegays, for Ariadne is in love with Simon. I even threatened her with this *exposé*, and she turned round on me, and said I should be a liar, for she *wasn't* in love with Simon. Then, I said, she might as well leave off taking the biggest half of the bed at night and all the looking-glass in the morning and first go at the bath, and other special privileges she has sneaked, because she is supposed to be unhappy. I am willing to make every allowance for one so persecuted by fate, but not for a woman who enjoys all the usual pleasures of her age and sex, as if nothing was the matter. Then she cried, and said I was unkind, that she wanted all the comfort she could get, and went off fishing with the Squire to spite me, that very afternoon! What can one do with a weathercock like that!

Then Church decorating came on, and Ariadne could do without the Squire. We worked all day, and in the evening we doctored our cuts and the places where the Lord had let us get bruised and scratched in smartening up His Church for His Harvest Festival. Ariadne had a big brown bruise done by a jagged pew on her upper leg shaped like a tortoise, and so we called it, so to be able to allude to it at all times and seasons.

At lunch, Christina used to ask Ariadne how her tortoise was, and Ariadne answered demurely that it was getting a nice pea-green, or a good strong blue, till Peter and the Squire were so much puzzled, that they teased Ariadne till she let it out, and then Peter teased her worse than ever.

Two local ladies hindered us at decoration and we could not get rid of them, as they had pulled their gardens about to give us flowers. But we had to make a rule that we wouldn't allow gentlemen in the church during decorations. It upset Miss Weeks so that she hammered her fingers instead of the nails, and put flowers into the men's button-holes instead of threading them into the altar-rails, in fits of absence. Miss Day, the other young lady, agreed with Christina that one must really keep a firm hand on Miss Weeks, and that she herself didn't care for so many men-folk about, talking their nonsense, and interfering with steady work, but she was sorry, her sailor cousin had just come home and she *reely* could not spare more than half-an-hour every other day away from him! We were only decorating for three days.

During the half-hour she did come, however, she and Miss Weeks got on very badly, finding they could not work together, and they had it out in the middle aisle every five minutes or so. Christina and Ariadne had taken the chancel, while these two were responsible for the font, so we did not get mixed up so very much. But when Miss Weeks boxed Miss Day's ears with a Scarborough lily, and Miss Day retorted with a double dahlia, the Vicar interposed, and ordered them out of his church just as the cook orders me out of her kitchen, and it is about as much their own, in either case.

Then we had some peace, and the Vicar used to come himself (he has no wife), and worked very hard at handing flowers to Ariadne, who did not look half bad on top of a ladder, a little weak and tottery, so that she had to be steadied by a strong hand now and then.

At home there was cooking to be done, cakes and pies and things for the village ball and tea-treat. We both cooked. Christina says there is a want of concentration about us, and that the trail of the flour-bin is all over her best chairs. She says it to callers to amuse them and to make them think her witty. Though really, Ariadne's untidiness is trying. We find baking-powder in our workboxes, and currants as book-markers, and butter— well, everywhere but in the butter-dish! Ariadne goes about with white hair, and Peter Ball complains that the door-handles are sticky. He says that Ariadne's cakes, when made, will form a capital hunting lunch, sustaining if eaten, and capable of breaking the nastiest fall.

Christina's cook (cooks are the same, I see, all over the world!) gave her annual notice which is never taken any notice of, just before the Festival, when all the servants are so overworked that they get fractious. Luckily this time something happened to put them in a tearing good temper again. Farmer Dale died, and Christina blessed him for giving us a good funeral to cheer the household up a bit. So the status was preserved.

On the Sunday morning, of course, we all attended Divine Service. Peter Ball came too and read the lessons. He is called one of the pillars of the church. He once spoke to some men who were lounging about outside while the service was proceeding, and told them that he looked to them to be pillars too. They sniggered, because they felt ashamed, and one of them said, "Ay, Sir, but aren't we men the buttresses a-leaning up against it and propping it up like?" Peter was only shocked.

We workers could not attend much on this particular occasion, any more than a cook can enjoy the dinner she has cooked. We could not take our eyes off our own special rail that we had wreathed, and kept hoping our flowers wouldn't topple suddenly because we hadn't tied them securely enough, or wilt during the sermon. I noticed a curious sort of doll, standing on the altar-steps, dressed in three tissue-paper flounces and a sash. As we came out I asked old John Peacock what it was, and he said, "Why, that wor t' Kern babby!" I was no wiser. But Ariadne, who dotes on superstitions, said she would ask the Vicar. She wrote him a pretty note in her all backwards hand, and said she felt sure the doll on the altar-steps was a heathen survival of some sort. This was his answer; he was pleased.

"My dear Miss Vero-Taylor,

"Your interest in the study of folk-lore is highly commendable in one so young. The little mannikin—or rather womankin—is, as you aptly conjecture, a remnant of a custom dating from a period of the very remotest antiquity. In our Northumbrian villages it is the custom, the moment the sickle is laid down, for the villagers to dress the last sheaf in tawdry finery and carry it through the streets, finally when it presides at the Harvest, or Mell Supper, and the people dance round it singing:

'Blest be the day that Christ was born!
We've getten Mell of *Ball's* corn!
It's well bun' and better shorn!
Hip! Hip! Hurray!'

"This custom was found, however, so prevocative of disorderly scenes that my revered predecessor here decreed that in future the Mell Doll (or Kern baby) should be simply placed on the altar-steps during Divine Service. Is it not wonderful to reflect that this grotesque image prefigures no less a personage than Ceres, the goddess of plenty, the Frigga of the Teutons, sometimes called Freia, Frey, conf. Grimm's Teutonic Mythology, passim—"

"Oh yes, pass him, pass him!" said Peter impatiently, who won't however let any one else make fun of the church, and scolded Christina for saying,

"Rather a come-down for a goddess, wasn't it?"

"Well," she remarked to Ariadne later on, "you had better be getting up your mythology" (meaning the Bible, only Peter didn't twig anything so wrapped up as this), "because you will be sure to be subpœna'd to take a class in the Sunday school after you have fished for it. *Nemo Dodd impune lacessit!*"

"Can't Dodd lace his boots with impunity?" I asked Peter. I knew it wasn't that, any more than *Res angusta domi* means "Please to keep Augusta at home," and some others like that I have made.

Sure enough, Mr. Dodd made Ariadne take a class in his Sunday school, and Christina chuckled. It is the price of Mr. Dodd's admiration, and he admired Ariadne very much. She is not really any happier for it, rather bored by it in fact. She spent three whole days getting up Sacred History for fear the school children, who have of course been properly brought up and grounded, should floor her, a poor feckless literary man's daughter. Peter Ball gave her a little arithmetic. She got as far as Proportion with him. There was one sum about how many men it would take to build a wall of so many feet in so many hours. If it was Inverse Proportion, which it might be, and then again it mightn't, you put the men under the wall and divide by the hours; as many of them as are left after such treatment is the answer. It came, stupidly enough, two-and-a-half, so I suggested to Ariadne, as I was helping her, to put *Two men and a boy*. Peter said she didn't repay teaching, and saw nothing to laugh at, though his wife seemed to.

Then Ariadne started an essay club with prizes. The Squire bought those for her in Morpeth when he went in to sell pelts and hides. Fancy touching his hand after that! They were bits of his poor beasts that he had killed! Billy Scott's short essay on the elephant, "*an animal with a leg at each corner and a tail at both ends,*" was funny; and Sally Moscrop's description of "*any animal she liked to choose.*" She invented "*The Proc,*" a beast with four legs, "*two of whom are bigger and longer than the others, for the Proc lives all around a hill.*" Grace Paterson's essay was quite long. "*The Pin is an exceedingly useful article. It has saved the lives of many men, many women and many children by not swallering of them.*"

Grace is fourteen and the beauty of the village. She has begun a tale in ten chapters. She has to write it up in the apple-tree, for fear her father should "warm" her.

She and Ariadne were the two belles of the Ball in the Parish Room on Monday evening. They both danced with the Squire, who said he was in luck to get two literary ladies to dance with him on the same night. But Ariadne walked home with him, and I went with Christina. Mr. Rochester had one of his own roses Ariadne had given him back, in his button-hole. She is so unhappy about Simon that she doesn't care who proposes to her. That is the way girls take it—a very selfish way, but they are selfish all through when they are in love. Ariadne actually thinks the Squire thinks he proposed to her going home that night. I don't. It was pitch dark as we went home, the village is not lighted, and it is a very wicked village. She says, long arms like tentacles came groping out from the wall in the dark, and the Squire dragged her past them. As the village young men couldn't see, they thought her one of their own sweethearts, for by then the party had broken up and was all over the place. The chucker-out had been very much occupied and had found the brook near the school-house door very handy.

But I don't myself think the Squire did propose. He offered to take care of her, past the tentacles, but not for life. I think if a girl is always dreading proposals and thinking of how men will feel it when refused, proposals never come to them. That is what Christina said, and that Peter Ball took her entirely by surprise, when he asked her. I knew better, for I had chaperoned that affair. She says Peter wears very well, and that there's some gilt left on the gingerbread still. The gramophone is still in all its glory, and when she was ill up-stairs, when Jim was born, Peter used to send up a message by the nurse for her to leave the door of her room open for half-an-hour before dinner, and then she would hear it. The nurse always forbade it, but Christina always insisted on it, to please Peter, and lay with her ears stopped up with sheet till the half hour was over. It is a new gramophone, not the one he had in Leinster Gardens. That shouted itself out, I suppose? Christina found an entry in his old pocket-book—

"July 19—a memorable year in my life. I bought a new gramophone and I got married. I won't say anything about my wife here, but the gramophone was a beauty when she was new——"

Ariadne was disgusted. She doesn't believe Simon would say such a coarse thing. Well, I wish she had some experience on the subject, what Simon would say, that's all!

When Simon did come over to shoot, Ariadne hardly spoke to him during the three days he was here. No one did, much. He is so fearfully eligible that all the nice girls feel they must snub him, and he hardly gets a cup of tea. If Christina hadn't known nice girls only, Ariadne would have had a better chance. What is the good of being a nice modest girl among other nice modest girls? And though Ariadne would not believe it, she did badly without her foil Lady Scilly, who showed up her niceness and made Simon draw comparisons. Then there was another adverse circumstance. The Squire came and followed Ariadne about with his eyes, till it really wasn't safe to sit in a line with them both. That put Simon off. He is too nice to prefer a girl because another man is making himself unhappy about her.

Indeed Simon looked most uncomfortably serious and even sad. He has got his first wrinkle fixed between his eyebrows. He looks at Ariadne often, but in a puzzled sort of way, and takes himself up with a jerk, shaking his head, that the curls are cut off from too short to waggle.

"He cares for me—yes, he cares desperately," said Ariadne one night, just as she was arranging her watch and her handkerchief on the chair beside our bed, and his photograph under her pillow. I have to take that away every morning lest the housemaid should see it and make fun of her. Ariadne forgets. We also arrange the strap of our box down the middle of the bed so that neither of us should encroach in the other's part, and all these arrangements take time. Ariadne, though she is so gentle and so in love, always looks sharply to her rights, and more than her rights, and I generally find myself lying on the very rim of the bed. She is the eldest, unfortunately, and once she took the strap out of the bed to me when I objected.

"He loves me—oh, he does!" she moaned, "only he is not free."

"He is in the power of a wicked witch, like the one who enchanted Jorinde and Joringel in Grimm!" I said, and tried to go to sleep and thought a little. Lady Scilly isn't old, like the German witch, but I remember what the Ollendorff man said to me about her being a "fairy," and I know there is some connection between them. Fairies are those who would do harm if they had the power; witches have the power, but only because they are old and don't care for the things they cared for when they were young. Ariadne will never be a fairy when she grows up, she will always be too silly, and get put upon in society, though in private life she is quite up to her rights, and talks as loud as any one and doesn't trouble to be die-away. Men never see that side of girls, mercifully they are able to keep it out of sight till they are at least married, and on the pig's back, as Peter says. It is the unromantic things they are ashamed of. Ariadne wouldn't mind Simon knowing she had appendicitis, but not for worlds that she had a corn on her foot and had to have it cut, or a chilblain, and it burst.

Presently she woke up and said, "Will any one tell me why a woman like that should be allowed to ruin his young life?"

"All young men have nine lives like a cat, there will be eight left for you to ruin, when you get him—but you never will." I always add this not to raise false hopes. "And, goodness me, you can't expect to get a young man all to yourself, as fresh and shining as a new pin!"

"Yes, I do!" said Ariadne crossly. "I want a safety-pin even. I am a new pin myself—I have never loved anybody but Simon, now have I?"

I didn't answer that, but said I did wish we might turn over and go to sleep, when Christina rapped on the wall with a hairbrush and begged us to be quiet.

"Yes. All right! We will!" I yelled, and I certainly wouldn't have said another word, but Ariadne began again, five minutes later.

"Tempe, why do these wretched married women— I'd be ashamed to be one—always want everybody at once? She has got Mr. Pawky, and——"

"Mr. Pawky is only for money," I said. I was not going to tell her about her dear Simon paying Lady Scilly's bills as well as poor Pawky.

"And Simon's for love, then—oh dear! And George for literature. I am prettier than her, Tempe? Say I am—oh say I am, I want to hear you say it."

"I won't say it. You are far too conceited already."

"That is the same as saying it," answered Ariadne, and got calmer. "And at all events I am real, and that's more than she can say. I don't have to peel off my charms and put them away in a drawer like she has to." (Ariadne is able to put her poems quite in grammar, but I suppose she thinks it unnecessary to be always at a stretch.)

"I don't believe realness counts at all with young men," I said. "I believe they really and truly enjoy kissing paint, and groping about the floor for pin curls when they've done, and powder on their shoulders when they go out into the street from calling."

"Goodness!" cried Ariadne, almost shrieking, "you don't suppose Simon ever went as far as kissing her? If I thought that, I'd——"

"What?"

"Never let him kiss me again. He hasn't of course, yet! Oh, Tempe, I wish he had!"

"There you go!" I cried out, sick of her changeableness. "First you want him not to, then you wish he had. And the poor thing must kiss somebody—

he's got no mother, and kissing Almeria would be like kissing a cactus or cuddling a porcupine. Do please keep to your own part of the bed, you don't respect the strap a bit! I shall be on the floor in a minute. I'm lying right in the hem of the sheet now."

Ariadne kindly made a little more room for me as I was patiently listening to her, and went on.

"Tempe, I have learned in three short seasons some of the bitter truths of so-called society——"

Just then, as any one could have foretold from the noise we were making, Christina walked right into the room.

"Will you two children be quiet! Why are you crying, Ariadne?"

Ariadne said she wasn't crying, and at the same time asked Christina to be good enough, as she was up, to get her a clean pocket-handkerchief out of the drawer, one of those tied up with blue ribbon, not pink, for they are larger and plainer. Christina got it and then came and sat on my foot, which she could scarcely help doing, as I was only just but tumbling out of the bed altogether. She was exceedingly nice and sympathetic and agreed that Lady Scilly ought to put Simon back, for he was too little a fish for her to hook, being only twenty-four and she thirty-eight. She assured Ariadne, much as Mother used to assure me, that there were no ghosts—then if there aren't, what are the white things one sees hanging about the doors of rooms?—that Simon didn't really care for an old thing like that, and that if he did, her attraction must naturally wear out in the course of ages, and that Simon wouldn't be so very old by the time that happened, and would know a nice girl when he saw one, with his unjaundiced eyes.

She also thought Ariadne should not put upon me so, and should give me a bigger piece of bed.

I was thinking all the time she was talking of George, and how Mother too as well as Ariadne was unhappy because of this evil fairy. I wished the Scilly motor-car might upset and spoil Lady Scilly a little sooner, and that Simon mightn't be in it when that happened.

When Christina had tucked me in, and kissed us, and gone away, I made Ariadne make me a solemn promise that come what would, if she were ever married to Simon Hermyre, or indeed to any one else, that she would let all the others alone and not poach; for even if a young man seems unattached, you may be pretty sure there's a girl worrying about him somewhere in the background. One woman, one man! That's my motto, and indeed a woman now-a-days is lucky if she gets a whole man to herself as Christina has Peter, and well she knows when she is well off, and only laughs when her Peter says, as he did at breakfast, when she offered him

Quaker Oats, "Woman, haven't you learnt that my constitution clashes with cereals?"

Ariadne woke up with a plan, and after Simon had gone back to his friends at Henderland without proposing, and a hearty breakfast, we went out into the village and bought sixpenny-worth of beeswax, and pinched it into the shape of a skinny woman like Lady Scilly as near as we could. Then we laid it in a drawer on one of Ariadne's best silk ties, and we stuck a pin into it every day. I don't know if it did Lady Scilly any harm, but it did Ariadne a great deal of good. She looked down the columns of the *Morning Post* every day to see if Lady Scilly was ill, or perhaps even dead? When we left Rattenraw she gave the waxen image to Christina, and asked her to be good enough to finish up the boxful of best short whites on it. Christina promised faithfully that she would, and said that we might rely on her, as she had a little private spite of her own to work off on that lady. I knew what it was, *i. e.* Lady Scilly's having tried to flirt with Peter, or at least Christina thinks that she did. Wives always think that only let them get into the same room with them, other women make a bee-line for their own particular dull husbands! Christina is nice, but she is just like another wife when it comes to preserving Peter.

The Squire saw us off, with an enormous bouquet, that we put under the seat, having started, and forgot. So did Ariadne forget the Squire. One can only hope that after a decent interval he will marry Grace Paterson.

She is a substantial farmer's daughter, in spite of her thinking she can write. But she can wring a fowl's neck, and make butter, two things that Ariadne never would be able to do, the one from disgust and the other from native incompetence and a hot hand. As regards the Squire's position, Grace is very nearly a lady, and he is very nearly not a gentleman, so it ought to turn out all right.

CHAPTER XVIII

LADY SCILLY has had three nervous chills this autumn, and one motor spill and a half, so I think that the sixpence was well spent on beeswax. Christina in her letter to us said that she had stuck the figure so full of pins that it had fallen apart, whereupon she had consumed the bits before a slow fire, muttering incantations the while. I asked her what she did say, afterwards, and she said that "Devil! Devil! Devil!" repeated quite steadily till it melted, seemed all that was necessary, and that the simplest, strongest incantations were the best.

Simon Hermyre comes here very often to call on Mother, whom he likes, if possible, better than Ariadne. He says that she is like Cigarette in a novel of Ouida's. I believe Cigarette was a Vivandière. I suppose it is Mother's neat figure makes him think of her as Cigarette. Simon adores Ouida, and Doré is his favourite artist. He has "that beautiful Pilate's wife's Dream" hung over his bed at home, he says. I always think it looks like a woman going down into her own coal-cellar and awfully afraid of beetles!

Christina came on to us for a few days after staying with her mother-in-law, and brought her sewing-machine, The Little Wanzer, and taught Ariadne and me to manage that wretched tension of which one hears so much. She nearly lockstitched one of my ears to the table, as I was learning with all my might, but it was worth it, and to Ariadne it was an advent.

Up to now, she has always thought she looked very nice in her bags with holes in them for the arms, and her twenty necklaces on at once, and her undescribable colours. Beautiful colours never seem to look quite clean, do you know? It is all very well for George, he is an author and not young, but young men like you to look fresh, and well-groomed, and above all to have a waist. Now a waist is not even allowed to be mentioned in our house. Mother left off hers, and her ear-rings too, at George's request, when she married him, and as she never goes anywhere, she does not feel the want of them, but even when Ariadne was seventeen, Elizabeth Cawthorne said that it was time that she began to see about making herself a waist, and although George laughed Ariadne to death about it when she told him what the cook had said, yet it sank in, and I used to wake up in the grey winter mornings and find Ariadne sitting up in bed like a new sort of Penelope taking tucks in her stays, which Mother made her take out again in the daytime, knowing how George would disapprove of it.

Ariadne managed to "sneak" a waist, and George never noticed. That is the odd part of it; we all think that that inch more or less makes such a difference, and we may be panting with uncomfortableness all the time, and to the outward eye look as thick as ever!

Ariadne's figure is not her best point. Her hair is. It is well to find out one's best points early in life and stick to them, as they say of friends. Ariadne trains hers day and night in the way it should go, but doesn't want. I wonder it stands it, and doesn't come out in self-defence! It is what they call Burne-Jones hair, like cocoanut fibre, *I* think, but Papa's friends admire it, and she gets the reputation of being a beauty on it in our set.

But in Lady Scilly's set, that is Simon's set more or less, they think her a pretty girl, badly turned out!

"Ah, you are your father's daughter, I see!" Christina said at once to her, when she caught her sewing a black boot-button on to her nightgown, because she couldn't find a white one. I did not mention that I myself had begun to sew one of Ariadne's iron pills on to my shoe, and only stopped because it didn't seem to have any shank. But I was saying, we have all the trouble in the world to tidy up Ariadne before she goes down to the drawing-room to receive Simon when he calls. Ariadne comes out of her room half-dressed, and somebody catches her on the landing and buttons her frock, and perhaps the housemaid on the next floor points out to her that she hasn't got on any waistband, and another in the hall sticks a pin in somewhere, that shines in the sun, when she gets into the drawing-room, and Simon puts his head on one side and looks at it fixedly.

"*Dégagée*, as usual!" he says in his bad French accent, and yet he was two years at a crammer's to get him into the Foreign Office, and one in Germany to get polish, all before we knew him. He has got something better than polish, I think, and that is breeding. He is not the least shop-walkerish, and yet they have the best manners in the world. Simon says the most awful things, rude things, natural things, but how can one be angry with him, when he says them with his head on one side? Not Ariadne, certainly, and yet she can't stand chaff as a general thing. Peter Ball could make her cry by crooking his little finger at her.

Simon has curly hair—not at all neat—which he can neither help nor disguise, though he forces Truefitt to shingle it like a convict's so as to get rid of the curly ends, which are his greatest beauty, in mine and Ariadne's estimation. "Can't help it. Couldn't bear to look like one of those chaps."

He means the short-cuffed, long-haired, weepy-eyed men he meets here sometimes; not so often as before though, for George is revising his visiting-list. Ariadne hates them too, she hates everything artistic now. She can't bear our ridiculous house, all entrances and vestibules, and no bedrooms and boudoirs to speak of. She laughs at the people who come to describe it and photograph it for the Art papers, and wonders if they have any idea how uncomfortable it is inside, and how different from Highsam that Simon is always telling her about. As for Simon, he seems to think it rather a disgraceful thing to get into the papers at all, as bad as getting summoned in the police court. His father won't let Highsam be done for *Rural Life*, or lend Mary Queen of Scots' cradle to the New Gallery. Mr. Frederick Cook offered to put Almeria's portrait in *The Bittern* with her prize bull-dog, Caspar, but Almeria wrote him such a letter, *almost* rude, giving him her mind about interviewing. She has a mind on most subjects and never drifts. Simon has the greatest respect for her views. On stable matters certainly, I grant her that, but what can a country mouse, however high-toned, know of the troubles of town? Her father trusts her to go to Wrexham and buy the carriage horses, for he is no judge of the "festive gee" now, he says. Almeria likes art, too, and buys up all the Christmas numbers, and frames the pictures out of them and hangs them on the walls of Highsam Hall. Simon has borrowed her opinions on art, and dress too, and they aren't the same as Ariadne's.

"Great Scott!" he said to Ariadne, when she came down to see him one afternoon when he called, wearing her best new Medicean dress that George had specially designed for her. "If Almeria saw you in that frock, with your sleeves tied up with bootlaces! I do hope you won't wear that absurd sort of fakement at my Aunt Meg's on the twenty-fourth! If you do, I swear I won't dance with you in it!"

Of course he didn't mean it really, he would have danced with Ariadne in her chemise, out of chivalry and cheek, but still Ariadne took it seriously, and set to work to quite alter her style of dressing to please Simon. The invitations to Lady Islington's dance had been sent out a whole month in advance, so you had to accept D.V. Ariadne had time to take a few lessons in scientific dressmaking, and then start on a ball-dress. Christina and I both helped her, for we are as keen on her marrying Simon as she is, and that is saying a good deal. We want her in a county family, not a Bohemian one.

Ariadne bought some grey and scarlet Japanese stuff that only cost ninepence-halfpenny a yard to make her ball-frock without consulting either of us. Christina said *Quem Deus vult*—and that though you might look Japanese for ninepence-halfpenny a yard, you never could look smart. And it was quite true. Ariadne's body was all over the place, with scientific seams meandering where they shouldn't. When it was basted and tried on, she looked exactly like a bagpipe in it. We were working in the little entresol half-way up-stairs, and though there are three Empire mirrors in that room, you can't see yourself in any one of them, so we had to tell her it didn't do, and never would do.

"Take the beastly thing off then!" said Ariadne, almost crying, and pitching the body across the room till it lighted on Amelia's head. (Amelia is the dummy, and the only good figure in the house.) "I won't wear anything at all!"

"And I daresay you will look just as nice like that!" I said to tease and console her, but she wouldn't be, and she left the body clinging to Amelia, and began to put on her old blue bodice again, and it was a good thing she did, for the door opened and George and Lady Scilly came in.

"Dear me!" Lady Scilly said, in her little drawly voice, that comes of lying in bed late. "You look like Burne-Jones' *Laus Veneris*—'all the maidens, sewing, lily-like a-row.' I persuaded your father to bring me up to have a look at you. He says you are so clever, Ariadne, and make all your own dresses."

So George had taken in that fact! I always thought he thought dresses grew, for he has certainly never been plagued with dressmakers' bills.

"The eternal feminine, making the garment that expresses her," said George.

"Ninepence-halfpenny isn't going to express me!" Ariadne said, under her breath. "It covers me, and that's all!"

"I always think," George maundered, "that the symbolic note struck in the toilette is in the nature of a signal, a storm-signal if you will, of the prevailing wind of a woman's mood. Her moods should be variable. She should be a violet wail one day, a peace-offering in blue the next, some mad scarlet incoherent thing another——"

"I don't see how you are going to do all that on ninepence-halfpenny," Ariadne said again, for George was too busy listening to himself to listen to her impertinence. "Why you can't even get the colour!"

"It is every woman's duty to set an example of beautiful dressing without extravagance!" and he looked at Lady Scilly's pretty pink fluffiness. Paris, of course. I hate Paris, where we never go.

"Oh, this," she said very contemptuously, looking down at it as if it was dirt, as all well-dressed women do. "This! This cost nothing at all! I have a clever maid, you know?"

"If all the women had clever maids that say they have," Christina whispered to me. "What would become of Camille, I wonder?"

George continued, inventing a hobby as he went on, "You must never quit an old dress merely because it has become unfashionable."

"My dresses quit me," said Ariadne, dipping her elbow in the ink-pot, so that the hole in it didn't show. "I'm jealous of the sofa! It's better covered than me."

I believe Lady Scilly noticed her do this, and though she is lazy, she is kind, and she asked Ariadne when she intended to wear "this creation."

"At Lady Islington's," Ariadne answered rather sulkily.

"Oh yes, I know. A Cinderella. It is far too good for that sort of romp, my dear child. I have a little thing at home I could lend you just to dance in—it is too *débutantish* for me, and I do wish some one would wear it for me. If I send it round, will you try it on? And if it will do, keep it, and wear it for my sake. When is the dance?"

"The day after to-morrow!" I answered for Ariadne, who was overcome with gratitude, for she knew what Lady Scilly's little dresses were like. Camille's "little" would beat Ariadne's biggest.

"Then you shall have it to-morrow, and if you can wear it, do; I shall be so much obliged."

Ariadne said "thank you," a little ashamed to think that Simon was coming to tea, and that the only reason she cared about the dress was to dance with Simon in it; but I thought the settling of Ariadne in life, and marrying into a county family, was far more important than Lady Scilly's little jealousies, and wanting to keep Simon to herself, when she got so many, including George, so I told Lady Scilly she was a brick and no mistake, and I really thought so.

But Christina thought Ariadne had better try to pull the first dress into some sort of shape, so that she could wear it if the other dress didn't come. "Put not thy trust in smart women!" she said, and as it happened, she was right, for the dress never did!

At five o'clock on the very day of the dance, there wasn't a sign of it, and Ariadne hadn't let herself worry over it, by my and Christina's advice. We told her that she had better keep all the looks she had to carry off the home-made dress, for it would require them. She didn't worry, but she was very angry with Lady Scilly, and anger made her eyes so bright, and gave her such a pretty colour, that I felt sure it would be all right. The dress wasn't so very bad either; we had given up all attempt at getting it to fit, and that was better, for you could tell that Ariadne had a very nice, simple girlish figure underneath. Elizabeth Cawthorne came up to see her "girl" when she was dressed, she nearly always does, and she thought the dress sweet.

"That'll get him, that'll get him, Miss Ariadne, you'll see!" she kept saying; it was very vulgar, but then, poor Ariadne was so much in love that she couldn't help liking it. She had taken particular care of her hair, and when she lay down to rest in the afternoon, she had put ten curlers in to make sure of it's looking nice. And it did, like Moses in the burning bush.

At nine she dressed and went, and Christina gave her a kiss for luck, and I went to bed, for it was quite ten o'clock. I was just jumping in (I always take a header off the chest of drawers to stop me getting stiff!) when I heard a great puffing and panting at the bedroom door. Elizabeth Cawthorne is getting fat. It goes with good-nature and beer. And she is learning to drop her h's in the south.

"'Ere!" she said. "'Ere!" and shoved a great cardboard box under my nose. "*With Lady Scilly's love and compliments.*"

I was out of bed again in two twos, and Elizabeth and I unfastened the string, and there was a ball-dress— *the* ball-dress!

I felt inclined to burst out crying, to think of poor Ariadne—so near and yet so far—dancing away, perhaps, and losing Simon Hermyre's affection at every step, because her dress hung badly, and looked home-made, and here was a perfect dream of a dress, lying quite useless on the bed in my room at home. Elizabeth would have it out to look at; I indulged her, keeping her rather dark fingers off it as well as I could. It was all white, and fluffy, and like clotted cream, and I do believe it was made on purpose for Ariadne. There was a note with it, addressed to my sister, which Elizabeth opened in her excitement. I forgave her. It said—

"DEAR CHILD,

"My frock, I found, was not quite suitable, your young waist must be larger than mine. So I have ordered one to be made for you, and I do hope it will fit and that you will look very nice in it, with my love. I hope, too, that your father will approve of my taste.

"Ever yours,
"PAQUERETTE SCILLY."

"That's all she cares about—that George should think her generous! But if she had wanted me or Ariadne to be grateful she should have managed to get it here in time. I don't care for misplaced generosity."

"Suppose, Miss," said Elizabeth, "that you was to take a cab and go to where Miss Ariadne is, and make her change! Better late than never, I say."

"My sister isn't a music-hall artist," I regret to say was what I answered, and Elizabeth agreed, and added too, that she hadn't altogether lost her faith in the other dress, and that it might get Ariadne an offer as well as a smarter. So then she went, and I laid the dress out on Ariadne's bed, and lay down, and tried to go to sleep with my eyes fixed on it, and I did and even dreamed.

I was woke by feeling a heavy weight on my chest. At first I thought it was indigestion, but as I began to get more awake, I found it was Ariadne, who was sitting there quite still in the dark. I joggled her off, and then I began to remember about the dress, but thought I would tease her a little first.

"Well, did you have a good time?" I asked her.

"Fairly," answered Ariadne.

"Did you have any offers—in that home-made dress? Elizabeth was sure you would."

"I believe I am all torn to bits?" said Ariadne, walking round and round her own train like a kitten round its tail, and not intending to take any notice of my question.

"Now don't expect me to help you to mend it. It will take days!"

Ariadne said, "I shall not touch it. I don't mean to wear it again, but hang it in a glass case and sit and look at it. It is a wonderful dress!"

"Don't drivel!" I said, "unless there is really something particular about the dress that I don't know."

She didn't even rise to that, so I said, "I wonder you don't light up, and have a good look at it."

"There is no hurry, is there, about lighting the candle?" Ariadne said, sitting plump down on a bureau, and looking as if she didn't mean to go to bed at all. I believe she smelt Lady Scilly's dress on her bed, and was keeping calm just to tease me.

"Did any one see you home?" I asked.

"Yes, some one did," she answered, still in a sort of dream.

"Did he kiss you in the cab?" I at last asked her, thinking that if anything would rouse her, that would. She was sitting, as far as I could tell, in the cold moonlight, looking fixedly at her hand as if she wanted it to come out in spots like Saint Catherine Emmerich. I was riled to extinction.

"Oh, for Goodness' sake, get to bed!" I cried. "And if you are going to undress in the dark, to hide your blushes, I should advise you to get into your bed very *very* carefully!"

That did it.

"You naughty girl," she said quite quickly. "Have you been putting Lady Castlewood there with her new lot of kittens? It's too bad of you!"

She lit the candle, and then I noticed that her ears were quite red. She saw the dress at the same instant and went across and fingered it.

"So you have come?" she said, talking to it as if it were a person. "You are rather pretty, I must say, but I have done very well without you."

"Well," said I, "you *are* condescending. Who tore your skirt, if one might ask?"

"Mr. Hermyre."

"Mister now! How intimate you have become to be afraid of his name! Ha! I believe she's shy? How often did you dance with *Mister* Hermyre?"

"Oh, don't tease me, Tempe dear. As often as there was, I am afraid."

"Afraid? Yes, you will be talked about, and he will have to marry you, there!"

"He is going to," said Ariadne, quietly letting down her hair. I didn't know my own Ariadne. She had turned cheeky in a single night!

I looked about for something to take her down with, and I found it.

"Did you—did you put your head on his shoulder when he had asked you, as we have always agreed you would?"

"I may have—I don't know—I hope not!"

"You hope you didn't, but you know you did! Well, I wonder it did not run into him, or put his eye out or something?"

"Beast, what do you mean?"

"Only that you have got a haircurler in your hair, near the left side, and I presume it has been there all the evening!"

Ariadne put out the light and came and sat on my bed after that, and told me all about it quite nicely.

As far as I could make out, Pique had begun it. There had been a slight difficulty with another man who was not a gentleman although he was a Count—fancy, at Lady Islington's?—and he had been rude to Ariadne about a dance, and Ariadne had appealed to Simon although he wasn't so near her as some other men, and Simon had at once insulted the other man, and had danced with Ariadne all the rest of the evening to spite him and Lady Scilly, who had brought him, and whose new "mash" he was. I believe he's the German chauffeur I saw in her car.

But Ariadne would have it that it was the fan business that had brought it on—that fan he gave her at Whitby he had broken at Whitby, and he had never bought her a new one. We had often talked about it, but of course never mentioned it to Simon.

Lady Islington is Simon's Aunt Meg, and he is awfully afraid of her. After the row with the chauffeur Count, Ariadne had felt quite strange and frightened— he made nasty speeches, as not gentlemen do when they are riled—and Simon had taken her to a window-seat in a long gallery sort of staircase. She sat beside him for a long while feeling as if she could not breathe, long after all fear of the other man had passed away. She thought it could hardly be that still, and yet she felt as if a cold hand or a key, like when your nose is bleeding, was being put down her spine, though of course there was none. Simon didn't say anything, he seemed to be thinking, but she dared not look at him for some reason or other. But she said she wished, as she sat there, more than anything else she had ever wished in the world, more than she had wished I would get better of the scarlet fever when I was a baby—that he would take hold of her hand that was lying in her lap. She kept on staring at it, imagining his taking hold of it, "willing" him to do it. She wanted him to do this so badly that she nearly screamed and asked him right out; but no, it would have been no good unless he had done it of his own free-will. The music had not begun, and she seemed to fancy it would not begin until Simon had done that silly little thing. She felt somehow that he was thinking of this too, or something like it— something to do with her, at any rate.

She hated explaining all this to me, but I made her, for she had always solemnly promised to me she would tell me exactly how her first offer took place.

Then the music began and the people on the stairs got up, and some of them were sure to come past where they were. She says she felt Simon take a resolution of some kind, and yet all he said was, "Have you got a fan?"

Ariadne didn't know in the least what he meant, but she knew it was all part of the thing that had to happen now, and at once answered quite truly—

"I haven't got one. You broke it."

"And didn't I give you a new one? What an objectionable brute I am! Well, then we must do without. I only hope my Aunt Meg doesn't see me?"

And he kissed her.

This was the strangest way for it to happen, as Ariadne and I agreed, quite different from all our plans and expectations. For of course he then told her he loved her, and wanted to marry her. It was very nearly all at the same time, but yet he kissed her first. Nothing can alter that fact, and it was in the wrong order, and so I shall always say, except that Ariadne has made me promise never to allude to it again. And of course, as she kept her promise, I shall keep mine.

Simon Nevill Hermyre and Ariadne Florentina Vero-Taylor are to be married in three months at latest, they settled it that very night, subject to parents. Sir Frederick may raise objections, but Ariadne was able to assure Simon that George won't, he doesn't care about keeping Ariadne a day longer than he needs to. As Mr. Simon Hermyre's *fiancée* she is only an encumbrance now, not an advertisement, for of course Simon won't let her do Bohemian things or dress queerly any more. And she is and will be as dull as ditch-water for at least a year, like all engaged girls. She bores me.

CHAPTER XIX

DEAR Simon let his hair grow comparatively long to be married to Ariadne in, to please me. I was chief bridesmaid, and stood next Almeria; Jane Emerson Tree was third bridesmaid, and behaved fairly well, though I am told she did bite off and eat the heads of the best flowers in her bouquet while the service was going on, and Jessie Hitchings, who stood next her, couldn't prevent it, for she hadn't a single pin on her she could get at. I expect Jane Emerson was very ill after all that stephanotis! I treated her with studied contempt, and only asked her what she thought of Ariadne's "waist" this time, and didn't she wish she could have one as above reproach when she was married, if she ever found time to get married between her great actings? Why, Ariadne's dress was made by Camille! I was as intimate as possible with Jessie Hitchings, the coal-agent's daughter from Isleworth. That did Jane Emerson good. Ariadne asked her to be one of her bridesmaids just to please Ben, who adores her, and doesn't see that she is a bit common. Men in love never do. Still, she is our only childhood's friend, so Simon and even Almeria didn't make the least objection to have her included in the procession. They are not snobs, and if they were, are high up enough to be able to afford to stoop, and know everybody. As for Almeria, she came out wonderfully, and I really don't mind her at all. As the bridesmaids' hat wouldn't set without a bank of hair or something on the forehead for it to rest on, she was sensible enough to buy a pin-curl at the Stores and stick it on under the brim for the occasion. Ariadne was very much softened towards her by that, and I promised to go and stay with her at Highsam later on and learn to ride.

George gave Ariadne his usual present, only more so—a set of his own works beautifully bound, and some of the old jewellery she has always had given out to her to wear, to take away for her very own. Mother gave her all her household linen, marked and embroidered by herself. Peter Ball gave her a gramophone, Christina a type-writer. The Squire gave her his mother's best salad-bowl. Lord Scilly gave her a great gold cup or beaker. I believe he was trying to atone for the low joke he had practised on her at the picnic. It was awfully good and valuable, Simon said. Lady Scilly gave her a Shakespeare bound in calf. I believe she meant a hint about calf love, just the kind of thing she would call a joke, and that *Punch* wouldn't put in; but Ariadne never noticed and was grateful, for she happens to like Shakespeare for himself. To Simon, I heard, Lady Scilly gave a queer sort of scarf or thumb ring, with the Latin word *Donec* engraved on it. I did not know what that meant, and Simon said he was blest if he did, and he hung it on his dog's collar afterwards.

Simon and Ariadne went to Venice for their honeymoon. She took note-books, etc., but could not write any poetry in Venice somehow, so shopped all the time, especially bead necklaces. She didn't care for her own hair any more when she came back, she said every other girl in Venice had it. She had put back her fringe, and wets it every morning to make it keep flat, to please Sir Frederick Hermyre and Simon, who owned, *after* marriage, to a weakness for smooth hair.

They are to live in Yorkshire at one of his father's six places. He has given it to Simon, and Simon is now the youngest J.P. on the bench, and is going to breed shorthorns. I am to go and stay there after Christmas.

George detests Christmas so much that he ignores it, and forces us all to do the same. We may not put up holly or mistletoe, or make a plum-pudding or mince-pies. We have mince-pies always at Midsummer, and plum-pudding on May Day, so one does not miss them altogether, but all the same, I have a sort of Christmas feeling come over me at the right time, and could enjoy a Christmas stocking or Santa Claus as much as any ordinary Philistine child. So could Mother. Elizabeth says it is all she can do not to give warning than stay in such a God-forgotten house over the time, and she makes a small plum-pudding for the kitchen and gets us all down, except George, to stir it on the sly. Up-stairs no one dares to mention Christmas. If we do, we are fined sixpence. We have all of us to pay a whole shilling if a pipe bursts? I don't know if George would insist on money down, if it happened, but it is an odd circumstance, that though of course if they do burst, it is nobody's fault but the plumber's, who came to put them right last time and carefully left something wrong ready for the next, now that this rule has been made the pipes contain themselves, and don't burst at all.

When Ariadne was here, she always contrived to send away a few parcels, and we received some, of course. We cannot help people, who respect Christmas, being kind to us then. George came in once while we were undoing a few, and damned "this whirling season of string and brown paper!"

"I resent the maddening appeals of an over-wrought post-office to post early. Why should I post early? Why should I post at all? I forbid all mention of the egregious subject!"

And he went out, and we asked Elizabeth to bring our parcels up to our bedrooms in future.

The Christmas after Ariadne left us, we didn't mind obeying him, we were so sad without her. I missed having some one to bully. George missed having two to bully instead of one. He has always sworn, but now he took to swearing as if he meant it, and saying bitter things to Mother, and poor Ben's chances of school are farther off than ever. He got quite desperate, did poor Ben, and asked Mother to make some arrangement by which she could give him less to eat and put what she could save aside for his schooling. He said he was willing to live on skilly if only he might go to school, and from what he heard, he wouldn't get much better there, so he might as well get used to it. Mother cried, and said no, she couldn't save off his keep, that she must make a man of him at any rate, and would try to save money some other way, or even make it? She would think till she thought of a plan. Meantime she would buy him some books, and Mr. Aix would look over his exercises if Ben went regularly to his rooms in Pump Court. Ben tried, but it is so awkward for him, since he started valeting George at Whitby. George can't do without him, and calls for him at all sorts of times, and Ben must be at call. George swears at his sulky expression while folding up coats, stretching trousers, etc., but I am afraid Ben will have the melancholia soon if he doesn't get what he has set his heart on. If Mother could only raise the money, she says she would go straight to George with it, and tell him that she meant to pay the cost of Ben's education, for it is money, she is sure, and nothing but money, which prevents his making up his mind which school? Gracious me! Schools are all alike, all beastly, and a necessary evil for the sons of men.

I often wonder if the people he goes among, and stays with—"he is the devil for country houses!" Mr. Aix says, "he has got them in the blood,"—I wonder if when they see him come smiling down to breakfast—he has to come down to breakfast in some houses, never at home—they realize that he has a wife and children and a secretary, and three cats depending on him? For I believe he is the kind of useful guest who has small talk for breakfast, which reminds me of those houses where the cook gets up early to bake the little hot cakes people like, and what it means to her, no one imagines! George stokes and talks at the same time, and that is one reason why they all love him and ask him madly for Saturdays to Mondays or longer.

George is not well just now, his voice is all in his throat, and husky. His hair is getting very grey, and suits him; his eyes are large, like a sad deer's. He is still as graceful. Mr. Aix says he has taken to wearing stays. I don't believe this. I am the only one in the house who sticks up for George. Ben hates him, so does Aunt Gerty. Ben will go on hating him till he is allowed to go to school. Mother never speaks of him, so I don't know how she feels about him. In cold weather he is always much nicer to her. He feels the cold of England. He has written about Italy till he is half Italian. He has got a new secretary, a "singularly colourless personage," whom Mother likes very much. She isn't half so amusing as Christina, but Lady Scilly says she is far more suitable.

After Christmas was over, George left us and went to "The Hutch," Lady Scilly's place in Wiltshire. Her novel is nearly finished, and Ben says she has piped all hands on deck—I mean all the people who are helping her have to be ready with their help. There is a lawyer and a doctor among the crew, but George is master-skipper. I believe that she will drop them all when once the book is done? George too, perhaps. Though I am not sure she likes him only for the sake of the novel? He can be fascinating when he likes, and he does like with her. It's such a good old title.

I think I am right, for he was away a long time, indeed he has never stayed so long at "The Hutch" before. He has his own suite there, and all the other rooms are called after the names of his novels or characters in them. Could any one pay an author a greater compliment?

Mrs. Ptomaine was not staying there—Never no more!—but she has a lady friend who was, and the friend says Lord Scilly is beginning to get "restive."

Mrs. Ptomaine comes to see us, at least to see Aunt Gerty, a good deal; she is no longer all in all with Lady Scilly since the Mr. Pawky episode.

"And I didn't make much of him, after all!" she told Mother and Aunt Gerty. "Lady Scilly had squeezed him nearly dry. He didn't trust women any more, always imagined they wanted money. And then dangled an empty purse at them, metaphorically. Poor old man, it is a shame to destroy any one—even a millionaire's— confidence in human nature. She borrows of every one, even the masseuse and the charwoman, my dear, it's quite awful! That poor, pretty young Hermyre! I was quite pleased when your sweet innocent daughter rescued him from the wiles of Scilly, and perhaps Charybdis— who knows? He looked weak!"

"And so secured a weak child to look after him and strengthen his hands!" said Mother. It is no use minding Mrs. Tommy, she isn't "quite eighteen carat," Aunt Gerty says, or else she would surely not discuss a woman's own son-in-law to her face. But, she is a journalist, and journalists know no laws of consanguinity or decency even. If one is to get any good whatever out of the press, one must accept it with all its inconveniences, and Aunt Gerty and Mother think everything of the press in these days. They ask Mrs. Ptomaine to dinner continually, and Mr. Freddy Cook to meet her. And Mr. Aix as a standing dish, and Aunt Gerty of course. Then they make a lot of noise and smoke all over the house except the study. Mother won't let them go in there at all while George is away. I hear them talking between the puffs—

"You can engage to work so and so, eh?" or "Have you got thingumbob?"

Mr. Aix is writing a play. He brings the acts over here as he writes them, and gets Mother to speak the woman's part for him, so that he sees how it goes. He says Mother is a great dear, and he tells her continually how she helps him, how she puts the right interpretation on him at every turn. I never should have thought Mr. Aix difficult to understand, but then a man has to be very modest to realize that he takes no understanding and is as plain as a pike-staff. And as Mr. Aix always speaks the brutal truth—he can't wrap anything up—he is as "crude as the day," so George often says—I don't see Mother's cleverness.

They talk of The Play as if it was a baby. "Mustn't christen it before it is brought into the world," and "One thing you can confidently predict about it, it can't be born prematurely!" and so on. They use the study in the mornings, and Mr. Aix sits in George's swivel-chair, and Mother takes the floor in front of him. She reads the woman's part out aloud and he criticises her. She must do it pretty well, for he often calls out, "Oh, you darling!" when she has said a particular piece. "What a divine accent you give it!" "That will knock them!" "Wicked to hide such a talent!" and praise like that. He never asks Aunt Gerty to read any, though she is a real actress and sits there and criticises Mother all the time.

"Pooh, pooh!" says Mr. Aix, "leave her to her intuitions! You battered professionals don't know the value of a new note."

So I see that Mother never was a Professional, even before George married her. And a good thing too!

Mr. Aix worked very hard at the play, and promised that it should be finished one day next week. When George came home, he would want his study of course, but we hadn't the remotest idea of his arriving when he did, late one afternoon just before dinner-time.

We were all hard at it in the study. Aunt Gerty was making a pink surah blouse all over the study table and being prompter as well. Mr. Aix was in George's swivel-chair, and Mother standing in front of him. George was on us in a moment, just as Mr. Aix had closed the manuscript with a slap.

"Our child comes on bravely!" he was just saying to Mother, as George appeared in the doorway with his cigarette in his mouth.

Aunt Gerty whispered to Mother, "I'll bet you Lord Scilly has had him kicked out of the house. Go on that tack!" and bolted into the hall, forgetting her pink surah spread all over the desk.

"Welcome back, old fellow!" said Mr. Aix, turning round in the swivel-chair and putting a protecting paw over Aunt Gerty's blouseries. They would be sure to irritate George, he knew; so they did. George turned quite white with temper and flung his coat off, and Mother caught it across her arm as if she had been a servant. There seemed to be a great noise in the hall, and Polly came in looking disgusted, as servants always do when it is a question of not paying one's just debts.

She began "If you please, sir, the cabman——" but her voice was quite drowned between the cabman relieving his mind in the hall outside and George inside. He seemed bewildered, but able to swear all the time.

"Won't you pay your cab, George?" said Mother gently, "and then you can abuse me at your leisure!"

Mr. Aix went to pay the man, and I thought I had better get out of the room with him. George was sitting bolt upright in his chair, and Mother like a little school-girl before him. I don't know what they said to each other, but George wouldn't come out to dinner, but had a plate sent in.

Mother didn't alter her habits, but went to the theatre with Mr Aix.

George's plate of dinner came out untouched. After all it was my own father, and he had come all the way from Wiltshire, and perhaps had been kicked out of "The Hutch" as Aunt Gerty said. I knew enough of Lady Scilly to know how changeable she is, and perhaps it was only her novel she cared for. I went to him, as bold as a lion.

He was sitting still where he had been before dinner, only his head was on his hands among Aunt Gerty's blouse trimmings.

"Shall I take these away?" I asked. "Don't they make you angry?"

"I haven't noticed."

I saw he was ill, not to mind all Aunt Gerty's horrid pink shape all over his papers! I sat down on the edge of the table and he didn't even scold me.

"Where is Lucy—my wife?" he asked me presently.

"My Mother?" said I. "She's gone to the theatre."

"Is that usual?"

"Quite usual. She generally goes with Mr. Aix, but to-night Aunt Gerty has gone with them."

"Chaperons them, eh?"

I didn't like to hear him call Mother and Mr. Aix *them* in that insulting bracketting way, so I said—

"Mother has stayed in all her life. She wanted a change."

"Aix?" said he, "for a change! God!"

"She's collaborating with Mr. Aix."

"Damn him and his play too."

"Oh, not his play, George. Mother would be *so* grieved."

Then George suddenly pulled a paper out of his pocket and said, "Read that aloud, child."

"Is it a bit of your new novel?"

"Yes, it is a bit of my new novel. Read."

I did.

"*We talk and talk, and never act. Oh, this curse of civilization! You make excuses for S——, for your bitter enemy. Magnanimous, but effete! He is behaving well, but so unpicturesquely. He offers a woman no excuse for staying with him. Oh, Italy! Italy! You, magician, have made me long for the life of Italy, the silver incandescent sands, the passionate brown of the olives—but why should I try to outdo you in your own imitable manner?"*

"*In*imitable, you mean, don't you, child? But no, we will not trust this white devil of Italy. Go and fetch me a plateful of cold meat. And here are the keys; go down to the cellar and get a bottle of Burgundy. Corton eighty-eight. You'll see the label. We will carouse."

I was delighted. George and I finished the bottle between us, and he ate a good supper, and said no more of Mr. Aix, or Mother either.

I almost liked George just then. I saw why Lady Scilly liked him. He is funny and gentle. I asked him to choose a school for Ben, and he said he would think about it. It is the oddest feeling to suddenly become "pals" with one's own father. I had never known it before. There is some good in George, and his eyes are very bright.

CHAPTER XX

MY mother is changed—not horrid, but quite changed. She goes out nearly every morning at ten, with Aunt Gerty, whose manners are worse than ever, and who has a little chuckling, cheerful way of going about that simply irritates me to death! There is a secret, evidently, and George and I are out of it. It brings us together. He is not happy, no more than I am, no more than Mother is. She is excited, not happy. She has taken to wearing her mouth shut lately; once we used to tease her because she kept it open, and looked always just as if she were going to speak, or had done speaking. But Mother is a good woman. Although she gads about so much, she doesn't neglect her household duties. She sees after George's comfort as much as ever, and keeps all onions out of the house as usual. The more she fusses over him, the less he likes it. He shook his head once, when Mother had tidied his writing-table for him—it took her two hours—and then he said half-laughing, "A bad sign, Tempe! Read your Balzac."

I don't read Balzac, and I don't know what George means. I don't try, and I find that is the best sort of sympathy one can give. At any rate, he likes it, and he is always having me in his study, and teaching me to type-write, and saying little things, like that I have put down, under his breath. He mutters a good deal to himself, not to me, and wants not so much some one to talk to, as some one to talk at.

We hear no more of Lady Scilly. She has not been here since Ariadne was married. Ariadne was an excuse. Mother never gave her an excuse to come to see her, she had never accepted her, or been rude to her either. She simply ignored her. So Lady Scilly not having Ariadne to come and fetch, had no particular reason for coming to us, unless she came to see George, and she could have seen him more easily at "The Hutch" or her town-house, till quite recently. She used to come here about her novel, but most uncomfortably, for Christina was a sad dragon, and looked down her nose at her. Christina could curl her nostril really, which very few women can do. It is a horrid thing to have done at you, and withers you soonest of anything. Now the novel is finished, and the type-written copy, tied up like Christmas meat, is going the social round of all the literary men who have been asked to her dinner-parties with a view to their favourable opinion. I know that Mr. Frederick Cook has had it, and written her a polite letter about it, though that won't prevent him slating it in *The Bittern* if he wants to. So Mrs. Ptomaine says.

I know that what Aunt Gerty said in spite, and to give Mother a stick to hit George back with when he came and found us doing dressmaking in his sacred study, was true. Lord Scilly had told George not to go to his house any more. Perhaps Lady Scilly had said he might? Having no more use for George, she may have given Lord Scilly a free hand with him, and perhaps a free foot, who knows? I think she is not nice. I am on George's side now, as far as outside politics go, though I shall never approve of the way he treats my brother Benvenuto.

Lady Scilly came to Cinque Cento House at last, and George didn't "look that pleased to see her," as Elizabeth Cawthorne said afterwards. Elizabeth Cawthorne has no opinion of her, nor of the way she goes on with that German fellow. She means the man who was so rude to Ariadne at the Islingtons', at least he was far too kind for politeness. He was a Count then, but he is also Lady Scilly's chauffeur. He was waiting outside on her motor at this very moment, quite the servant. She took him to her aunt's ball for the fun of it, I suppose, and it was easy to pretend he was somebody, for he looks quite military and distinguished.

Elizabeth showed her into the study, saying gruffly, "A female to see you, sir."

"Paquerette!" said George, in real amazement, as she floated in, and when the door had closed on Elizabeth Cawthorne, went a little down on one knee and looked up into George's face, saying, as I have heard the French do to their professors of painting or music,—"*Cher maître!*"

George had taught her to do this in the days when he was really her professor, and she wanted to do everything as Bohemians do in the Quartier Latin, but only the way she looked at him as she said it I could tell that she had no further use for him.

I was sitting at the type-writer, in the corner of the room, as if I were in my castle, and I stayed there. It was getting dark and they didn't think of turning on the electric light. Besides, George had at first made me a little sign which I understood, because of the *entente cordiale* we had had for some time, to stay where I was, and I like doing what people seem to want, especially when it goes with what I want myself. Then he forgot me altogether. Lady Scilly, I believe, never saw me at all, for she never said how-do-you-do, or looked my way, and yet we had not quarrelled. George put on his "pretty woman" manner, and raised her, and made her sit in a nice high-backed chair that suited her.

"How nice of you to come! My wife is out. By the way, I may as well tell you, she is leaving me."

I nearly fell off my chair. Lady Scilly looked upset; for she hadn't come to see Mother, and hadn't thought of asking whether she was out or not. She collected herself, and said to George with some dignity—

"You put it crudely."

"I do. I never mince my words, except in books. It is as I say. I shall not oppose it. I hope that my unhappy partner may one day come to know the bourgeois happiness I have been unable to give her. Unlucky fellow that I am—*cœur de célibat*, you know; an Alastor of Fitz John's Avenue, the Villon of Maresfield Gardens——"

"No woman's such a fool as to leave a place like this——"

"What does Shelley say? *Love first leaves the well-built nest——*"

"You certainly are a most extraordinary man!" she mumbled. George puzzled her by changing about so.

"Yes," he answered her, smiling. "Come, take off your furs and make yourself at home. Compromise yourself merrily. I suppose now, by all the rights and wrongs of it, I ought to invite you to bolt with me, but I am weak, I shall not."

"Are you quite sure you won't be stronger by the end of this interview?"

"Oh, is this an interview? Ah, why be formal and boring? Why stable the steed after the horse—I mean the novel is out? It will be a huge success, so your enemies predict. Frederick Cook of *The Bittern* writes me that this, the latest output of a militant aristocracy, seeking to beat us with our own weapons, is chockful of cleverness and primitive woman. What more do you want?"

"D. the novel! I want *you!*" she said, stamping her foot.

"Oh, throw away the fugitive husk and the rind outworn—the creed forgotten—the deed forborne—

how does it go? Give a poor author a chance, now that you have sucked his commonplace book dry, and torn the heart out of his theories, butchered him to make a literary agent's holiday."

"You *are* unkind."

"Don't say that. It is unworthy of you. Stale! like the plot of the new novel you propose we should work out together."

"I am prepared to go all lengths to assert——"

"Your powers of imagination. I don't doubt it. But I have been thinking it over, and I find it a ghastly, an impossible plot. No, it would never do, not even if we made a motor-motif of it. It won't go on all fours. It would not even begin to sell. It has none of the elements of popularity. To begin and end with, there's not an atom of passion about it, not even so much as would lie on twenty thousand pounds of radium, and you know how much that is!"

"Don't imply that I am incapable of passion in that insulting way!" she said quite angrily. "It shall never be said——"

"It will never be said, unless we run away and apply the test of Boulogne and social ostracism. Believe me, Paquerette, things are best as they are—going to be. There's true evolution in it. When the feast is over, you put out the fluttering candles, tear down the wreaths, open the windows. When the novel is done——"

"I hate you to talk like this!" said she, making a cross face.

"Women hate realism."

"Women hate lukewarmness. Pull yourself together, George, and let us lay our heads together to make Scilly—look silly. He's mad just now, but it will pass off, he will get over it, and you will come down to us at 'The Hutch' as usual and more so. Dear old Scilly will be the first to climb down——"

George shook his head.

"No, no, *non bis in idem*. Not twice in the same place." (I wasn't sure if he was alluding to the kick Lord Scilly had given him or not.) "Go now, you sweet woman. I want to be alone. You are staid for."

"Yes, yes, I must go. You remind me. The Count will be so deliciously irritated. Thanks so much, so very, very much, for all your help and timely assistance, your——"

"Has the play been worth the scandal?" George asked her, while he was kissing her hand to hide how much he loathed her, and was glad she was going. He knew, as well as I knew, that she was the kind of woman who kicks away the ladder she has just got up by with a toss of her fairy foot, and that he would never be asked to "The Hutch" again. Mr. Aix would, more probably, because he may chance to review what George has helped her to write. And it seemed to me that she has been massaged so much or so long or something, that her cheeks are like flabby oysters, and her figure brought out in all the wrong places. She was too pretty to last kittenish and fluffy as she was when I saw her come out of the public-house that first day.

"Good-bye—then—George!" she said, with something between a sneer and a sob. "We meet again— in society, not under the clock at Charing Cross."

What should take George and her there I cannot imagine, but George bowed, and led her out, and I followed them. There was her chauffeur in the car as large as life—and as a German. Though indeed he is very good-looking.

"I can see that he is cross in every line of his back," Lady Scilly whispered to George as she left him on the steps, and tripped down them, and got in beside her crabstick Count. He received her most coldly, and it was easy to see he was her master more than her servant.

George grunted as he fastened the door. There was an east wind blowing, and he was afraid of catching cold after standing there bareheaded.

"She will probably bolt with him before the year is out," he said, as we went back to the study shivering. He played cat's-cradle with me till dinner-time. It was all he was good for, he said, and as the game appeared to amuse him, I didn't mind making a fool of myself for once.

About Mother's going away that he spoke of to Lady Scilly! I believe it really is with Mr. Aix, as George is so very civil to him. I don't see who else it could be, for we see more of him than of any one else. He is George's greatest friend, as well as Mother's, and people don't run away with perfect strangers, as a rule.

Mother was certainly up to something, for her eyes were as bright as glass, and she had hysterics two days running. Aunt Gerty used to say while these were going on, slapping Mother's palms and vinaigretting her—"It is natural, you know—the excitement." The excitement of running away, I suppose. She used to make her lie down a great deal, and "nurse her energy," for she "would want it all!" Mother was by far the most important person in the whole house in these days, and instead of George being out late, and needing his latch-key, it was Mother who was always on the go, and dining with the Press every other night of her life. At least, I suppose Mrs. Ptomaine and Mr. Freddy Cook are the Press, they are certainly nothing else of importance. Mother joined a club, and stayed there one night when there was a fog.

George never asks her any questions. He is too proud, and of course he knows that she is too. She wouldn't stand having her movements questioned, any more than he would. But he began to look ragged and grey, and to have indigestion. He lived chiefly in his study. He fenced a good deal, with Mr. Aix. He asked Mr. Aix to leave the button off his foil, but Mr. Aix would not. George's other distraction is Father Mack, who comes to see him a good deal, and when George goes out now, which he seldom does, it is to see Father Mack. Father Mack is not oppressively stiff. Once George came back from confession and set us all to try and translate "The Survival of the Fittest" into French, a problem Father Mack had asked him. Father Mack also gave Mother the address of a very good little dressmaker. He lent George the *Life of Saint Catherine Emmerich*, a lovely book. She was one of those women who can think so hard of something that it comes out all over their bodies, in spots. People came from far and wide to look at her and admire her, and her family allowed it, instead of getting a trained nurse at five-and-twenty shillings a week, and giving her a free hand till Catherine was cured. It is my belief that she did not want to be cured, she liked being praised for having so many spots that you could fancy it was all in the shape of a crown of thorns. Still it is a nice romantic story, and the poor woman meant well.

Aunt Gerty says George is going to be a 'vert, and that I shall have to be baptized over again, and not buried in consecrated ground when I die. She said I need not bother to go on with preparing for my confirmation, as all that would be stopped. I was hemming my veil and

I went on, for I believed she was teasing. And as for Father Mack, he is quite a nice man, and George doesn't swear half so badly since he came under his influence.

One of these nights, when Mother had gone off to dine at some restaurant or other, with a merry party, Aunt Gerty said, I had a talk with Ben. George, as usual now, dined in his study alone. Ben told me some things Mother had been saying to him, about better times coming, and darkest before dawn, and so on. He wanted me to explain her, but I couldn't, for the only fact I knew, viz. her going to Boulogne with Mr. Aix, would not do Ben any good that I could see? It is really no use trying to find out what grown-up people mean, sometimes, it is like trying to imagine eternity; one has nothing to go on.

We went to bed early, but I couldn't sleep; after what Ben had said I felt I must see Mother again that night. I kept awake with great difficulty till I heard the swish of her dress on the stairs, and then I slipped out of bed and faced her. She was too tired to scold, she had trodden twice in the hem of her dress going up-stairs. When we got into her own room, she let her cloak slide off on to the floor, and came out of it like a flower, and looked awfully nice in her low neck and bare arms.

"Oh, my pretty little Mother," I said. "I do love you."

"You are just like every one else," she answered me pettishly.

"I'm not," I said, but of course there is no doubt about it, one does love people more in evening dress and less in a nightgown.

"Did George ever see you like this?" I asked.

"Often. Is he gone to bed?"

"Yes, with a headache."

She took a candle and we went on tiptoe to his room, Mother first taking off her high-heeled shoes, for they would tap on the parquet and make a noise. George was asleep. He had eaten one of his bananas, and the other was still by the side of his bed.

"Hold the candle, Tempe!" Mother said quickly. It was that she might go down on her knees beside George. She then buried her head in the quilt and cried.

"Oh, George, I am doing it for the best—I am, I am! For my poor neglected boy—my poor Ben."

She upset and puzzled me so by alluding to Ben, after my conversation with him that very evening, that I dropped a blob of candle-grease on the sheet near George's arm, and I was so afraid I had awakened him, that I at once shut the stable-door—I mean blew out the candle and made a horrible smell. Mother jumped off her knees as frightened as I was—Father Mack hasn't cured George quite of swearing!—and we made a clean bolt of it back to her room, where she re-lit the candle and began to get out of her dress as quickly as she could, while I sat in a honeypot on the floor, and kept my nightgown well round my legs not to catch cold, and talked to her nicely, so as not to startle her.

"Of course, Mother dear, you are doing it for the best, even if it is to run away."

"Run away! Who says I am going to run away?"

"George."

"He told you?"

"He told Lady Scilly."

"Did he, then? He deserves that I should make it true." She laughed, a laugh I did not like at all. It wasn't her laugh, but I have said she was quite changed.

"Oh, Mother, don't laugh like that!"

"You are like the good little girl in the play, who preaches down a wicked mother's heart! Well, my dear, I'll promise you one thing. I will never run away without you. Will that be all right?"

"That will be all right," I answered, much relieved. For although I am so much more "pally" with George and sorry for him, I don't want to be left with him. Perhaps I shall be allowed to run over in the *Marguerite* from Boulogne sometimes on a visit? Then I could darn and mend for him, as Mr. Aix would not be able to spare Mother from doing for him. I did not mention Mr. Aix to her. I thought she would rather tell me all in her own time.

I often wonder if we three will be happy in Boulogne, or wherever it is social ostracism takes you to? I fancy the inconvenience of running away is chiefly the want of society.

That is the only want Mother will not feel after all those years buried away in Isleworth. Ariadne is now happily married, so it won't affect her, though I suppose that if this had happened a year ago, a mother-in-law spending her days in social ostracism would not have suited Simon's stiff relations. It might have prevented him from proposing. I see it all; Mother unselfishly waited.

One thing really troubles me. Why does not Mother do some packing? I hope that she is not going to run away in that uncomfortable style when you only throw two or three things into a bag? A couple of bottles of eau-de-cologne, and some hair-pins, like Laura in *To Leeward?* I, at any rate, have some personal property, and I shall do very badly without it in a dull, dead-alive place like Boulogne. But I will be patient. Whatever Mother does is sure to be right, even running away, which gets so dreadfully condemned in novels.

George's new secretary is quite utilitarian and devoted to him, she is not so *farouche* as Christina, Mr. Aix says, or so charming. George keeps her hard at work typing his autobiography, and doesn't go to see Father Mack any more. I asked him why he was "off" dear Father Mack, and he says last time he went to see him it was the Father's supper-time, and he saw a horrid sight. He could not think, he says, of entrusting his salvation to a man whom he had seen supping with the utmost relish off a plateful of bullock's eyes. Just like George to be put off his salvation by a little thing like that! Though I always felt myself as if Father Mack was not quite ascetic enough for a real right-down sinner like George.

Tickets have come to George for the first night of Mr. Aix's play. George calls it Ingomar, which vexes Aix, because Ingomar is a certain old-fashioned kind of play that only needs a pretty woman who can't act, as "lead."

"Who's your Parthenia?" he asked him.

Mr. Aix answered, "Oh, a little woman I unearthed for myself from the suburban drama—the usual way."

"Any good?" asked George casually.

"I am telling her exactly what I want her to do, and she looks upon me as Shakespeare and the Angel Gabriel in one," said Mr. Aix, glancing across at Mother, who pursed up her lips and laughed.

"I will take Tempe to your first night," said George suddenly.

"A play of Jim Aix's for the child's first play!" cried Mother in a fright. "I shouldn't think of it."

"Children never see impropriety, or ought not to," George said. "But if you don't wish it, I will take Lady Scilly and the Fylingdales instead. It will do the play good."

"It's a fond delusion," said Aix, "that the aristocracy can even damn a play."

Of course I understood the impropriety blind. Mother wanted me to be free to go away with her, and the twenty-sixth was to be the night, after all. I thought of the crossing by the nine o'clock mail that we should have to do, and that I only know of from hearsay, and wondered why they must choose such an awkward time? Perhaps we should not after all cross that night, for surely Mr. Aix would want to come before the curtain if called, and that wouldn't possibly be till about ten o'clock, too late for the train?

Perhaps we should stay the night at an hotel? I should simply love that.

CHAPTER XXI

"SHALL I type your Good-bye to George?" I asked Mother. She said, "What do you mean?" I said, "The one you will leave pinned to your pincushion in the usual place?"

She laughed, and I again thought her most fearfully casual. There was no packing done, although one would have thought she would have liked her clothes nice and fresh and lots of them, so that she shouldn't feel shabby at Boulogne, and let Mr. Aix and herself down. As for my clothes—I really only had one—one dress I mean—and it was hanging loose where it shouldn't, and with a large ink-spot in front nobody had troubled to take out with salts of lemon or anything.

But I began to think some things had been sent on beforehand, as advance luggage or so forth, for Mr. Aix came in one evening, and when Aunt Gerty raised her eyebrows at him, he said "A 1!" That I fancied was the ticket number for the luggage, so I felt more at ease.

One eventful evening, after Mother had been lying down all day, I was told to put on my sun-ray pleated, and to mend it if it wanted it. I did mend it and I put a toothbrush in the pocket of it, and I kissed all the cats until they hated me. Cats don't like kissing, but then I didn't know when I should see them again? I supposed some time, for running away never is a permanent thing.

People always come back and take up housekeeping again, in the long run.

The funny thing was, they had chosen the day of Mr. Aix's first night to run away on. I suppose it was in case he was boo-ed. Then the manager could come on and say, "The author is not in the house, having gone to Boulogne with a lady and little girl, by the nine o'clock mail!" That, of course, was the train we were to catch. I looked it out, I am good at trains.

George took Lady Scilly to dine at the Paxton that night, and on to the theatre where some others were to meet them. I have never been to a theatre myself, only music halls. At six o'clock George went off, all grin and gardenia. The grin was as forced as the gardenia. I observed that.

Aunt Gerty badly wanted to go with Mr. Aix and hold his hand, as he was as nervous as a cat. But he wouldn't have her with him, and I don't wonder. It would have been impossible to shake her off by nine o'clock, and he would have missed the boat-train, and Mother and me.

After our dinner, Mother went up to her room and put on her hat, and told me to go to mine and to put on my Shanter. I didn't intrude on her privacy. I daresay she was saying a long good-bye to her old home, as I was. I filled my pockets with mementoes. I took Ernie Fynes' list of horses—for after all he is the only boy I ever loved, and it is my only love-letter. I wondered what Mother would take? However, she came out of her room smiling, and her pockets didn't stick out a bit. She is calm in the face of danger; just as she was that awful day when I supplied a fresh lot of methylated to a dying flame under our tea-kettle straight from the bottle, and she had to put out the large fire I had started unconsciously.

"Goodness, child, how you do bulge! Empty your pocket at once!"

I did as I was told. We must buy pencils over there, I suppose, but I held on to the toothbrush.

"Now you are not to talk all the way there and tire me!" Mother said, as we got into a hansom.

"I won't; but do tell me where we are to meet Mr. Aix?"

"Mr. Aix? I am sure I don't know. He will be about, I suppose, unless they sit on his head to keep him quiet! Don't talk."

She put her hand up to her head, not because she had a headache, but to keep her hair in place, as it was a windy night, and I couldn't help thinking of the crossing that I had never crossed, only heard what Ariadne said about it, when she came back from her wedding-tour. Ariadne tried seven cures, and none of them saved her.

It was ridiculously early, only seven o'clock. As we drove on and on I began to hope that we were going to lose Mr. Aix and go alone. But it was no good. We stopped at a door that certainly wasn't the door of a station, and Mr. Aix came out to meet us. He squeezed our hands, and his hand was hot, while his face was as white as a table-cloth. We went in, up a dirty passage, and into a great cellar where there seemed to be building constructions going on, for I noticed lots of scaffolding and that sort of thing. There were also great pieces of canvas stretched on wood, and one very big bit lying there propped against the wall had a landscape of an orchard on it.

"What is it?" I asked one of the people standing about—a man in a white jacket.

"That, Missie—that's the back cloth to the first scene," and then he mumbled something, about flies and their wings, that I did not chose to show I didn't understand.

"Oh, yes, quite so," I said to the dirty man in the white (it had once been) jacket, and got hold of Mr. Aix, who was mooning about in evening dress, quite unsuitable for a journey. But he was always an untidy sort of inappropriate man.

"Where's my mother?"

"Oh, your mother! Yes, she's gone to her room. I'll take you to her."

"But are you going to make us live *here?*" I asked; but bless the man! he was too nervous to take any more notice of me and my remarks. We muddled along; I tumbled over a lump in the middle of the floor with grass sown on it, and caught my foot in a carpet, made of the same. Mr. Aix quite forgot me and I lost him.

"Mind! Mind!" everybody kept saying, and shouldering past me with bits of the very walls in their arms. They left the brick perfectly bare, as bare as our old coal-cellar at Isleworth. (The one in Cinque Cento House is panelled.) I saw an ordinary tree, as I thought, but I was quite upset to find it was flat, like a free-hand drawing. My eyes were dazzled with electric lights, mounted on strings, like a necklace, only stiff, that they pushed about everywhere they liked. There were things like our nursery fire-guard all round the gas, that was there as well as electric. I noticed a girl go and look through a hole in a bit of canvas or tapestry that took up all one side of the wall, and went near her.

"Pretty fair house!" she said. She was a funny-looking little thing, with hardly enough on, and what there was was dirty, or dyed a dirty colour. In fact no two persons there were dressed alike; it was like a fancy-dress party, such as the Hitchings have at their Christmas-tree. The noise was deafening, they were shoving heavy weights about here and there, without knowing particularly or caring where they were going. My new friend had an American accent, and was as gentle as a cat. She went a little way back from the curtain with me and stood by a man she seemed rather to like, though he didn't seem to like her. He was very tall and big, and when she had been talking to him a little while, she said suddenly—

"Excuse me! I must not let myself get stiff!" and took hold of a great leather belt he wore, and propped herself up by it and began to dip up and down, opening her knees wide. The man didn't seem to like it much, but he was kind and chaffed her, till I got tired of her see-sawing up and down, and talking of her Greekness, and asked one or the other of them to be kind enough to take me to my mother.

"Certainly, little 'un," said the man; "kindly point the young lady out to me. There's so many in the Greek chorus!"

"It is Miss Lucy Jennings' daughter," said somebody near.

"I'll take you to her after my dance," said the girl. "Wait. Watch me! I go on!"

It was a sort of hop-skip-and-a-jump, like a little spring lamb capering about the fields and running races with the others as they do, but not more than that. They made a ring for her, and we all stood round and watched her, and somebody sang while she was dancing. She had no stockings at all on her clean manicured feet, but a kind of open-work boot of fancy leather. She came back as cool as a cucumber, and no wonder, for she had nearly stayed still, not so much exercise as an ordinary game of blindman's-buff, and said to me, "Now, pussy, I will escort you to your mommer."

She took me to the edge of the wall where a little stairs came down, and on the way we passed a boy with one side of him blue and the other green, and another man with wattles like a turkey hanging down his cheeks and a baby's rattle in his hand. I hated them all, they were streaky and hot, like a nightmare, and simply longed for my nice, clean, natural mother.

But when we got to a door and knocked, a woman like a nurse came and answered it, and through her arm I could see my mother, standing in front of a looking-glass, under a gas globe with a fender over it, and she was streakier than anybody. She had a queer dress on too, with a waistband much too low, and a skirt, shortish, and her hair was yellow!

That finished me, and I screamed, "Oh, Mother, where have you put your black hair?"

Aunt Gerty, who was sitting on a large cane dress-basket, told me to shut my mouth, and Mother turned round and said—

"It is only a wig, dear, and the paint will wash off, and then I will kiss you. Meantime, sit down and keep still!"

So I did, and watched the nurse arranging Mother as if she was a child, nothing more or less. I turned this way and that, trying to get the effect, but it was no use, I still thought she looked horrid.

The others didn't think so. Aunt Gerty kept saying, "Really, Lucy, I wouldn't have believed it! A little make-up goes a long way with us poor women, I see. More on the left-hand corner of the cheek, Kate. The lighting is rather unkind here, I happen to know."

So Kate put more on, and Mother kept taking more off with a shabby bit of an animal's foot she kept in her hand. She never looked at me at all, she was much too busy. Then suddenly a little scrubby boy came and said something at the door—"Garden scene on!" and went away. The nurse called Kate threw a coat over Mother, and we all three went out and down the stairs.

Then for the first time I twigged what it was—a *Theatre!* The people were acting all round us. I knew acting well enough when I saw it, but what I didn't know was behind the scenes, and goodness me, I have heard Aunt Gerty talk about it enough! I was ashamed of having been so stupid, and terribly disillusioned as well.

The play was all the running away there was to be! Mother was going to be no more to Mr. Aix than taking a leading part in his play amounted to. My toothbrush literally burned in my pocket. I had been made a fool of.

But when I came to think it over quietly, I did not know but what I was not rather glad. It would have been a horrid upset, this running-away idea, and I believe George secretly felt it very much, though he did swagger so and pretend he didn't care. The only thing was, perhaps he would mind Mother going on the stage even worse than running away? I longed to see him and hear what he had to say about it.

Mr. Aix was standing quite near us, between a flat green tree and the wall of a temple. He looked almost handsome; I suppose it was the aroma of success, for certainly this *was* a success. The audience seemed delighted with Mr. Bell, a great fat actor in boots, with frilled tops like an ancient Roman, who stood in the very middle of the stage raging away at Mother about something or other she had done.

"Bell's in capital form to-night," said Mr. Aix, quite loud. "I'm pleased with him."

"I hope I shall content you too," said Mother, who was shivering all over, and I don't wonder, for the draughts in this place were terrific. Kate handed her a bottle of smelling-salts.

"Better by far have a B. and S.," said Mr. Aix.

"No Dutch courage for me, thank you!" said Mother. "Tell me at once, is George and the cat in the box?"

"They are, and Mr. Sidney Robinson and the Countess of Fylingdales. You must buck up, little woman, and show them what you can do!"

"And what you can do!" she answered politely. "I shan't forget you have entrusted me with your play."

"And, by Jove! you'll bring it out as no other woman could. You can——"

"I'm on!" said Mother, suddenly, and shunted the shawl, and pushed forward and began to act.

They clapped her at first and nearly drowned her voice, but she went right on and abused Mr. Bell in blank verse. I was glad Mr. Aix hadn't made her a laundress or a serio, but something nice and Greek and respectable.

I stood there with Kate and Mother's shawl and Aunt Gerty, and never knew what it was to be so excited before! The Greek girl came up to me and said—

"Say, your mommer'll knock them!"

Then they seemed to come to a sort of proper place to stop, and the curtain began to rattle down, and Mother and Mr. Bell were holding each other tight, like lovers, only I heard her say in a whisper, "Mind my hair!"

They stayed there a long time looking stupid, even while the curtain was down and people were clapping all round. Then I saw why they did it, for it went up again, and again, and then they parted and took hands the last time, and looked straight in front of them and panted, while people shouted their names. Then the curtain came down again and Mr. Bell limped off, for, as he said, politely, Mother had been standing all the while on his best corn. She was so sorry, and he said it didn't matter, and he hoped he hadn't disarranged her hair.

Oddly enough the clapping began again. Aunt Gerty jogged Mother, who stood near me looking quite giddy, and said "Take your call, silly!"

Mr. Bell took her by the hand and made her walk along in front of the curtain that a man held back for her by main force, and then we heard the people roaring again, till it seemed more as if they thirsted for their blood than wanted to praise them. This happened twice. When they didn't seem inclined to clap any more she went off to her room with Kate, while Mr. Aix thanked her for making his play.

"Come and look at them!" said Aunt Gerty to me, and we went and looked through the rent in the curtain, for that was the hole in the wall the girl looked through. There was George and Lady Scilly talking away as if Mother and her triumph hadn't existed. I think George was cross, but I really couldn't tell.

Mother wouldn't have me in her room at all this time, and I lounged about with Aunt Gerty till it all began again. Mother didn't do this next act so well, at least Aunt Gerty said not, and scolded her.

"I can't help it, Gertrude," Mother said. "I thought George would have——"

"Never fear! He'll hold out till the end of the play. Then he'll be round here bothering as sure as my name is Gertrude Jenynge!"

And her name is Gertrude Jennings, which is pretty near, and in the third piece of acting, when Mother was not on much, I heard George's voice asking to be taken to her.

"Miss Jennings left word she was not to be disturbed this wait."

"I'm her husband."

"Very likely, sir!" The man sneered.

He didn't get in, and he stood there neglected by the staircase till the beginning of the next and last act, as they said it was. I dared not go and speak to him, for he looked so cross, and I was also afraid he would carry me away to the box with Lady Scilly, so I just slipped behind a bit of scenery and observed.

Presently Mother came softly out of her room and passed George leaning on the rail of the staircase leading to her dressing-room.

She nodded and laughed.

"Wait for me, George, please. Kate, take this gentleman to my room——"

And she went gaily on to the stage.

I followed George and Kate to Mother's room, and discovered myself to him. He made no fuss, simply looked right through me, and began walking up and down while Kate sewed a button on to something.

We heard the clapping from the front quite distinctly. George ground his teeth. Then Kate slipped out and Mother came in alone, panting, and took hold of the dressing-table as if she was drowning.

"I've saved the piece!" said she almost to herself, and then to George, "I'm an artist. Oh, George, why weren't you in front to see me in the best moment of my life?"

"When I married you, Lucy——" George stuttered.

"Yes, but that wasn't nearly such an occasion! Oh, George, forgive me, and don't spoil all my pleasure."

"Pleasure!" said George, as if he was disgusted.

"Here comes Jim Aix to congratulate me. Poor Aix, he is so pleased...."

She burst into tears as Mr. Aix came in. He took absolutely no notice of George, but just caught hold of Mother's hands and said several times over—

"Thank you! Thank you! Bless you! Bless you! Good God! You are crying——"

"It is my husband there, who grudges me my success! He does, he does! Oh, George, for shame! I did it for Ben—for our son—to be able to send him to college. I have made a hit—quite by accident—and you grudge it me!"

"He doesn't, he doesn't grudge you your artistic expansion!" said Mr. Aix, and went to George and put his hand on his shoulder. "Old George is the best sort in the world at the bottom. Pull yourself together, dear old man, and be thankful you have a clever wife, as well as a good one. She's a genius—she's better, she's a brick. I can tell you she's a heaven-born actress, and you know what sort of a wife she has been to you. Speak to her, man, don't let her cry her heart out now, in the hour of her triumph. What's a triumph? At the best but short-lived! Don't grudge it her! Congratulate her——"

George came out of his corner and took Mother's hand and kissed it nicely, as I have seen him kiss Lady Scilly's hand, but Mother's never.

"One can only beg your pardon, Lucy, for this, and everything else. Can you forgive me?"

I re-open my MS. to add a few facts of interest.

1. Ariadne got a baby in June; his name is Almeric Peter Frederick.

2. Aunt Gerty got her brewer, and Mrs. Bowser has left the stage.

3. Ben was sent to school, and they say he is clever, though I never could see it.

4. Lady Scilly has run away with the chauffeur and, so far, hasn't come back.

5. I am going to stay with Ernie Fynes' mother, Lady Fynes, at Barsom. Ernie will be away at Eton, but he loves me.

THE END

www.ingramcontent.com/pod-product-compliance
Lightning Source LLC
Chambersburg PA
CBHW031154050726
47495CB00019B/1706